Arkansas Summer

Anne Moose

This story is dedicated to my parents, who taught me, very early on, to line up on the side of justice.

✳

Chapter 1

Los Angeles, 1986

After the call came, Hannah fell into a long, grim silence. She could have spent hours in the refuge of that silence, but eventually she watched her hand dial the number that would bring her mother's voice. As Hannah listened to the dial tone, and stared at the wall by her phone, she wondered how she would survive the unwelcome blur of rituals that would follow, and then, once it was all over, how she would face life without her father.

CB

Hannah and her mother were devastated by her father's death, but there was an obituary to write, a funeral to plan, and seemingly endless other details to attend to. Hannah had a hard time comprehending that they were expected to produce a multi-media event in the midst of processing their unimaginable loss, and yet here they were, trapped in a series of commitments that seemed custom-designed to keep them from doing the only thing they really wanted to do, which was sleep.

Besides their own grief, Hannah and her mother had to deal with the grief of a law firm that was now reeling from the loss of its founding partner. Hannah's father's heart attack had happened at a charity fundraiser sponsored by his firm, so many of his closest friends and colleagues had witnessed his collapse. Hannah and her mother would normally have been there, but this year Hannah had been busy preparing for court, and her mother was home with a cold.

In the midst of all the turmoil, Hannah struggled to accept her father's disappearance from her life. She was part of his law firm, which split its time between cases that paid the bills, and civil rights cases, which were the real purpose of the firm. She'd loved working with her father, and having a profession that made a difference. But now he was gone, and she was so stricken by the loss that she felt paralyzed, untethered.

Sitting in bed in her small Los Angeles apartment, reading and rereading the words that she would try to deliver at her father's memorial, Hannah wondered how she could possibly go back to work and deal with the stacks of folders piling up on her desk. And her poor mother, who was trying so hard to put on a brave face. What was she going to do? Hannah's father had been the great love and mainstay of her mother's life. How would she cope once all the hubbub was over?

ೞ

It was noon, the funeral and other assorted obligations were now finally behind them, and Hannah was at her parents' house, waiting to take her mother out for a walk on the beach. As Catherine was in her bedroom getting ready, Hannah perused the fireplace mantel, bookcases, and other assorted surfaces filled with family pictures. She picked up a photo of her parents that had been taken in Colorado just a few months back, and felt the familiar upwelling of emotion and sting of tears. Her father appeared to be the picture of health, as lean and handsome as ever. How could he possibly have had died?

She studied her mother's image. At fifty-one, she was still a beautiful woman. Hannah couldn't help but wonder if she'd find love again, or be one of those women who would be content to live the rest of her life alone. She guessed she'd eventually want to find another companion, but it was hard to picture. Her parents had been so solid, so perfect together.

Catherine was quiet on their drive to the ocean, and Hannah sensed that she was far away. She'd been noticeably distant for days, and Hannah was starting to worry about her. Just as they were arriving at the beach, Catherine broke the silence, seeming to come back from wherever she'd been. "There's something I want to talk to you about, Hannah," she said.

Something in her voice made Hannah's imagination take flight. "What is it, Mom? What haven't you been telling me?"

She nodded out the window. "Let's go walk."

Hannah parked the car, and she and her mother removed their shoes and headed across the sand for the surf. The beach was mostly deserted, and the crashing of the waves was soothing to Hannah's frayed spirit. It was warm for February, but breezy, and the morning fog had given way to blue sky, which, at present, was enlivened by scattered seagulls.

At the water's edge they turned left, then walked for a time before either of them spoke. Hannah said finally, "So what is it, Mom?"

Catherine looked out over the ocean, then turned back to her daughter. "There are some things that happened before you were born that it's time I told you about."

"Like what?" Hannah asked, her curiosity rising.

"Well, it's kind of a long story, and I've been trying to think how to tell you."

"We've got all day and a long stretch of beach," Hannah said, looking at her mother expectantly. She wondered what was coming, but guessed it had something to do with her father.

Catherine's expression was sober. "I've been wanting to tell you this for years," she said, "but, I don't know, maybe this

3

is not the best time. You have an awful lot to deal with already."

"I'm fine," Hannah said. "Just tell me."

Catherine pulled an elastic band from her pocket and tied back her hair, which was flying every which way in the wind.

"All right," she said. "I just hope you'll forgive me for keeping this from you for so long."

Chapter 2

Arkansas, 1955

Stepping off the bus was like walking into a steam bath. Catherine had been warned, but she could never have imagined the intensity of the heat that assaulted her as she left the stifling atmosphere of the bus for the even more oppressive air of the terminal yard. Suddenly it was clear why so many of her memories of her grandparents' farm involved playing in sprinklers and pitchers of lemonade.

It had been many years since she'd visited or even spoken to her grandparents. She had last seen them the summer she was nine, so her memories of both her grandparents and their farm were fading. She had a hazy memory of picking strawberries and feeding them to a tortoise that lived in a wide open yard. She remembered trees with stringy moss hanging from the branches, clothes lines with laundry blowing in the breeze, and playing with the children of a black woman named Sally, who cooked and did chores for her grandmother. A string bean of a boy named Jimmy figured prominently in her memories, and she recalled playing school with a couple of shy little girls whose faces she'd forgotten. The children had come and gone in a rickety horse-drawn wagon, and Catherine remembered feeling envious of that old wagon, which looked to her like a big adventure.

The death of her grandfather was the reason that Catherine was finally returning to Arkansas. She had not gone to the funeral. Not even her father had gone to the funeral. Her family had been estranged from her grandparents since the summer of their last visit. But Catherine's father was here now, and since Catherine was home from college for the summer, she was joining him to help him assess his mother's situation, and, if necessary, move her off the farm—to an Arkansas retirement home, probably, though there was some discussion of bringing her back to their home in San Diego.

Catherine's parents were never specific about the fight that had led to her father's alienation from his parents, but it was no secret that her grandfather had been a hateful man, and had taken a particular dislike to Catherine's mother, who was not one to kowtow to an ignorant old drinker who treated his wife and everyone else with disdain. Catherine's grandmother, or *Mama Rae* as she was known by most everyone, had been more or less caught in the cross-fire. She was now in her seventies, and her health was fading, so Catherine's father had it in his mind to patch things up—or at least try, now that her "Lord and Master" was dead.

Catherine was just noticing the *Whites Only* sign on what appeared to be the main entrance to the bus station when a red-faced version of her father stepped up to meet her. "Sweltering enough for you?" Ben asked, planting a kiss on her cheek. Catherine smiled, then gave her dad a sweaty hug.

The bus driver began throwing luggage from under the bus onto the hot pavement, and Catherine and her father had to jump out of the way to avoid being hit. "I can't believe how hot it is," Catherine said, wiping her hairline with a handkerchief that her mother had given her for the trip. "But to tell you the truth," she added, lowering her voice, "it wasn't much better on the bus. With all the fanning that was going on, it was like being in a windstorm of hot B.O. Some of these people are in serious need of deodorant."

Ben laughed and grabbed Catherine's suitcase, then steered her towards a nearby truck. "You don't smell so great yourself," he said, throwing the suitcase in the back. "When we get to your grandmother's house, the first thing I'm going to do is point you to the bathtub. Later tonight it'll cool down. And just wait until you see the fireflies."

Ben rumbled the truck to a start, and suddenly they were moving down a dusty Main Street that stirred memories of a diner with a checkerboard floor, a movie theater, and a hardware store in which the proprietor had erected an elaborate electric train set.

Soon they turned off the main drag and were on a two-lane highway that headed out of town. "Besides the windstorms of hot B.O., how was the bus ride?" Ben asked. "Did you manage to stir up any controversy?"

Catherine was preoccupied in an attempt to un-stick her exposed lower thighs from the seat of the truck. "It was mostly pretty uneventful," she said, placing her hands under her legs as a buffer between her skin and the seat. "But I did give the bus driver a dirty look in some hick bus station when he pointed to the three Negro passengers on the bus and told them, 'It's time for y'all to move on back now. We've passed into Texas.' Then, sure enough, he put up a sign on the back of one of the seats that said *Whites* on one side, and *Colored* on the other."

Catherine's father had told her about seeing signs like this appear and disappear on trains while traveling with his family between Northern and Southern states, but seeing it played out in real life—bearing witness to the humiliation of the passengers—had made Catherine feel sick to her stomach.

"Welcome to the South," Ben said.

After a few miles they turned left onto a narrow road that led them up into some low hills. They passed a couple of ramshackle houses, saw horses grazing in a green field, and finally came to a large pond that Ben identified as *Granddaddy's fishing hole*. Suddenly Catherine had visions of worms on hooks, red and white bobbers, and a snapping turtle that reportedly ate small children. Ben pulled off and parked under some trees.

"I can't believe I'm back here again," Catherine said. "We used to fish and catch tadpoles here. And I remember Granddaddy had an old rowboat he'd take us out on."

They got out of the truck and walked to the edge of the pond. The area was lush with greenery, and alive with birds and buzzing insects. "When I was a teenager, we had a rope swing over on the other side," Ben said. He pointed across the pond, where, in addition to a large stand of trees, there was a skinny pier that Catherine remembered.

Catherine kicked off her shoes and stepped into the water. Her feet sank into soft, slippery mud, and she made a face. "The bottom's slimy."

Ben smiled. "It's better farther out. Maybe later in the week we can come back and go swimming."

"It's beautiful here," Catherine said, looking around to take in the surroundings. She bent down and splashed water over her bare arms and legs. "The water's not real cold, but it feels pretty good." She stepped cautiously into deeper water. "Are there really snapping turtles, or was that just a tall tale?"

"You remember that, do you?" Ben said. He took off his baseball cap and wiped his brow with a bandana pulled from his back pocket. "Your grandfather was big on terrorizing children."

"What happened between you and your dad, exactly?" Catherine asked. "I know something happened that last summer we were here, but I was never clear on what it was."

"We can talk about that another time. For now, I just want to enjoy the place."

"How's Mama Rae doing? Was she glad to see you?" Catherine rolled up her shorts as far as they would go and stepped farther out, eying the depths suspiciously.

"I think so, although it's a little hard to tell. I think she's afraid I might try to force her to leave her house, so she's a little frosty."

"Well, aren't you maybe thinking of doing that?"

"Only if she isn't safe to live alone."

"Well, then you are thinking of it."

"Yeah, I suppose. But I don't feel like I have much choice. We're the only family she has now—besides Sally, I guess, who's practically family at this point."

"I remember Sally," Catherine said. "So she's still around after all this time?"

"Not as much as she was in the old days, but she still drops by a couple times a week to do some cooking and cleaning, and she kind of looks after your grandmother a little bit. She helps her with shopping and things like that." Ben put his cap back on and stuffed the bandana back into his pocket. "That woman is a saint as far as I'm concerned. I don't know how she put up with my father all those years."

"How's Mama Rae adjusting to Granddaddy being gone?"

A flock of birds startled across the pond, and Catherine and Ben looked up. The sky was a deep blue, and massive clouds in the distance threatened a summer storm.

"She seems okay," Ben said. "Better than I expected. But there is one thing I want to talk to you about." He picked up a stone and tossed it in the water. "It's possible you might hear her say some things you're not going to like. And you're going to see and hear some things around town that you'll have a hard time with, too. You know, like the bus driver, and signs and things. Not much has changed since the last time we were here. Jim Crow is still the reality, and I'm afraid it's all Mama Rae has ever known."

"So is she pretty bad?"

"Well, she's not like your grandfather was, but she's a Southerner, and they have a perverse way of looking at things. I've had to bite my tongue more than a few times already."

"Maybe you shouldn't bite your tongue. You know what I mean? Things are never going to change if people don't get called out."

"I hear you," Ben said. "And I have been talking to her some, but it's probably a little late for her at this point. She's an old lady, and set in her ways."

Catherine and her father were just getting ready to leave the pond when a rusty red pickup drove up and parked, and two young men in cutoff jeans and no shirts jumped out. The tallest, a rangy blond with a crew cut, walked up and eyed the two of them. "How y'all doing?" he said, directing special attention to Catherine. "My name is JT, and this here is my friend Teddy."

Teddy sidled up and said, "Hey." He was shorter, and had brown hair combed back into a duck tail. "Y'all from around here?"

"No, we're visiting from California," Ben said. "But I grew up just up the road a ways."

10

"Well, how 'bout that," JT responded. "California." He grinned at Teddy, then looked back at Ben. "You look to be about my daddy's age. Maybe you know him. The name Jesse Taylor ring a bell?"

"Oh yeah, I remember Jesse," Ben said. "He was a year ahead of me in school. What's he up to these days?"

"He's a deputy sheriff," JT boasted. "You'll probably run into him if you spend much time on the highway. He's got a speed trap just outside of town."

"Well, that's good to know," Ben chuckled. "Thanks for the tip."

JT turned to Catherine, his eyes doing an exaggerated survey of her legs. "How long y'all going to be around for?"

Catherine started to answer, but was interrupted by Ben. "Not long," he said. "And I'm afraid we're going to have to run off now. We've got people waiting for us." He put his hand on Catherine's back and directed her towards the truck.

"Yeah, well I hope we see you around," JT hollered after them.

Catherine and Ben climbed into the truck and the boys turned and dove into the pond. "Did you notice the way that guy was leering at me?" Catherine asked when they were back on the road.

"I noticed," Ben said, looking into the rearview mirror. "And, knowing his father, it doesn't surprise me." He shot Catherine a look. "Jesse Taylor was a scary guy."

cs

When Catherine and Ben arrived at the farmhouse just a couple of minutes later, Mama Rae was sitting on the front porch, anticipating their arrival. The clapboard house and expansive surrounding yard were almost exactly as Catherine remembered, and so was her grandmother.

Mama Rae stood up and waved. She was wearing a light cotton dress, and her white hair was pulled up in a loose bun. "You're finally here!" she called from the porch. "What took you so long? I was getting ready to call out the hounds!"

Ben collected the suitcase, then he and Catherine headed for the house, where Catherine was met with an energetic embrace. "Oh my good Lord," Mama Rae said in a rush of enthusiasm. "Will you look at this girl all grown up? *And what a beauty!*"

Catherine was relieved at the warm welcome. "It's so nice to see you, Mama Rae. And you're looking pretty good yourself, although you're a lot smaller than I remembered."

"Well," Mama Rae chuckled, "you've grown a mile, and I've probably shrunk since the last time you were here." She beamed at Catherine. "I'm sorry I'm not gonna get to see your mother this time. I hear she's teachin' this summer. But I sure am glad you're here. Now come on in the house and have some supper. I hope y'all are hungry."

Mama Rae pulled open the screen door and disappeared inside. Catherine and Ben followed her through a dim living room and then on into the kitchen, where a table with a red checkered tablecloth was set for three, and a figure Catherine recognized as Sally was standing in front of an antique stove, turning chicken in a hot skillet. She was a handsome woman, with smooth dark skin and a straight, sturdy frame. "Well, look who's finally arrived," she exclaimed with a welcoming smile. "Your poor grandma's been so excited, waitin' out there on that porch. And just look at you now," she said to Catherine. "The last time I saw you, you was just a tiny little thing!"

"It's wonderful to see you, Sally," Catherine said, reaching for Sally's hands. "I have such fond memories of you and your children. Do you remember how we used to play hide and seek, and play school out on the front porch?"

"I surely do," Sally replied. "And I remember you sitting right here at this table helping me shuck corn and snap green beans. You were quite a little helper, yes you were." She shook her head and grinned, as if reliving an old memory. "It's right nice to see you again, Catherine. I'm so glad you come. And your grandmother... Well, she ain't talked about much else besides you visitin' for at least a week." She turned her attention back to the chicken. "Now, if you and your daddy want to go get washed up, I'll have supper ready for y'all in just a minute."

"Is it okay if I take a quick shower before we eat?" Catherine asked, noticing that she did, in fact, smell.

"That'll be just fine," Mama Rae said, "except we don't have a shower. You'll have to make due with a tub. Come on back and I'll show you to your room."

ↄ

After Catherine was bathed and changed, she returned to the kitchen and found her father and Mama Rae sitting at the table, talking about some of the things Ben planned to fix around the house. Sally was at the stove placing the chicken onto a platter. Out the window over the kitchen sink Catherine could see that it was starting to sprinkle, and she thought she heard some thunder off in the distance. Her father had told her a number of dramatic stories about Arkansas storms, and she wondered if they were in for one. She hoped not, but welcomed the rain, which would surely cool things down.

"Set yourself down and let's eat," Mama Rae said. Catherine obeyed, taking a seat next to her father. Sally placed the platter of chicken on the table next to some cornbread and a bowl of lima beans, then went to the refrigerator and pulled out a pitcher of water. She poured water into three tall glasses on the table, then returned the pitcher to the refrigerator.

"This looks wonderful, Sally," Catherine said, reaching for a piece of cornbread.

Sally smiled. "Well, I hope y'all enjoy it." She took off her apron and hung it on a hook by the stove. "My son should be here soon to pick me up, so I'm just going to go out on the porch and wait. I know y'all have a lot to talk about."

Catherine's ears perked up at the mention of Sally's son. "By any chance is it Jimmy who's picking you up?" she asked. "Because if it is, I'd love to say hello to him when he arrives, if that's okay. I have so many fond memories of him."

"Catherine," snapped Mama Rae, "that was a long time ago, and you were children. You got no business with that boy now that he's grown. You need to leave him be."

Catherine and Ben exchanged a look, and Sally started towards the door. "I best hurry on," she said. "I'll remember you to him, and that'll be fine."

After Sally left, the subject of Jimmy was dropped, and they turned their attention to the food, and to some of the chores that Catherine and her father would attend to the next day. It was decided that Ben would do some work on the front porch, and Catherine would drive Mama Rae into town to see her doctor. Afterwards, they'd go to the grocery store and pick up some food for dinner, which Catherine volunteered to cook.

When they were finished eating, Catherine did the dishes while Ben and Mama Rae watched *The Honeymooners* on the TV in the living room. Standing at the sink, looking out at rain falling lightly in the yard, Catherine thought about Jimmy, and all the fun they'd had together as children. In a book tucked in her suitcase, she had a photograph that her mother had taken of the two of them sitting on top of the horse that had pulled his family's wagon. Wearing a wide grin and baggy white t-shirt, Jimmy looked so happy. She wondered what he was like now. He'd been such a lively little boy—so funny, and full of laughter. Having grown up hearing her father talk about the cruelties of the South, Catherine had an inkling of what his life might be like. She hoped that he'd somehow managed to retain his exuberant spirit, but there was no telling how he might have changed. In any case, Catherine wanted to see Jimmy again, and find out for herself, and it made her both sad and angry to realize that, in Arkansas, this desire on her part was subversive. Maybe even dangerous.

When she was finished drying the dishes and tidying up the kitchen, Catherine joined her father and Mama Rae, who were now outside on the porch watching the rain. The moment she closed the screen door the sky lit up and a violent boom of thunder shook the house. Then, just as she was registering alarm, it happened again. Terrified, Catherine clutched her father's arm.

"There's nothing to be afraid of," Ben said, pulling her close. "This is just a good old fashioned Arkansas thunderstorm."

The thunder and lightning continued in spectacular fashion for the next half hour, with a level of intensity unlike anything Catherine had ever experienced. Once she was able to calm down, she actually enjoyed the show, feeling a part of the universe as never before. When the spectacle was finally over, she said good-night to her father and grandmother, and they all went off to their separate rooms. Not long after, Catherine climbed into bed, then fell asleep to the sound of gently falling rain.

Chapter 3

Catherine was awakened the next morning by a rooster crowing, and was amused by what felt like the movie version of waking up on a farm. 'Farm' was actually something of an overstatement. Her father's family had once owned a much larger piece of land, but most of it had been sold off long ago. What remained, and now belonged to Catherine's grandmother, was a house, a weather-beaten barn, and two or three surrounding acres that were mostly pasture and trees. When Catherine's father was a boy, they'd had a vegetable garden and a few horses and chickens, but her grandfather had never made his living from the property. He'd mostly worked as a loan officer at a bank in town. Nevertheless, her father had grown up feeling close to the land, and Catherine knew that, for him, the "farm" was the best thing about his childhood.

The rooster crowed many more times before Catherine finally got out of bed. She heard activity in the kitchen, but the smell of coffee is what eventually motivated her to get up. When she was dressed and mostly put together, she entered the kitchen and was surprised to find Sally, whom she hadn't expected to see again for another couple of days.

"Good morning, young lady," Sally said cheerfully. "I'm fixin' to make you some breakfast, so I hope you woke up hungry."

Catherine eyed the coffee on the stove. "Breakfast sounds great, thank you. And, also, if you could point me to a cup, I'd love some coffee."

Sally produced a cup, and Catherine got some milk from the refrigerator. "Where is everyone?" she asked.

"Your father's taking your grandmother to her doctor's appointment, and they're going to stop off at the market afterwards and do some shopping. They told me to tell you that Mama Rae got the time wrong. Her appointment was at 9:00, and not 2:00 like she thought. Luckily, the time was written down on the little chalk board she keeps by the back door."

Catherine sat down at the table. "It's awfully nice of you to cook me breakfast." She wanted to ask Sally about Jimmy, but was hesitant. She took some sips of her coffee. "How is your family?" she asked finally. "I remember that you had at least three kids—Jimmy, and two younger girls. What were their names?"

"Martha and Delilah," Sally said. "We used to call Delilah *Little Dee*."

"Oh yeah, now I remember." Catherine was suddenly struck with a memory that forced her to stifle a laugh. "Little Dee was the younger one, right?"

"That's right; she was my baby. Now that she's older, we mostly call her *Dee*. She gets mad when we call her *Little Dee*. She says it's a baby name." Sally chuckled, then walked to the sink and began rinsing dishes. "The girls are teenagers now. Dee's fifteen and Martha's sixteen, almost seventeen. Then there's Jimmy, he's twenty, and I have an older son who's grown. George is twenty-six. He works for the railroad, and mostly stays in Chicago now."

"What about Jimmy?" Catherine asked. "What's he doing these days?" She tried to picture Jimmy as a twenty-year-old, but it was hard to let go of the little-boy image she remembered so fondly.

Sally turned around and beamed. "Jimmy's my college boy," she said, her voice filled with pride. "He's home for the summer, but he's been off studying at Oberlin College, in Ohio."

Catherine felt a surge of shame for being surprised, but besides being surprised, she was thrilled. All her fears about what might have become of Jimmy were gone, replaced in an instant by the picture of a dignified college student. And Catherine had heard of Oberlin. It was a liberal college famous for being the first to admit both Negroes and women. Catherine smiled at the thought of Jimmy in that environment. "Did you ask him if he remembered me?"

"Oh, he remembers you, all right. I told him you were asking about him, and he started asking about you." She lowered her voice and added in a conspiratorial tone, "He's out back in the garden right now. I put him to work gathering up some greens for dinner, and this morning your father asked him if he wanted to do some work around the place, so you'll be seeing him around." She smiled, then turned back to the sink. "If you want, you can go on out and say hello. I'm pretty sure he's out there waiting for you."

&

Catherine quickly brushed her teeth, brushed her hair, and examined her reflection in the mirror. Then she took some deep breaths and started anxiously for the backyard, where she found Jimmy sitting on a bench next to a pail of leafy vegetables. The instant she saw his familiar grin she felt at ease.

"Well, look who's finally come back after all these years," Jimmy said, rising to greet her.

Catherine wanted to hug her old friend, but she settled for a handshake and met his smile with one of her own. "Jimmy," she said, with earnest affection. "I'm so happy to see you. And look at you," she added, *"You're gigantic!"*

"You're looking pretty grown up yourself," Jimmy said, still holding her hand. He had an air of confidence that pleased Catherine, and though he was almost six feet tall, she recognized the feisty ten-year-old she remembered.

There was a brief silence while they took each other in, and Catherine could feel herself blushing. "Look what I have," she said finally. She handed Jimmy a small photograph, and he immediately laughed.

"I remember this. Your mother took this picture." He looked at the photo intently, then handed it back to Catherine. "That was a long time ago," he said, "but I've never forgotten my little friend from California."

"I've never forgotten you either," Catherine said. "When my parents told me we weren't coming back here anymore, I cried for days. And it wasn't because I was going to miss my grandparents." Catherine pointed to the picture. "Just look at you. You were adorable!"

"Well, you were pretty cute yourself," Jimmy said, smiling at the photo. "With your pigtails, and cartwheeling all around the yard, and the stories you'd read to the girls on the porch. You were a natural little teacher."

"I don't know if you remember this," Catherine said, feeling bold, "but at one point I proposed to you, and you accepted. I think it might have been the same day this picture was taken. I remember we were eating popsicles, and you were wearing that same white t-shirt. I told you that I wanted to marry you when I grew up, and you said okay. Then we turned on the sprinkler and pretended it was Niagara Falls."

Jimmy laughed. "No wonder your family never brought you back. I can't picture your grandparents attending that particular wedding."

Jimmy sat back down on the bench and Catherine joined him, feeling a little embarrassed. She decided to change the subject. "You mother told me you're going to Oberlin College," she said. "How do you like it there?"

"It's good," Jimmy said. "The college, the town..." He looked out over the green pasture beyond the yard, then back at Catherine. "It's not perfect, but it's worlds better than this here." He gave Catherine a serious look. "This is the second time I've been back home since I been gone, and coming back is hard." He looked down at his feet. "*It's hard.*"

Catherine was touched by the emotion in Jimmy's voice, and by his quickness to honesty, and trust.

"I can't do what a colored man has to do here to survive," he continued, his brow furrowed. "Not anymore. I never could, really. I had to get out of the South. But, look," he said, brightening, "tell me about you. Your daddy tells me you're going to college in San Diego."

Suddenly Sally was at the back door. "Why don't you two come on in the house," she called. "I have breakfast waiting for you, and it's best if y'all finish before Mama Rae gets back."

❧

Catherine and Jimmy sat down to a hearty breakfast of fried ham, scrambled eggs, and buttermilk biscuits. The conversation started out casual. They talked about Sally's cooking, and reminisced about some of the things they'd done together as children.

After a few minutes, Sally wiped her hands on her apron, sat down at the table, and gave each of them a serious look. "I know this is old home week for y'all," she said, "and I don't want to spoil the party, but you need to mind yourselves, and not go getting yourselves into trouble."

Jimmy started to say something, but Sally interrupted him. "I'm not finished, son. You need to let me speak my piece."

Catherine had some idea what was coming, and she felt the blood rushing to her face.

"Now, Jimmy, I know I don't need to tell you this, but I'm going to tell you anyway. We are not in Oberlin, Ohio, and we ain't in California neither. Where we are, colored boys get themselves killed for just thinking about a white girl. Now, I know y'all been readin' in the newspapers about Emmett Till—dead because of some silly thing he said to a white woman. But I can tell you, *because I know*, history is filled with Emmett Tills that ain't never been in the newspaper, and some of them have been right here."

She paused for effect, and her face was dead serious. "Now, you two are old friends. I understand that, and that's fine. I'm not saying you can't be friends, or shouldn't be friends. But you need to be sensible, and keep things out of view. I don't want y'all going near that road together. If you want to talk with one another, you need to stay right here. And I want you to be careful around Mama Rae, too. There's no need to go upsetting Mama Rae. Y'all gotta remember, she's just lost her husband. And he was no prize—Lord knows he was a difficult man. But he was all she knew, and now that he's gone, it's an adjustment. And we're in *her* home."

Sally looked at Catherine, and then focused hard on Jimmy. "If some white boy gets exercised about you and this pretty girl here, you could get yourself killed."

CB

21

Shortly after breakfast Ben and Mama Rae returned, and everyone turned their attention to the various chores that were on the agenda for the day. Jimmy would help Ben do some repairs on the front porch, and Mama Rae had expressed a desire to "get rid of stuff," so Catherine was tasked with helping her go through closets, drawers, and cabinets for the purpose of deciding what to keep, what to give to the Salvation Army, and what to throw away. Ben had come back from town with a truck full of empty boxes, and it was his hope that, by the end of the day, they would be filled up and ready for delivery to the dump.

Catherine's job sounded simple enough, but she soon realized that it was not going to happen quickly. The objects, clothes, and papers that resided in every nook and cranny of the house represented Mama Rae's life, and she agonized over things that Catherine would have tossed without a thought. "I wore this to church most Sundays for probably a good twenty years," Mama Rae said, holding a small hat that had once been black, but was now faded to gray. "I know it's silly to want to hold onto something like this, but sometimes it's hard to let go of things."

"I understand," Catherine said. "They hold memories, so of course it's hard."

There were numerous frayed and faded items that were too precious to let go, but Catherine found Mama Rae's sentimentality endearing, and it was a pleasure to see her brighten at the sudden appearance of some relic or knick-knack that she hadn't seen in years. Luckily, there were a lot of things about which she was not sentimental, so the 'throw away' and 'give away' boxes were steadily filling up.

"Oh my good Lord," Mama Rae said with excitement when Catherine handed her a very old-looking baby doll that she found wrapped in a shoebox. "That belonged to my mother when she was a child." She stared at the doll tenderly, then passed it back to Catherine. "I always meant to give this to you, so you can keep it. It's for you."

"She's beautiful, Mama Rae," Catherine said, touched by the gesture, "but are you sure?"

"Sweetheart," Mama Rae said, tearing up, "it's the least I can do. The absolute least."

She paused for a moment to collect herself, then continued. "I'm not normally one to do a lot of apologizing, but I need to tell you that I'm truly sorry about what happened between your grandfather and your father, and for not speaking to y'all for all these years. If I'd had anything to say about it, all that would 'a never happened. It was all your grandfather's doing. And I'm sad to say it, but he was a horse's ass."

Catherine laughed.

Mama Rae laughed, too. "He was. He was a *horse's ass*. But I was his wife, and there was nothing I could do but go along. But now that he's gone, I intend for things to be different. I'm glad you and your daddy are here. And I'm grateful, too."

Catherine started to say something, but Mama Rae stopped her. "I'm not finished yet," she said, looking serious. "I want to say something to you about that boy out on the porch."

Catherine held her breath.

"Your father and I had a long talk this morning, and he explained to me that you and that boy were friends when you were youngsters, and you intend to be friends now. And I remember the two of you running around thick as thieves. It's what started all the nonsense between your daddy and your granddaddy in the first place. But that's past history. For the here and now, I want you to know that I don't intend to interfere. Y'all have a different way of viewing things, and I accept that. But I hope that you can accept that I was raised to have certain views and beliefs myself, and those are not likely to change."

Catherine wasn't sure how to respond, so she just said, "Okay." Then they went back to sifting, sorting, and tossing. But for the rest of the day Catherine was thinking about what Mama Rae had said—that the problem between her father and her grandfather had had something to do with her friendship with Jimmy. This was the first she'd heard of this, and she was anxious to talk to her father about it.

By the end of the day there were enough old magazines, ratty clothes, empty coffee cans, and other assorted refuse to fill the back of the truck, so Catherine and Ben decided to take a trip to the dump and reward themselves afterwards with a swim in the pond. Jimmy had long since gone. Catherine regretted that she hadn't had the chance to speak to him again, but she was assured by Ben that he would be back the next day.

ᘓ

Catherine and Ben had dumped the *'throw-aways'* and were on their way to the pond when Catherine decided to ask her father about Mama Rae's remark. "I had kind of a nice talk with Mama Rae today," she said, "and she apologized for everything, and told me that Granddaddy was a horse's ass."

"There's an understatement," said Ben, who was never one to hide his contempt for his father. "But I'm glad the two of you are getting to spend some time together. Since you're her only grandchild, the rift in our family was hard on her. I know it means a lot to her to have you here."

"She said that the fight you had with Granddaddy had something to do with Jimmy and me. Is that true?"

"Well, he didn't like you running around with Sally's kids, and Jimmy was closest to your age, and your favorite, so yeah,

24

it bothered him. He told Sally to stop bringing them around, and she told him that if she couldn't bring them, she'd have to quit."

Ben slowed down and swerved to avoid a pothole in the road. "When Mama Rae got wind of what was going on, and found out that Sally was threatening to quit, she pitched a fit." He glanced at Catherine. "Mama Rae almost never stood up to the old man, but she did that time, and she won. But my father was not happy, and he said a lot of ugly things. To put it in his words, he didn't like his granddaughter "getting so friendly with that little nigger."

"So he said that, you got in a fight, and then you decided never to speak to him again?"

"Well, it wasn't quite that simple. There were some other things said, and an incident, but that was the basic gist. But I should never have brought you here to begin with. It was a mistake to expose you to that type of talk, and attitude. I only did it because of Mama Rae. But after that last summer, I knew we couldn't come back here anymore."

"But you never even talked to them again. Couldn't you have at least talked to Mama Rae?"

"Well, it was your grandfather who really cut things off. He forbade Mama Rae to talk to us, and that was it. I did speak to her a couple of times on the phone when my father was in the hospital, but she mostly did what she was told. She was always under his thumb."

Now at the pond, Catherine and Ben got out of the truck and stripped down to their swim suits. It was not as humid as the day before, but it was hot, and they were looking forward to cooling off. Catherine stepped into the water and Ben followed her, then they both plunged in. Soon the two of them were floating happily in deep water.

"How did you manage to turn out so well?" Catherine asked, treading water next to her father. "I'd have thought that, coming from Granddaddy, you'd be like him, but you're the exact opposite. How did that happen?"

"Well, I was always at odds with my dad," Ben said. "He was a bully, and I never liked the way he treated my mother, or anyone really. So he wasn't any kind of role model."

Ben swatted at a horsefly that was hovering near his face. "I left home when I was eighteen and went to college in California, and that was an eye-opener, especially coming from the South. Later on, when I was in the Navy during the war, that brought me into contact with a lot of different people, and that had a big impact on me." He took another exasperated swipe at the horsefly, then continued. "Anyway, I guess between all that, and, of course, meeting your mother and raising you, I kind of evolved. But, trust me, I was never anything like my father, or most of the people around here, really. I was never cut out for the South."

Catherine and Ben spent the next twenty minutes swimming and soaking in the natural beauty of the place. In addition to bird songs and the buzzing of dragon flies and other assorted insects, Catherine detected the chirping of frogs, which brought back memories of catching tadpoles and keeping them in buckets. "I can see why you wanted to bring me here," she said, pulling herself up onto the pier at the other side of the pond. She remembered sitting in the same spot with Jimmy, watching red and white bobbers attached to bamboo fishing poles.

Ben got out and sat on a large rock next to the pier. Though he was now well into his forties, his body was still relatively youthful. His face, too, belied his age, even sporting two day's growth of beard. Catherine suddenly pictured him in the faded green swimming trunks that had been his summertime trademark when she was young. "Do you remember teaching Jimmy and me to fish?" she asked.

"Of course," Ben said. "And, as I recall, you did pretty well."

Catherine smiled and pointed to a swarm of minnows swimming beneath her feet. "We definitely caught our share of fish," she said, feeling a dreamy sense of nostalgia. "It was so exciting to see the bobber go under. I liked that better than actually catching the fish. I wasn't that crazy about the fish, or the worms." She laughed out loud at a recollection of Jimmy chasing her with a worm. Savoring that and other memories that suddenly came to mind, she was flooded with affection for her old friend.

She and Ben were mostly silent for the next few minutes, content to quietly enjoy the warmth and sounds of the teeming world that enveloped them. The spell was broken when Ben stepped back into the water and announced that it was time to get going. Catherine stood up, dove off the end of the pier, then followed her father back to the other side of the pond, where they quickly got out and dried off.

When they were dressed and back on the road, Catherine asked, "What was the incident?"

Ben was quiet.

"You know," Catherine continued, "the incident that you said happened between you and Granddaddy that contributed to the big split."

"It's not really important," Ben said, but Catherine persisted.

"You can't just tell me that there was some big incident, and then leave me in the dark. Come on, what happened? If you don't tell me, I'm going to ask Mom, and she will, so you might as well just tell me now."

"Please don't badger me, Catherine, I shouldn't have even mentioned it."

"Just tell me. Come on. Then no more badgering."

Ben was hesitant, but clearly not in the mood for an argument. "*All right,*" he said finally.

Catherine looked at him expectantly.

Ben took a deep breath, then exhaled. "I'm not a hundred percent certain about this..." He stopped, shot Catherine a serious look, then continued, slowly, "I'm not a hundred percent certain about this, but at the time, I believed that your grandfather may have tried to drown Jimmy."

Catherine was not expecting an 'incident' of this magnitude, and she was stunned. "*What?*" she cried. "Are you saying that Granddaddy tried to *kill* Jimmy?"

"Well, I can't say for sure what was in his mind, but one day I happened along the pond when he was fishing, and he appeared to be watching Jimmy in the process of drowning."

Ben stopped the truck and turned to face Catherine with a sober look. "He claims that he was going to pull him out, but I saw no indication that he was going to. I jumped in and pulled him out myself. When I asked Jimmy what had happened, he told me that your grandfather threw him in."

Catherine stared at her father in disbelief.

"Your grandfather's story was that he was teaching Jimmy to swim. He said it was how his father taught him—by just throwing him in deep water. But it sure looked to me like he was letting him drown."

℘

Catherine had a hard time processing what she'd learned about her grandfather. She finally decided to simply put it aside for the moment. But she planned to ask Jimmy what he remembered when the time was right, and she was anxious to hear his version of the story. In the meantime, she focused on the dinner she'd promised to prepare that night. Her father had gone to the store when he was out earlier with Mama Rae, but since they hadn't discussed what Catherine would cook, he'd bought little beyond a few staples, so Catherine wanted to drive into town and buy some more food.

Mama Rae objected when Catherine announced her intention to make a run to the store. "We have plenty of leftovers," she insisted. "We have fried chicken and cornbread and a whole garden full of vegetables right out the back door."

But Catherine was determined. "It's not a big deal," she argued, "I'll be back in a jiffy."

Ben was also in favor of leftovers, but he knew not to argue with Catherine when she had her mind set on something, so he gave her some money, some simple directions, and relinquished the keys to the truck. He also offered to drive her, but Catherine assured him that she knew where she was going, and was fine on her own.

"Well, watch out for the speed trap!" Ben hollered from the porch as she climbed into the truck.

"I will, I promise," Catherine called back. Then she closed the door, rolled down the window, and took off down the driveway towards the road.

Navigating to the small grocery store was simple, requiring only one turn off Main Street, which was a straight shot from the highway, where Catherine cautiously avoided speeding and kept an eye on the rearview mirror. It was Saturday, and getting on towards evening, and there were surprisingly few cars on the road, or people out on the street. The phrase *'sleepy town'* came to mind as Catherine drove slowly past sights and people that seemed both tired and vaguely familiar. She passed a drug store, a small diner, and a furniture store that she remembered. She also recognized the movie theater, which advertised *The Night of the Hunter* on its time-worn marquee. She recalled seeing Abbot and Costello in that theater one summer after a campaign of relentless begging, and being told by her parents, when she'd asked why all the Negroes were sitting in the balcony, that it was a Southern tradition. At the time her reaction was to be envious, since, to her, the balcony looked like the better deal.

Up the street from the movie theater she passed a hardware store that lived vividly in her memory. She resolved to go back there when she had more time, and with her father, who would, no doubt, also be interested in whether it still hosted the elaborate train set that had run all around its walls, and over the front door. Catherine couldn't remember his name, but she could picture the white-haired proprietor of the store. She wondered if he were still alive.

Farther up the street was a barber shop that Catherine recalled had catered to Negroes. She remembered its hallmark barber pole, and being told by her mother that this is where Sally's husband had worked before he'd been killed in some type of accident. Catherine had been upset to learn that Jimmy and his siblings had no father. She felt a renewed sadness now to think that Jimmy's father hadn't lived to see his children grow up, or Jimmy go to college.

She smiled at the thought of grown-up Jimmy, and felt impatient for their next chance to talk. She recalled Sally's warning about the danger their friendship posed, and it brought a flash of anger. She was contemplating the anger that must live inside Jimmy all the time when she turned right and suddenly saw the store that she'd known as the source of popsicles and penny candy.

She parked the truck and walked into the market through a screen door that jingled to announce her entrance. The store was mostly deserted, the only other patrons being an old black gentleman in a fedora and a couple of teenagers who bought cigarettes, then exited soon after she arrived. Not wanting to waste any time, she quickly located the items she was looking for, then headed for the checkout, where a middle aged woman with fleshy arms and orange checkered shorts was flipping through a magazine, looking bored. "Find everything all right?" she asked as Catherine approached.

"Actually," Catherine said, doing a showy about face, "I just thought of a couple things I forgot." She then went searching the aisles for what she'd need to make a pineapple upside-down cake, which was her father's favorite dessert. A few minutes later she returned to the checkout, where the old man in the fedora was now placing canned goods on the counter. When the woman saw Catherine approach, she abruptly moved his items to the side, then motioned for Catherine to step up.

Catherine froze.

"Come on over, he can wait," the woman snapped, as though the old man weren't even there.

"*No… Please*," Catherine said, blushing with alarm. "Finish with this gentleman first."

"Suit yourself," sniffed the woman. Then she finished ringing the man up, but with an air of contempt.

Catherine burned with embarrassment and shame, but said nothing. When the man left the store, the woman turned her attention to Catherine's items, mumbling some things under her breath that Catherine couldn't make out. "You're not from around here, are you?" she asked icily, just as she was finishing up.

Catherine responded with equal chilliness. "No, just visiting." Then she paid for the groceries and hurried out the door.

Just as the bell was tinkling behind her, she heard the woman call, with obvious sarcasm, "I sure do hope you enjoy your stay."

ɔഽ

When Catherine arrived home she made a simple dinner that received overblown but much appreciated accolades from both her father and Mama Rae. She had decided it was too late to make a cake, so after dinner they enjoyed vanilla ice cream out on the front porch, which was still in a state of partial repair. The day was now turning to night, and the air was warm and fragrant.

Ben went inside, then returned with a cold beer. "Look," he said, pointing out into the yard. "See the fireflies?" He sat down next to Catherine in a squeaky porch swing that she remembered fondly from her visits as a child.

"Oh my gosh," Catherine said, now aware of tiny lights beginning to flicker in the darkness. She pressed her memory for a moment. "Did we used put them in jars?"

"You surely did," Mama Rae answered. "And so did your father when he was a boy. He was always catching some type of critter. That boy brought home frogs, snakes, lizards, bugs of all kinds." She slapped her knee and laughed heartily. "He once about frightened me to death with an enormous grasshopper. He walked up with that big ol' thing on the end of a stick, and it jumped right at me. Nearly gave me a heart attack!"

They all laughed, and Catherine was happy to see how much her grandmother was enjoying herself. Perhaps now that Mama Rae was free of her husband, she'd be able to find some pleasure in life, and some peace.

Soon, Mama Rae retired for the evening, and Catherine and her father were alone on the porch. Between the fireflies, the stars, and the rhythmic chirping that Ben identified as frogs at the pond, the night had a magical air. "It's amazing here at night," Catherine said.

Ben yawned. "Nighttime was always the best time in the summer. Or, at least, it should have been. With my father around, things were never very pleasant."

"Mom says he was a big drinker."

"Yeah, he liked to drink. And it brought out the worst in him, so you'd want to avoid him when he was drunk. But he wasn't any picnic when he was sober, either."

"Why do you think he was like that?"

"I don't know. I think maybe this area just breeds bitterness. To be honest, I don't think a lot of people in the South ever got over losing the Civil War. And, of course, my father lived through both World Wars, which produced some pretty tough times. He never went to war himself, but probably his favorite brother died in World War One, and his mother died in the big flu epidemic of 1917. And then there was the Depression, and that was hard on him, because he was out of work for a number of years."

Ben took a pull on his beer. "I was here during the Depression, and that was a pretty terrible time. Lots of people suffered a lot during those years, the Negroes especially. I can remember seeing people walking down the road wearing nothing but rags. *Just rags.* Many with no shoes, skinny as could be." Ben's voice cracked with emotion. "It was awful, seeing people like that. Mama Rae used to feed some of them when she could."

He took another drink. "We were relatively lucky, because when your grandfather was out of work, we at least had food. We had chickens, and a couple of cows, and we always had a large vegetable garden. So people would sometimes come around, seeing if they could do some kind of work in exchange for food. Mama Rae would give 'em vegetables, and a few eggs, or maybe some milk. But only when my father wasn't around to see. If he was here, he'd tell her he didn't want her *'feeding the animals.'*"

He shook his head in disgust. "There's no excuse for that kind of behavior. I don't care how many wars or Depressions or whatever he might have lived through. That was just blind, ignorant hate. But that's who he was. He was a hateful man, and he made everyone's life miserable."

"It makes me sad to think of you as a little boy, having such an awful father," Catherine said.

"Well, I don't dwell on it. These days I feel lucky more than anything else. I have a good life, and the most wonderful wife and daughter in the world, so I'd say I came through it all pretty well intact." He gave Catherine a squeeze.

They sat quietly for a moment, then Catherine told her father about the incident at the grocery store checkout.

"Unfortunately, you're going to see a lot of things like that around here," Ben said. "Besides the actual laws they have here to enforce racial segregation—like the ones that mandate separate schools and bathrooms, and things like that—there are a whole bunch of unwritten laws and customs that are designed to humiliate Negroes. Waiting on white people first in stores is one of them. It's not universal, but it's common. It's also common to see Negroes stepping off the sidewalk to make way for whites. I used to see that in town a lot when I was a boy, and I don't know, but I assume it probably still goes on now. Then there are the so-called *rules* about what you can call people. I remember being told growing up that I should never call a Negro man 'Mister,' and that a Negro woman should never be called a 'lady.' And, of course, a lot of people around here are in love with the word *'nigger.'* My father was one of those. And there was no reason for it. No Negro ever did *anything* to my father."

Ben drained the last of his beer, then shook his head. "Like I said, this area just seems to breed a type of hatred. I don't pretend to understand it, but I'm damn glad to be away from it." He stood up and stretched. "It pains me to expose you to some of these things, but it's real life, I guess." He turned to Catherine with a sad expression, then looked back out over the yard. "With all the fireflies and stars and whatnot, it might look like a fairy tale, but I'm afraid that real life here is not a pretty picture. Not by a long shot."

Chapter 4

The next morning Ben took Mama Rae to church and Catherine slept in, finally succumbing to the relentless crowing of the rooster around 9:00. According to Mama Rae, the rooster belonged to an abutting farm that had once been owned by a family that had six boys. "Your father was friendly with a couple of 'em when they were small," she'd told Catherine, "but they grew up pretty wild, so as they got older, he generally tried to avoid the whole bunch."

Catherine took a bath, then went into the kitchen and heated up the coffee that was left on the stove. She was starting to think about breakfast when she heard knocking at the back door. She could see through the glass at the top of the door that it was Jimmy, and she was both pleased and surprised to see him. She hadn't expected him to arrive until later in the day.

"You're just in time for breakfast," Catherine said, opening the door with a smile.

"Well, I wasn't coming here looking for food," Jimmy said, smiling back. "I'm looking for your father. But if you're offering some of that Northern hospitality I've been hearing so much about, I guess I'd be a fool to turn it down—as long as you think your daddy and grandma won't mind."

"They're off at church, so it's just me," Catherine said, ushering him in. "I'm going to make some eggs and toast, and I can make some bacon too, if you like bacon."

Jimmy followed her into the kitchen. "You feed me bacon, I'll be your friend for life." He sat down at the table and Catherine set to work making breakfast. They made light conversation, and Catherine was happy to have Jimmy watching her cook. She could feel his eyes on her as she moved around the kitchen, and she couldn't help wondering what he was thinking.

While she was turning bacon and scrambling eggs, Catherine told Jimmy about watching fireflies with her father, and about some of her communion with Mama Rae the previous day. There were lots of other things she wanted to tell him, and ask him, but she held back, hoping that, in time, the conversation would naturally turn to more serious topics. Jimmy didn't say much during most of Catherine's cheerful chatter, but he made good-natured comments, and looked pleased to be sitting in her sunny kitchen. When everything was ready, including a pot of fresh coffee, Catherine put a plate and cup in front of him, then sat down with a plate of her own.

Jimmy tried the eggs. "*Mmm, mmmm,*" he said, with exaggerated pleasure. "And I haven't even gotten to the bacon." He picked up a piece of bacon and took a slow bite, then beamed a look of delight. Catherine dug in herself, and then had a memory that caused her to lean forward with excitement. "Do you remember the little fort we built over near the pond?" she asked.

Jimmy grinned. "Of course. Fort Apache."

"That's right, Fort Apache!"

"To this day, whenever I eat a Moon Pie, I think of Fort Apache."

"You do not," Catherine laughed.

"I do too. Moon Pies and Mars Bars always remind me of Catherine and Fort Apache." He picked up a piece of toast. "You gotta understand, we didn't normally get that type of food at home, so coming here when you were visiting was like

Christmas. I bet if we were to go out and look for the ruins of old Fort Apache, we'd find a mountain of candy wrappers."

"We sure had a lot of fun together," Catherine mused. "Pretending we were Indians. Fishing. Do you remember chasing me with worms?"

Jimmy chuckled. "Oh yeah. It was fun makin' you run."

He took another bite of eggs. "It about broke my heart when summer came and you didn't come back. I really looked forward to your visits. And it wasn't just the Moon Pies."

He flashed a smile. "I don't know how many times it was you visited, but I kinda got used to my little California friend. Of course, in those days, I was too young to understand the danger of that type of friendship. It was an innocent time."

Catherine smiled and nodded in accord. "There's something I want to ask you about," she said.

"Keep feeding me and you can ask me anything," Jimmy said brightly.

"Well, this is kind of a serious question." She hesitated, wondering if she were making a mistake, but decided to continue. "My father told me that the last summer we were here, my grandfather threw you into the pond. Do you remember that?"

"Yeah, I remember."

The matter-of-fact nature of Jimmy's response didn't square with Ben's story, so Catherine was confused. "What do you remember exactly?"

"Well, let's see… I think you and I had been playing. Probably eating Moon Pies up at Fort Apache." He smiled. "You ran back home for some reason or other. I don't remember why. Maybe to go to the bathroom or something. Anyway, I went down to the pond, and your granddaddy was there fishing in his rowboat. I decided I wanted to catch some tadpoles. Remember how we used to catch tadpoles in paper cups?"

Catherine nodded.

"Well, the cup I wanted to use blew into the pond, out of reach, and I asked your granddaddy if he could get it for me, because it wasn't too far from where he was fishing. He told me to jump in and get it myself, and I told him I couldn't swim.

"He said, 'What do you mean you can't swim? You're down here all day playing at the pond, and you can't swim?'

"I said, 'No, I can't swim.' So he asks me, 'Do you know how my daddy taught me how to swim?' I said, 'No,' and he told me that his daddy taught him to swim by just throwing him in the pond. Then he says, 'Come on, hop in the boat. I'll teach you how to swim.'"

Now Catherine was shaking her head.

"I didn't really want to get in the boat, but I was taught to mind white folks, especially your grandma and granddaddy, so I got in the boat. He said he was going to throw me in, but if I needed help, I could grab the paddle. He said he'd put the paddle in the water. Then he just tossed me into the water."

Jimmy smiled. "I was scared, and thrashing around pretty good, but I was determined not to grab the paddle. The next thing I knew, your daddy pulled me out and took me back to your house."

"So, you didn't think my grandfather was trying to drown you?" Catherine asked.

Jimmy looked surprised. "Is that what your daddy thought?"

That's what it looked like to him."

Jimmy wrinkled his forehead. "Well, I don't know. I was just a little boy, so I can't say for sure, but I didn't *think* he was trying to kill me. I thought he was trying to teach me how to swim."

಼

When Ben and Mama Rae returned from church, everyone went back to their respective chores. Jimmy and Ben were going to attempt to finish up on the porch, and Catherine and Mama Rae decided to tackle a pair of closets that contained all of her grandfather's clothes and numerous boxes filled with *'Lord only knows what all.'* Their plan was to fill the truck with items that could be delivered to the Salvation Army the following day.

Catherine thought discarding her grandfather's clothes might spur emotion in Mama Rae, but she appeared matter-of-fact, instructing Catherine to simply pile them on the bed, hangers and all. "We'll let your father take everything out to the truck later on," she told Catherine. "There's no need for you to do any heavy lifting."

Catherine removed the clothes in several large bundles, each time holding her breath against the musty old-man smell that all but rose from the clothes in waves. Mama Rae appeared oblivious and unsentimental with respect to both the articles and their essence.

Catherine was just adding the last armful of clothes to the pile when Mama Rae seemed to read her mind. "You probably think I should be crying and fussing over these clothes," she said, "but I'm too old to put on a big show. The fact is, I don't feel much more than a great sense of relief when I see these things heading for the door, and I'm not inclined to pretend I feel any different."

Catherine sat down on the bed. Mama Rae was in a faded armchair next to a window overlooking the backyard. "Were you and Granddaddy ever happy?" Catherine asked.

Mama Rae pursed her lips, and Catherine studied her face. It was weathered, and deeply lined, but she had delicate features, much like Catherine's, and it didn't take much imagination to see that she'd once been an attractive woman.

"When I married your grandfather," Mama Rae said, "I barely knew him. I was nineteen years old, and when he came courtin', all I saw was a handsome man who looked good on a horse. He seemed as good a man as any, so when he asked me to marry him, I said *fine*, and off we went to the Justice of the Peace." She fiddled with a lace handkerchief, and Catherine kept quiet, not wanting to break her train of thought.

"Of course, like any girl," she continued, "I had romantic ideas about love and marriage, and for a while, when things were new, I was hopeful. But it didn't take long to figure out that your grandfather was a selfish man. As far as he was concerned, I was more or less a servant, and mostly I didn't measure up. In the early years, I did my share of cryin' and regrettin', but over time I guess I just accepted things the way they were. I was never one to stir the pot, so I learned to just go along, and not expect too much."

She fiddled some more with the handkerchief, drawing Catherine's attention to her hands, which were frail and heavily veined. "I guess I had some happiness when your father was a boy," she added. "I had a purpose, and a life apart from your grandfather. I wasn't the greatest mother, probably, but I loved your father something fierce. Taking care of him was the most important thing in the world to me. But your grandfather spoiled everything, because, being like he was, he was jealous. He wanted to be the only center of my universe, and when he wasn't, it brought out the worst in him. He started drinking more and more, and got more and more ugly, and that was it, that was our life. He was a terrible father, and I regret that more than anything."

Mama Rae's lips trembled. "When things fell apart for good between your father and grandfather, it was wrong of me to go along, but I didn't know what else to do. My way was always to try to keep the peace, and avoid conflict, because I just couldn't stand it when your grandfather was mad."

She dabbed her eyes with the handkerchief. "I wasn't like you, Catherine—questioning things, and not going along when you think something's wrong. I admire that in you. I do. I was a coward. *A coward and a fool.* I lived practically my whole life catering to a man that I could not stand. And now, almost all I have to show for it is a pile of stinky clothes that I simply cannot wait to get rid of."

C3

It was past noon, and Catherine and Mama Rae decided it was time to take a break. Mama Rae wanted to rest, so she settled into the easy chair in the living room. Catherine went out onto the porch, where she found Jimmy working on the steps and her father replacing the light fixture by the front door. It was another hot, sticky day, and both of them were visibly sweating.

"Hey you two," Catherine said, taking a seat in the porch swing. Jimmy stood up, and Ben wiped his forehead on the shoulder of his t-shirt.

Catherine flashed a smile at Jimmy, then looked at her father. "We have a bunch of stuff ready for the Salvation Army. It's mostly piled up on Mama Rae's bed. I was going to bring it down to the truck, but Mama Rae said to let you do the heavy lifting."

"How's she doing?" Ben asked. "She okay?"

"She's a little tired, but she's fine. She's resting in the living room."

Catherine gave the swing a little push and raised her bare feet in the air. Then she turned her attention to Jimmy and they exchanged another smile. "You look like you could use a cold drink," she said. "I'm going to bring you guys something to drink, then I'll make some lunch."

Catherine went into the house and returned shortly with two large glasses of lemonade. Afterwards, she went back to the kitchen to make sandwiches. She was just finishing up when Jimmy walked in to return the glasses. His cotton shirt was wet with perspiration, and the scent of his sweat was both strong and appealing. Catherine's father often had a similar smell after mowing the lawn, or playing basketball. Catherine's mother called it 'that manly smell,' and frequently confessed to liking it. Catherine liked it now on Jimmy, and thinking about it made something inside her stir.

Jimmy took the glasses to the sink, rinsed them, and placed them in a drying rack on the counter. When he was finished, Catherine nodded at the kitchen table. "Have a seat. My dad won't mind if you keep me company while I make lunch."

"Your daddy's a fine man," Jimmy said, pulling out a chair. "I've never met anyone quite like him before. He's got a way of putting you at ease."

Catherine cut the sandwiches into triangular halves, then placed them onto four small plates. "It's probably because he's a teacher," she said. "Both my parents are teachers, and I think it gives them a special understanding of people."

"No wonder you were always wantin' to play school," Jimmy said. "It's the family business."

Catherine opened the refrigerator. "I guess you could say that." She paused for a long moment to enjoy the cool air, and was aware of Jimmy watching her with an amused look. She acknowledged him with a grin, then grabbed a jar of pickles and closed the door.

"You thinking of becoming a teacher too?" Jimmy asked.

"I haven't decided yet, but it's definitely a possibility."

She tried, without success, to open the pickle jar, then handed it over to Jimmy, who immediately popped off the top. He raised his eyebrows comically, then offered the jar back to Catherine.

She smiled and placed the pickles on the counter next to the sandwiches. "What about you? What do you plan to do?"

Jimmy's eyes met Catherine's with a look that made her heart flutter. "I don't want to make you laugh."

She was charmed by his feigned modesty. "Come on," she said, sitting down next to him. "Tell me."

"Well," he said, with a half-smile, "I'd like to become a lawyer if I can find a way to pay for all the school."

Catherine felt a rush of admiration, and an emotion resembling love, and Jimmy appeared affected as well—as though, despite making light, he'd shared something deeply felt. Catherine was eager to respond, but her father walked in and interrupted them.

"So," Ben said, looking at his daughter expectantly. "What's for lunch?"

CB

After lunch Mama Rae said she wasn't feeling well, so Catherine asked Ben to move the clothes off her bed and into the truck so that she could lie down. Catherine was worried. Mama Rae seemed listless, and refused to eat, but she insisted that it was just the heat, and that she'd be fine after some rest. When her bed was all clear, Catherine helped her lie down, then put a cool cloth on her forehead and a tall glass of water on her bedside table. She also placed an electric fan near her bed.

"That's enough fussing over me," Mama Rae snapped, making a shooing motion at Catherine. "I'm just an old lady who needs a nap, so just go on now and leave me be."

"I'm leaving," Catherine conceded, "but I'm keeping your door open, so if you need anything, just holler."

Catherine went back to the front porch and found her father out in the yard instructing Jimmy about some repairs he wanted to make to the roof. He looked up. "How's she doing?"

"I think she's probably okay, but we should keep an eye on her." Catherine sat down on the porch swing. "What are you guys up to?"

"Well," Ben said, "we were just talking about some things we want to do next week, but since it's Sunday, I'm thinking we should call it a day."

Catherine and Jimmy glanced at one another, and Catherine wondered if Jimmy knew what she was thinking. In any case, her father may have known, because after a moment, he added, "The two of you can take a walk around if you want to. I'll stay close to Mama Rae in case she needs anything."

Ben walked up the front steps and opened the screen door. Just before he disappeared inside, he instructed Catherine in a low voice, "Keep away from the road."

Catherine looked at Jimmy hopefully. "Can you stay for a while?"

Jimmy looked pleased. "I'll stay if you don't mind, but I'd like to go around back and wash up a little if that's okay."

"You can come on in the house," Catherine said. "You don't have to go around back."

"Naw, the yard'll be fine," he said. "It'll be like the old days."

Jimmy retrieved a fresh shirt from his car, then Catherine followed him around to the backyard, where the hose was attached to a sprinkler in the vegetable garden. "Here's our old friend," Catherine reported, hit suddenly with memories of the two of them frolicking in the water as children. She picked up the hose, carried it to the center of the yard, and unscrewed the sprinkler head.

Jimmy turned on the water. At first, it came out warm. When it was cool, Catherine ran water over her hands and forearms before passing the hose to Jimmy, who seemed hesitant at the prospect of taking off his shirt.

"I'll go in and get you a towel," Catherine said. She bounded for the house, but before stepping inside, she turned to see Jimmy pull off his shirt, then bend over and hold the hose over his head before rubbing water over his face, arms, and underarms. The sight slowed her progress considerably, inspiring both a smile and feelings that were becoming harder by the minute to suppress. Soon she returned with a towel, and Jimmy dried himself, then put on a clean white shirt.

"That's a little better," he said, rolling up his sleeves. "Though, in this heat, I'll be back where I started in no time."

Catherine took stock of the natural beauty all around them. "It's so pretty here," she said, "but I don't know how people can stand the humidity."

"I guess you get used to it," Jimmy said, looking striking under the canopy of blue sky. "But I sure don't miss it."

Moments later, they crossed the yard and passed through a gate to the pasture, which was overgrown with green weeds and wildflowers. There was an antique barn to their left, and a grove of trees to the right. Catherine recalled that a trail through the trees provided a back route to the pond. At present, the heat drove them in the direction of the barn, where they hoped it might be cooler.

Jimmy opened the barn door, and he and Catherine stepped inside to find a dim interior streaked with narrow beams of sunlight. "Wow," Catherine whispered, entering what looked and felt like a dream.

The barn was mostly empty, but an old car was parked in one corner, and two dilapidated stalls and various horse-related relics were a reminder that horses had once been kept there. The air had an earthy smell that Catherine found pleasant, and floating all around them were particles of shimmering dust.

Catherine began moving her hands in and out of the beams of light. "Feels kind of magical, doesn't it?"

"Yes it does," Jimmy agreed, his face alternately dark and illuminated as he moved slowly through the glimmering rays.

Catherine looked at Jimmy, so handsome in the enchanted surroundings, and was suddenly filled with affection. She had adored him as a child, and now, it was as if all the love and sweetness she'd felt towards him then were reconstituted. She knew that what she was feeling wasn't sensible, given the circumstances, but what she mostly felt was a strong desire to be close to him.

Catherine walked over to the horse stalls, enjoying the sensation of the sun's rays as she passed in and out of the light. Jimmy followed her, and then, like a cat, hiked himself up onto one of the dividers.

"That was impressive!" Catherine cried at Jimmy's sudden feat of agility.

"Yeah, well let's just hope this thing'll hold me," Jimmy said, wobbling to keep his balance. "I don't think you'll be too impressed if I come crashing down on my behind."

Catherine was smiling so hard that her face was beginning to hurt, and Jimmy was grinning right back. A silence fell between them, and Catherine was tempted to look away, but she decided to be bold and simply keep smiling. It was Jimmy who finally broke the spell. "Do you still like climbing trees?"

Catherine chuckled at the memories that suddenly came to mind. "My tree climbing days are pretty much over," she reported. "I fell out of a tree and broke my arm when I was twelve, and that more or less ended my tree climbing career."

"If we have the chance, we should see if we can find that big old tree we used to climb," Jimmy said. "Remember when we stole your granddaddy's cigarettes and went up there and smoked?"

"Oh my God, I do remember that. What a couple of imps we were!"

Jimmy's grin widened. "I'm pretty sure it was your idea. You were the mastermind behind most of the questionable things we did."

"Well, I remember you having a few ideas yourself," Catherine said. She thought for a moment, then laughed out loud.

Jimmy laughed back. "What?" He was smiling so luminously that Catherine made a mental note to remember his face just at that moment. He was positively glowing, sending her feelings for him into the stratosphere.

"Come on," Jimmy pressed, "*What?*"

"This is a really bad one," Catherine said, shaking her head. "Do you remember making a 'milkshake' out of milk and mud and grass and sticks and worms—and I don't know what else—and trying to get your sisters to drink it?"

Jimmy began laughing so hard that he almost fell off his perch, and Catherine became all but hysterical. "I can't believe we did that!" she cried.

"I'm pretty sure that was your idea too," Jimmy said with raised eyebrows when he finally stopped laughing.

"For sure the worms were you," Catherine countered. "You know how I was about worms."

Jimmy hopped down, and they continued communing in the sun-streaked barn, sharing more laughter, and unearthing other long-forgotten memories. Catherine had the strong impulse to take Jimmy's hand, but she resisted, hoping he might initiate contact. She also fantasized about kissing him, and wondered if he were thinking the same thing. Her instincts told her that he was feeling what she was feeling, but she understood why he'd probably resist moving their relationship in that direction. It made her both sad and angry that their attraction was out of bounds, even dangerous, but she tried to push those feelings from her mind and focus on the magic of the moment. And it really did feel magical. On impulse, she asked him, "Do you have a girl back in Oberlin?"

Seeming suddenly nervous, Jimmy put his hands in his pockets and looked at his feet. Catherine instantly regretted asking the question. "I'm sorry," she said. "I shouldn't be so nosy."

"No, it's fine," Jimmy said, now looking at Catherine. "There is a girl back at school. *Sort of.*"

Catherine felt a surge of adrenaline. She tried her best to be unaffected, but she was betrayed by a knot in her throat, and her face was suddenly hot. "That's nice," she said, willing herself to sound normal. She knew she probably didn't, and cursed herself for being so silly, and so emotional.

Jimmy remained still, as though he didn't know what to say. Uncomfortable with the silence, and deciding to come clean, Catherine added, "I guess I'm a little jealous."

Jimmy looked at her with a quizzical smile. Then, seeming uncertain, he asked, "Are you really jealous?"

Catherine was embarrassed, and now she was the one looking at her feet. Jimmy touched her shoulder and she looked up. It was the first time he'd touched her since shaking her hand that first day in the garden.

"Catherine," Jimmy said, looking into her eyes. "I've taken a girl to the movies a few times, but there's not much more to it."

His face changed, and he suddenly looked sad. "To tell you the truth, I know there's no point, but you're all I've been thinking about since you got here."

Catherine's knees went weak, and as much as she tried to hold back, her eyes filled with tears.

"I'm not exactly sure what's going on in your head right now," Jimmy said, "but what's going on in mine is I've been wantin' to kiss you since about the first minute I saw you in your grandma's backyard. And I know it's a bad idea. Aside from the fact that we'll both be going back to school in a couple of weeks, there's people who would kill me for even thinking this way."

Catherine stepped closer to Jimmy and reached for his hand. Then, in what felt like a scene right out of a fairy tale, they kissed in the middle of all that magical light. And they kept kissing, and talking, and touching, until the sunbeams were gone, and they knew it was past time to get back.

Chapter 5

That night Catherine found it almost impossible to sleep. After returning from the barn, she'd somehow managed to behave casually, telling her father that she and Jimmy had enjoyed their opportunity to share old memories, and talk about college. Mama Rae was feeling better, so the three of them watched the news on TV, then ate left-overs that Mama Rae had insisted on preparing. They had a second night of ice cream on the porch, and fireflies, but Catherine was anxious to be alone, so she told her father and Mama Rae that she was exhausted, *probably from the heat*, and went off to her room early. But she hadn't wanted to sleep. All she'd wanted was to mentally re-play her experience that afternoon with Jimmy. And that's what she did. She ran it again and again like a movie, not wanting to forget a single word or touch. But eventually her thoughts turned to the impossible nature of their situation, and especially to the danger their attraction posed to Jimmy.

The news she'd watched on TV that night had included a story about Emmett Till, the fourteen-year-old Chicago boy who had been murdered and beaten beyond recognition for making a remark to a white woman in Mississippi. Catherine had sought refuge in the bathroom at the first mention of his name, because her heart began racing, and her face was heating up. She knew what she and Jimmy were risking, and about all the lynchings and violence that blacks suffered in the South. Her father, himself, had borne witness to violence on more than one occasion. He'd once seen a black man pulled from his car and savagely beaten for honking his horn at a white man.

Her grandfather had laughed about it, and called the man an "uppity nigger" for having the temerity to be driving a new car. It was one of the most traumatic events of her father's childhood, and one of the major contributors to his desire to leave the South.

What would her father think of her, Catherine wondered, if he knew that she might be placing Jimmy's life in jeopardy? And what would Sally think? Catherine knew that she and Jimmy were probably being reckless, but she also knew that it was wrong that they should have to be afraid. And for what crime? For having a natural attraction to one another? It was a sobering insight into what life was like for black people in the South who lived *every day* with injustice, humiliation, and fear.

Catherine wrestled with her thoughts and emotions all night long, feeling as though all the sins of her race had come to rest squarely on her shoulders. She had spent her whole life hearing from her father about crimes and cruelties that seemed never to let him rest. It was part of his fabric, and it was part of her fabric too. She had no doubt that her feelings about the South made her feelings for Jimmy more poignant. Her attraction to him felt natural, but also profound—like she were part of healing some centuries-old wound. She wondered how it felt on Jimmy's side of things, and she kept wondering, and worrying, and replaying until the rooster started crowing, and it was time for another day.

ଔ

Catherine was in the kitchen drinking coffee when both Jimmy and Sally arrived the next morning—Sally ready to fix a big Southern breakfast, and Jimmy ready to start work. Catherine and Jimmy were just greeting each other, trying to subdue their enthusiasm, when Ben walked into the kitchen, said

Good Morning to everyone, and then whisked Jimmy back outside to talk about the roof.

"Your daddy is a good man," Sally remarked, putting on her apron. "We could use more like him around here."

Mama Rae came in and sat down at the table, still in her robe and slippers.

"Ain't that right, Mama Rae?" Sally continued. "Your son is a good man, and I know you're proud of him."

"I am proud of him," Mama Rae said. "And I'm proud of this one, too," she added, taking Catherine's hand and giving it a squeeze.

"How are you feeling this morning, Mama Rae?" Catherine asked. "Did you sleep all right?"

Mama Rae pulled back her hand and waved it dismissively. "I'm not a great sleeper, but it's nothing to fret about. When you get this old, life is pretty much one big downhill slide, and sleep is no different." She picked up a cup that Sally placed in front of her. "Being an old lady is not for the faint of heart. You'll see someday."

Mama Rae went off to get dressed, and Catherine set the table and helped Sally make breakfast. Soon the kitchen sideboard was covered with platters of scrambled eggs, buttered grits, fried ham and bacon, sliced melon, and buttermilk biscuits.

Catherine went outside and found her father on a ladder and Jimmy up on the roof. "It's time to eat," she called.

When she returned to the kitchen Sally was regarding the kitchen table with a look of concern. "I know you mean well, Catherine," she said, "but you got too many places set at this table. I ain't here to eat, I'm here to cook. And I'm not sure Mama Rae is ready to sit down with Jimmy, neither." She raised her eyebrows. "I know it may be different in California, but around here, white folks don't eat with colored folks."

Catherine was considering how to respond when Mama Rae walked in. "Sally," she said, coolly, "It'll be just fine if you and Jimmy want to help us eat some of this feast you and Catherine have prepared."

Catherine and Sally were exchanging a look of surprise when Jimmy walked in and lit the room with his smile. "Good morning, ma'am," he said, turning his attention to Mama Rae.

"Good morning, young man," she replied, matter-of-factly. "Now go on over and load up a plate before all this food gets cold."

∞

Much to everyone's delight and relief, breakfast went smoothly, with none of the awkwardness that might have been predicted. Ben set an easy tone, first complimenting Sally and Catherine on the food, then moving on to praise Jimmy for his great work and good nature, making Sally positively glow with pride. In no time they were all eating and conversing like the old friends and family that they were. Mama Rae mostly listened, but she seemed pleased to be in everyone's company, and Catherine caught her looking at Jimmy once or twice with a look of subdued astonishment, if not respect. She'd spent a lifetime being schooled on the inferiority of blacks, and this articulate young man, answering questions about his college courses and aspirations for the future, did not fit the picture. More than once while Jimmy was talking, Catherine and her father exchanged looks, each knowing what the other was thinking. This was a new experience for Mama Rae, and by all appearances, she was embracing it.

Catherine and Jimmy mostly behaved themselves, trying hard not to look at each other too long, or smile too much. At one point Catherine engaged Jimmy in a little under-the-table foot-play, but Jimmy eventually shut it down, which was just as well, because Catherine's heart began speeding up, and she was in imminent danger of blushing.

When breakfast was finished, Catherine and Ben headed for the truck, needing to do some shopping and make a run to the Salvation Army. Jimmy was just starting to climb back onto the roof when Catherine managed to catch his eye and shoot him a smile. They'd had a hard time all morning finding a moment alone, but they did finally manage to talk, and they agreed that, no matter what, they'd find an excuse to get away again. It was clear to Catherine that Jimmy shared her fears, but they were convinced that they could find a safe way to meet. They would simply need to stay close to home and out of sight.

Now in the truck and headed up the road towards town, Catherine commented on Mama Rae's seeming conversion. "Not more than forty-eight hours ago, when we were talking about Jimmy, Mama Rae told me that her *views and beliefs* weren't going to change. But this morning I think she did all right. More than all right, actually."

"I agree," Ben said. "I've been talking to her a lot since I've been here, and we've had some pretty serious discussions. Maybe things are finally starting to sink in."

Catherine rolled down her window. "Yesterday she basically told me that she hated your father. Maybe now that he's gone, she'll blossom into a whole different person."

"Well, that's a little optimistic," Ben said with a smile, "but breakfast was definitely a good sign. It was one of Mama Rae's finest hours, and I think she knew it."

They passed the pond, and the smell of the air and warm wind blowing in through the open window gave Catherine a feeling of deep contentment. She closed her eyes and was once again transported back to the barn.

Ben brought her back. "That Jimmy is quite an impressive young man. I've been enjoying the chance to get to know him a little bit. Did he tell you about his scholarship?"

"No," Catherine said, her interest piqued. "But I was wondering how he was paying for college. They can't have much money."

"It seems that he was such a good student, one of his teachers encouraged him to enter a writing competition for a scholarship, and he got it. I mentioned it to Mama Rae, and she said there'd been a story about it in the newspaper."

Catherine tried her best to convey just the right level of enthusiasm. "I sure like seeing him doing so well," she said. "I have a feeling he's going to do great things."

"It wouldn't surprise me," Ben said. "He's a fine young man."

They were getting close to town when Catherine noticed a sheriff's car parked off the road behind a faded billboard for the Glory of God Baptist Church. She nodded at the car. "I wonder if that's your old buddy's speed trap."

"I don't want to find out," Ben said, checking his speed.

"Do you think he'd remember you?"

Ben glanced up at the rearview mirror. "I'd be surprised if he didn't. I had a reputation for being what you might call a *non-conformist*. I kept to myself a lot, and didn't go along with a lot of things, as you know, so it made me a target for bullies, and he was definitely a bully."

"Did he ever beat you up, or anything like that?"

"No, but I had a couple of run-ins with him over the years. Nothing he'd necessarily remember, but I'd rather not meet up with him again if I can help it. Especially now that he's armed." He shook his head and grimaced at the thought.

In another minute they turned off the highway, then drove through town before turning onto a dusty street that Catherine didn't recognize. They were passing into the "colored" part of town, characterized by streets with no sidewalks, dilapidated shops and churches, and tiny rough-hewn houses. At one point they passed a weary looking clapboard structure surrounded by a low chain link fence that appeared to be an elementary school. Scores of children running and playing in the yard belied the meager surroundings, and Catherine couldn't help but be struck by the irony of the time-worn signboard out front that read, in faded block letters, *Bethlehem Colored Academy: Shaping Bright Futures*.

Shortly, they came to the Salvation Army, which was a shabby cinder-block building surrounded by a large dirt and gravel parking lot. A sign instructed them to drive around to the back. There, they were met by a young black man who directed them to park beside some large bins near an open back door. Two old men in overalls were sitting in kitchen chairs near the door playing checkers on a stack of wooden crates. Three small barefoot children played under some trees nearby.

Ben parked as directed, then got out of the truck as the young man stepped up. "Good morning," Ben said. "I've got some old clothes and a few boxes of odds and ends we'd like to give you, if that's all right."

"Yes sir," the young man said. "That'll be all right."

Catherine wanted to give the man a friendly acknowledgement, but he avoided looking at her and quickly got to work removing items from the back of the truck. Ben started to assist, but was waved off by a second man who emerged from inside the building to help.

Catherine looked at the second man, then over to the men playing checkers, hoping to offer someone a smile or gesture, but they all appeared oblivious. She turned her attention to the children, two little boys and a girl who looked to be around four or five years old. They had sweet faces and bright eyes, and Catherine was fascinated by the little girl's hair, which was pulled into scores of tiny braids fixed with multi-colored barrettes. She was just wondering if anything among the items they were delivering might be of interest to the children when another truck sped around the corner and stopped abruptly with a flurry of flying gravel.

"Hey! Boy!" hollered an angry voice from the truck. "Come unload this junk my wife put together for y'all. I don't have time to wait around, I got things to do!"

The men playing checkers showed little ostensible notice, and the children looked up briefly, then turned back to their play. Catherine burned with anger, and she knew that her father was feeling the same way. The young men were just removing the last box of items from their truck when the man roared again, *"Hey! I'm talking to you, boy! Don't you dare ignore me!"*

The workmen seemed determined neither to react, nor rush to his bidding. Finally, after more yelling and some ugly name-calling, one of the men walked over and started pulling bags from the roughneck's truck. The other approached Ben.

"I'm truly sorry about that," Ben said, motioning towards the menace, who was now shouting another harsh directive. "You shouldn't have to put up with that kind of treatment."

The young man nodded, and Ben extended his hand. After a moment's hesitation, the man shook it. Then, before turning to go, he finally glanced into the truck at Catherine. She wanted mightily to communicate how much shame and anger she felt at seeing him treated so despicably, but all she could do was offer a smile, trying, with a single look, to acknowledge his humanity.

"That was unbelievable!" Catherine cried as they drove off. "What a jackass!"

Ben shook his head. "I don't know what to tell you, except some people around here are just raised to hate. I don't know how the Negroes manage to take it. I guess they're just conditioned, early on, not to react, because if they do, the white man will always win. Everything is stacked in their favor." He looked at Catherine with pain in his eyes. "People like that sad excuse for a man have total power to say and do whatever they want."

ʚ

Soon Catherine and Ben arrived at their next destination, which was the hardware store that Catherine remembered so fondly. Unfortunately, both the train and its owner were history. Catherine was reading a framed newspaper memorial near the store's entrance when someone walked up and poked her in the side.

"Hey there, California," said a familiar voice.

Catherine turned her head to see JT, whom she immediately recognized from the pond. In addition to a wide grin, he was wearing a name tag that identified him as an employee of the store. She was startled by the poke and dismayed by its source, but she was determined to be polite. "Hello," she said. "It's JT, right?"

"That's me," he replied, clearly pleased to be remembered. "I don't think I got your name."

Catherine was reluctant, but saw no alternative to answering. "It's Catherine," she said.

She turned back to the newspaper, which included a photo of the old man with his hand on the train, which, according to the story, he'd called *Old Bessie*. "My father used to bring me here when I was little," she said. "I'm sorry the train's not here anymore, and sad to learn the old man died."

"Yeah, all the kids loved that old guy and his train," JT said. "When he died, his son sold the store, but he wouldn't let go of the train. And it's too bad, 'cause it was a big draw." He stepped closer. "We get people coming in all the time looking for that train, but most ain't as pretty as you."

Catherine was stepping back when her father walked up. "Hey," she said, happy to be rescued. "You remember JT from the pond?"

Ben glanced at JT's name tag. "Small world."

JT shot Catherine a toothy smile. "Small town, you mean." He turned back to Ben. "Did you find everything you were looking for?"

"Mostly," Ben said, lifting a bag filled with items he'd purchased. "But I put a few things on order. I'll come back later in the week to pick them up." He gave JT a quick smile, then ushered Catherine towards the door as she half-heartedly raised her hand in a good-bye gesture.

"Well, I hope you both come back," JT called after them. "I'll be lookin' out for y'all."

Back in the car, Catherine shook her head and had to laugh as Ben pulled away from the curb. "What were the odds?"

"That's life in a small town."

"Well, needless to say, I'll be letting you come back here on your own."

"Catherine the heart breaker," Ben teased. "Turning heads wherever she goes."

"Well, that's one head I'd rather not turn," Catherine remarked with a chuckle. Then she turned her thoughts to their next errand, which was to pick up some groceries—including and especially, she hoped, some Moon Pies.

附

When Catherine and Ben got back to the farm, Jimmy was just coming around from the back, where he'd obviously been cleaning himself up, because he was wearing a fresh shirt. "I think everything is patched up pretty good now, sir," he reported. "I replaced the rotten shingles, and I think I fixed the leaks." He glanced at Catherine, who was holding a bag of groceries and wearing an impish smile. "I guess we won't know for sure about the leaks until the next time it rains," he continued, "but I think I got everything all right."

"Good job," Ben remarked brightly, patting Jimmy on the back. "I didn't think you'd finish so quickly."

"Well, it wasn't that bad," Jimmy said. "But I left the ladder up in case you want to go up and take a look around."

Ben shook his head. "That's all right. I trust your judgment better than mine."

Catherine looked at her father expectantly. "I think Jimmy's earned a break, don't you?"

"Absolutely," Ben said.

Mama Rae appeared at the screen door. "Well, it looks like the troops have returned." She opened the door and stepped out onto the porch. "Can I get y'all something cold to drink?"

"No, you sit down right here, Mama Rae," Catherine said, pointing to the porch swing. "I'll bring you a drink and maybe think about fixing everyone some lunch."

Mama Rae obediently headed for the swing. "Catherine, I don't need a thing," she said, lowering herself cautiously onto the sun-bleached seat.

"I don't need anything, either," Ben said, heading inside. "I'm still full from breakfast. But I am going to go splash some water on myself and change my shirt. This humidity's killing me. Afterwards, I'm going to help Mama Rae fill out some insurance forms."

"By the way, sir," Jimmy called after Ben. "My mama's gone home, but she said to tell you that if you need her for anything, she can come back."

Ben waved his hand. "We're all set here."

Catherine turned to Jimmy. "Are you hungry?"

"Naw, I'm fine," he said. "But some water might be nice if you don't mind."

Catherine gave Jimmy a look of enthusiasm. "Of course I don't mind. Come on inside. I have something else for you too. A surprise."

Catherine turned to Mama Rae to see if she would react, but she appeared oblivious. "You kids go on," she said, noticing Catherine looking at her. "I'm just gonna sit right here and enjoy the peace."

"All right, Mama Rae," Catherine said. "But you just holler if you need anything."

Catherine contemplated her grandmother, dainty in a cotton dress and terrycloth slippers, and was impressed by her seeming state of serenity. *She's not looking for trouble,* she thought. *She simply wants to enjoy her new-found freedom from tyranny.* She opened the screen door, and Ben reappeared.

"Why don't you go ahead and take the ladder back to the barn," he said to Jimmy. "I don't think we'll need it anymore today."

"Be happy to, sir," Jimmy answered. Then he grabbed the ladder and started off in the direction of the barn, turning to give Catherine a quick look over his shoulder as he went.

A few minutes later, he joined Catherine in the kitchen. He was just stepping in close, looking around to make sure they were alone, when Catherine placed something in his hand. He chuckled when he realized it was a Moon Pie. "I'll get to this in a minute," he said, putting it down on the table. He looked towards the kitchen door, then steered Catherine to a spot in the kitchen where they weren't visible through the window. Pipes squealed at the back of the house, signaling that Ben was in the bathroom. "This okay?" Jimmy whispered, searching Catherine's face for permission to kiss her.

"Yes please," she replied, feeling a rush of desire.

∽

When Ben was finished cleaning himself up, he entered the kitchen, where Catherine was rinsing a glass, and Jimmy was sitting at the table, unwrapping a Moon Pie. Catherine's heart was racing and her emotions were high, but she tried to appear normal. Jimmy looked calm, though he and Catherine had been kissing only seconds before.

"I see you got your Moon Pie," Ben said cheerfully. "I thought Catherine was going to do a cartwheel right in the store when she found those."

Catherine blushed. "He's exaggerating, but only slightly."

Jimmy grinned. "I haven't had one of these in years." He closed his eyes and took a bite. "*Mmmm...delicious*. Just as good as they were back then." He shot a quick look at Catherine, then swallowed and turned to Ben. "Is there anything else you'd like for me to do today?"

Catherine tried to seem disinterested, but she was holding her breath, praying that her father would let Jimmy go.

"Well, there are a couple of other small projects that I'd like you to help me with, if you want to," Ben said, "but some of the materials we need are on order and won't arrive for a day or two." He thought for a moment. "There's something that maybe the two of you can work on together, if you want to."

Catherine was heartened, but remained stoic, forcing herself not to look at Jimmy.

"I took a walk through the woods a few days ago," Ben continued. "You remember that old trail that leads to the back part of the pond?"

Both Catherine and Jimmy nodded.

"Well, there's litter and soda bottles all over the place from years of kids running around back there. Maybe you two can take a walk around with a couple of big bags and clean things up a little. That's our property, and it bothers me to see it looking like a garbage dump."

Catherine was ecstatic. "We can do that," she said, trying to sound matter-of-fact.

Jimmy looked at Catherine with a hint of a smile, then said to Ben, "That'd be fine, sir."

"Great," Ben said. "You can get started whenever you want. I'm going to go on out now and see if Mama Rae's ready for me to help her with her paperwork."

Catherine and Jimmy wasted no time. No more than two minutes later, they were headed across the pasture in the direction of the trees and the old path to the pond. At first, they kept their distance from one another, but as soon as they entered the grove, and were certain they were alone, they came together like magnets.

They kissed with sweaty abandon, then finally paused to look at one another. Catherine was breathless, and aware of her body as never before. She was exhilarated, but also a little frightened by the intensity of her feelings. She'd been with other boys, but never felt such an overpowering physical and emotional reaction.

Jimmy smoothed back a loose strand of her hair. "I don't know about you, but since yesterday, I feel like I don't know if I'm coming or going." He smiled and shook his head. "I probably couldn't even tell you my name right now." He studied Catherine's face. "You're something," he said. "I do know this is crazy, though."

Catherine was brimming with so many emotions that she was uncertain how to respond. "I know it's crazy," she said finally. "But I also know that I've never felt like this before."

"I've been thinking and thinking about this," Jimmy said, "and no matter which way you look at it, it's hard to see how things can work out for us. Even if you put all the obvious problems aside—and there are some big problems—in less than two weeks, I'll be in Ohio and you'll be in California. And we both have at least two years of school ahead of us."

Catherine gazed at Jimmy, so handsome in the muted light of the rustling trees. "What are you saying?" she asked. "Are you saying that we should stop?"

"Well, I can't really say I want to stop," Jimmy chuckled. "I'm not sayin' that. But I think we need to think this through."

He sighed, then took Catherine's hand and thought for a moment. "I'd like to spend as much time with you as I can," he said, "but I think we need to be realistic about the future."

Catherine was uncertain what to say. She'd begun fantasizing about following Jimmy back to Ohio, but she knew she was probably romanticizing what would be a hard reality, even in the North. And it would be Jimmy who would risk the most. Would it be fair for her to ask him to make that kind of sacrifice? Why should he upend his life, with all its promise, for her?

Jimmy appeared to sense her conflict. "I could easily fall in love with you, Catherine. I may be there already. But I think we both know that, even outside of the South, a couple like us would face a lot of opposition. I don't want to do that to you, and, to be honest, I don't know if I want it for myself." His face took on a pained expression. "As strong as we might feel right now, I think we'll both be better off if we don't get too carried away."

Catherine fought back tears. It's not what she wanted to hear, but she understood, and knew his misgivings were sensible. She asked, with no malice, "So are you saying that after this summer we should try to forget each other?"

"I could never forget you," Jimmy said earnestly. "But, for now at least, I think we need to think of this as a special time that we'll always remember, but be ready to let it go when the time comes. I'm not saying it'll be easy, but nothin' else makes sense."

Catherine looked down, embarrassed by the force of her emotions. Jimmy lifted her chin and looked into her eyes. "I know this feels really strong, and really romantic, like we're some kind of black and white Romeo and Juliet."

Catherine gave a chuckle of recognition, because that's exactly how it felt.

"You'll always be my Juliet," Jimmy said tenderly. "But, in reality, this thing between us is more dangerous than romantic once you take it out of the shadows. Out of the shadows, things could get really ugly."

Catherine knew Jimmy was right, but it hurt. "Okay," she said, trying to smile. "This will be our special time."

They kissed some more, this time with a heightened sense of urgency. Eventually, they reluctantly detached and set about filling their bags with bottles, wrappers, and other types of refuse that were strewn here and there throughout the trees. The physical separation it required gave them the opportunity to think, and talk, and Catherine felt an ease with Jimmy that she attributed to their closeness as children. "Do you think our attraction to each other has mostly to do with when we were kids?" she asked, thinking out loud. "Because I know it sounds strange, given how many years we've been separated, but I feel like I've known you my whole life."

"I know what you mean," Jimmy said. "I feel like that too. But besides that..." He paused. "I don't know, there's just something about you. An openness, I guess, and a sweetness." His expression brightened to a grin. "You're pretty hard to resist."

Catherine looked at Jimmy, lean and beautiful in his moist t-shirt, and she felt suddenly overcome with thoughts and feelings that were all mixed up. She decided to open the floodgates and see what would come out. "There are so many things I want to tell you, and ask you," she said, throwing her sack by a tree, then sitting down next to it.

Jimmy joined her under the tree. "Go ahead," he said. "I'm listening."

Catherine looked up at the sun sparkling through lush leaves and branches and felt a rush of love for the beauty that surrounded them. Then she looked back at Jimmy, with his dark eyes and radiant smile, and wanted so much for him to know her thoughts, and understand her longing to love him.

"I don't know how this is going to sound to you," she said, "but it's hard for me to separate my affection for you from the pain and shame that I feel when I see how you've had to live because of the ignorance of white people. It's like all my feelings about things are mixed up together, and it's so strong that it's almost overwhelming."

She paused, trying to make sense of what she was feeling. Uncertain how to put words to her thoughts, she turned her attention to his side of the equation. "How does this feel on your side?" she asked. "And how have you managed to live among people who treat you so terribly and not go crazy?"

She shook her head. "I know the kind of humiliation you're forced to live with. How have you managed to survive it without going crazy with bitterness? How have you become so good?"

Jimmy was silent, and Catherine apologized. "I'm sorry," she said. "I'm turning something really nice into something awful."

"No, it's fine," Jimmy said. "You don't have to be sorry. I can talk about it."

He stretched his long legs out in front of him and thought for a moment. "I think maybe I've managed," he said, "because early on I decided not to let white people define me, or make me feel bad about myself. I realized that they could hurt me the most by making me hate myself, so I just decided not to let them do that to me."

He thought some more, and then went on. "I've been called names, and humiliated. I've been threatened. Like all Negroes in the South, I've been subjected to endless indignities and injustices." He raised his eyebrows. "I even got beat once pretty good." He shook his head. "It's hard not to react in a way that'll get you hurt, or killed, but you learn not to react as a matter of simple survival."

He looked down. "I haven't always been so good at that, I guess. *It's hard.* But whatever happened, I never let anyone touch me inside. And I simply refused to be broken. I always had self-respect, and I have my mama and a couple of teachers in particular to thank for that. They taught me not to limit myself based on the stupidity of ignorant white folks. They also encouraged me to read books, and I think that reading and understanding the power of books has probably helped me more than anything."

He paused again, and Catherine could see that he was filling up with emotion. "This life here does do a lot of damage to black folks," he said. "Some get so beat down, they end up tailoring their aspirations to the limitations imposed on them by whites, and believing that they're less than whites. It's the worst thing about the life here. Some people are ruined by all that hate. Fortunately, I was never like that. To survive, I kept my head down when I had to, but I never doubted that I would make something of myself." He looked down at his hands. "I'm not so special. Lots of black folks are getting out of the South, trying to make decent lives for themselves."

He picked up a leaf and twirled it. "It's no paradise for Negroes in the North. They don't have the Jim Crow laws like here, but there are lots of ways that whites keep black folks down. *Lots of ways.* You should hear my brother George talk about tryin' to find a decent place to live in Chicago. In cities like Chicago and Detroit and New York, Negroes are crammed into certain areas like sardines, because white folks won't let 'em live most places, even if they have the money. But it's better there than here. At least there a man has a fightin' chance."

"What about my other question?" Catherine asked. "What's it like for you to have feelings for me? It has to be, I don't know... I can't even say what I'm thinking. I feel like a terrible person for putting you in this position."

"You're not a terrible person," Jimmy assured. "And I understand why your feelings about me are mixed up with other stuff. In a way, our attraction is profound, because love is nature's way of solving the great racial divide. The fear of *this right here* is why black men are punished so severely for even looking at white women. The white man figures that if they let nature take its course, people will inevitably fall in love, and intermarry, and white men simply cannot stand the idea of their women being with black men."

He took Catherine's hand and caressed it. "I think the fear of interracial love is one of the most basic reasons that whites try so hard to keep Negroes poor, and under-educated. They figure that if we're allowed to live and work on an equal footing, eventually the races will blend. But just like I refuse to let whites make me hate myself or feel inferior, I refuse to let 'em tell me who I can and cannot love."

"But what about what you said before?" Catherine asked. "You said that you didn't want the kinds of problems that a relationship like ours would cause."

Jimmy sighed, then lay back and looked up at the sky through the trees. "I did say that," he said, "but I don't like saying it, and I'm not a hundred percent sure I mean it." He sat back up. "To be honest, I don't know what to say about all this."

He leaned over and kissed Catherine. "For now, how about we enjoy today and worry about everything else when the time comes?"

Catherine agreed, and after a few more sweaty kisses, they reluctantly resumed their clean-up, but with the motivation of working their way as quickly as possible to the pond, where they could cool off. They knew that the pond was a dangerous place to be seen together, but there was a part that was not visible from the road. They felt that they'd be safe there for at least long enough to splash some water on themselves. If a car drove up, they figured they'd hear it, and it was unlikely that anyone would approach the pond on foot. In any case, it was hot, and humid, and their motivation to find some relief was strong, as were their sentiments towards the place where they'd spent so many happy hours together as children.

As they neared the pond, they were on the lookout for remnants of their old "Fort Apache." Between the two of them, they did manage to find some dilapidated playing cards, a squirt gun that Catherine thought she remembered, and some moss-covered two-by-fours that were probably part of its ruins, but those were the only signs of the shelter they'd erected and enjoyed more than a decade earlier.

When they finally reached the pond, they were pleased to discover that their memories were correct. There was a sizable area where they would be out of view should anyone approach from the other side. Giddy with delight, Catherine quickly took off her sandals and rolled up her shorts. Jimmy removed his shirt and shoes, then rolled his long pants up above his knees. Soon they were ankle deep in mud, splashing cool water over their exposed parts. In short order they began discussing the pros and cons of jumping in, clothes and all.

"I don't think my clothes would take that long to dry," Catherine said, looking down at her shorts and light cotton top. "But I don't know about your pants. How do you feel about swimming in your underwear?"

Jimmy looked doubtful. "I don't know," he said. "Just being caught with you here would be enough to get me killed. Being caught with you in my underwear would probably get me *tortured* and killed." He laughed nervously.

"That's not funny," Catherine responded. "But it's decided. You're keeping the pants on."

A moment later, she plunged forward, immersing everything but her head in the cool water. Jimmy hesitated, looked around to make sure they were alone, and then he, too, dove in, disappearing under the water for several seconds before reappearing several yards away.

"It looks like you finally learned to swim," Catherine said, swimming to where Jimmy popped up.

She initially resisted the urge to attach herself to him, but they eventually came together in an underwater tangle of arms and legs that brought their physical intimacy to a whole new level. Catherine's light clothing clung to her body, leaving little to the imagination, but she felt no modesty, which surprised her as much as she imagined it surprised Jimmy. He did not touch her in sensitive places, but she wanted him to, and it made her desire him so forcefully that she knew she'd make love to him, given the chance. "Jimmy," she whispered. "I think you'd be shocked if you knew what I was thinking."

"I think you'd slap me if you knew what I was thinking," he laughed.

"No chance," Catherine said. She wrapped her legs around his waist and kissed him deeply. They were just entering unknown territory when they were startled into sobriety by the sound of a car on the other side of the pond. They looked at each other in a shared state of terror, then quickly but quietly went about exiting the pond, gathering up their things, and moving as silently as possible away from the water and back into the trees.

As they were scurrying to safety, they heard the doors of a vehicle open and close, voices talking and laughing, and then the sound of bodies hitting the water as the interlopers dove into the pond. As Catherine and Jimmy disappeared, barefoot and half clothed into the woods, they knew that it might be seconds before they were in view of the swimmers. Terrified that their movements would be perceived if they continued running, they stopped and lay down behind a mound of debris piled up against an overturned tree. They were a fair distance from the edge of the pond, but, given the light and the density of the trees, they knew they might be detected should the swimmers be alerted by any sound or activity.

"I'm so sorry," Catherine whispered, her heart racing. She felt as if all her worst fears were coming true, and she hated herself for behaving so recklessly. Jimmy gave her a look of sympathy and understanding, but put his finger to his lips as a sign to be silent.

Catherine peeked over the mound and could see the bois- terous swimmers, who were now in full view, splashing and carrying on like children. There were two of them, and Cathe- rine thought one might be JT's friend Teddy. The other she didn't recognize.

"I think we're okay for now," Jimmy whispered. "But we might be in trouble if they decide to swim over to the pier."

Catherine was afraid to breathe, and her heart was beating so hard that her chest hurt. Her wet clothes still clung to her body, but they were now covered with dirt. Jimmy was shirt- less, and his pants were equally coated with debris. They were both shoeless. They had grabbed their things before running for the trees, but as Catherine assessed the items lying beside them now, she realized with horror that she was missing one of her sandals. They had also not taken their bags of litter. Those were still leaning against a tree by the shore where they'd left them. Catherine prayed that the bags would not be noticed and inspire curiosity, and she worried especially about the interest that might be generated if her lost sandal were spotted. She closed her eyes and began silently whispering, *"Please God, please God, please God, please God..."*

Minutes passed, and the swimmers did eventually make it over to the pier. Catherine and Jimmy looked at each other with a sense of helplessness. They realized, with some relief, that they were still out of view, but they were now much closer to their visitors, and they knew that if, for whatever reason, the boys should decide to venture into the trees, they would surely be discovered. They also knew that in their new proximity, the boys were more likely to notice the bags of litter, or Catherine's sandal. Catherine buried her face into Jimmy's chest and continued praying: *"Please God, please God, please God..."*

The boys were laughing and clowning, and Catherine tried to calm herself with the thought that their ruckus made them unlikely to be tuned in to anything but their own antics, but her fear continued unabated. Finally, after what felt like forever, the boys dove back into the water, and it appeared as though they were swimming back across the pond in the direction of the road.

After another couple of minutes it became clear that Catherine and Jimmy were probably safe, but they didn't move until they heard car doors slam and an engine start. At that point Catherine broke down, and it took her some time before she was relatively calm. Jimmy held her and comforted her, but the rapid beating of his heart made it apparent to Catherine that, despite his brave face, he was equally affected.

"I am so sorry," Catherine said when she was settled down enough to talk. "This is all my fault. I could have gotten you killed."

Jimmy pulled her close. "This is not your fault," he said. "There are two of us here, remember? You didn't make me do anything I didn't want to do."

They continued holding each other for a time. Then, when they were both reasonably steady, they stood up and tried to brush the dirt and grit off one another. In frustration, they eventually returned to the pond and did their best to clean themselves in the water. Afterwards, Jimmy put on his shoes and retrieved the bags of litter while Catherine located her lost sandal.

When they had gathered all their belongings, and were as cleaned up as they were going to get, they headed back through the trees, moving slowly in the hope that their clothing would dry in the still-stifling heat.

"What do you think your father would say if he knew about all this?" Jimmy asked, stepping momentarily off the trail to pick up a Coke bottle that they'd missed on the way in.

"I've been worrying about that," Catherine said. "But not for the reason you might think."

They had been walking single file, but now the path widened and Catherine moved next to Jimmy and took his hand.

"My dad's not a hypocrite," she said. "I don't think he'd be upset about our feelings for each other, at least not in principle. He knows you, and he's told me several times how much he likes you. But I think he'd be disappointed in me for putting you in danger. And probably pretty mad. And, let's face it, he'd have a point." She squeezed his hand. "I was definitely being reckless back there, and you could have paid for it with your life."

Jimmy stopped Catherine and gently turned her to face him squarely. "Like I told you before, that was not just you. And if anyone should have known better, it's me."

"Well, nevertheless, I think my father would be upset with me, and your mother would probably want to kill me."

The thought of what Sally would think filled Catherine with dread, and Jimmy let the subject drop, so Catherine decided not to push it. He plainly didn't want to talk about it.

Before moving on, they agreed to maintain their resolve to make the most of the time they had left, and to try to put the incident at the pond behind them. When they arrived at the end of the trees, their clothes were still wet, so they decided to seek refuge in the barn until they appeared more presentable. As they approached the barn door, they each instinctively looked around to make sure no one was observing them. When they felt certain that no one was watching, they stepped in, and were enveloped, once again, in a world of darkness streaked with shimmering light.

Catherine passed her hand through a sparkling sunbeam. "Here we go again," she said, her fears dissolving in the dreamlike atmosphere. "Can you even imagine a more romantic setting? It's like some kind of special little universe, just for us."

She wrapped herself in Jimmy's arms. "Isn't life strange? Here we are in this incredible place, feeling all these positive feelings for one another, and there are people who would literally kill us for it."

"Well," Jimmy answered softly, "how about for now we forget about those people."

Catherine turned and looked up into Jimmy's face. "How am I ever going to say goodbye to you?"

"*Shhhh,*" he said, pressing his finger to her lips. "We can worry about that later."

Once again they kissed and caressed, this time with less restraint than the day before. They did not make love, but they explored each other's bodies with an increased sense of ease, and Catherine's instincts in the direction of total intimacy were strong and clear.

When it began to get late, they reluctantly returned to the real universe in which they lived—dry, happy, and already hungry for their next encounter.

ⱌ

Now home, Catherine dropped the bags of litter on the porch, opened the screen door, then hurried straight for the bathroom, hollering, "*I'm going to take a bath,*" as she went. She didn't know the whereabouts of her father or Mama Rae, but she was happy to have dodged them, along with any questions that might have been raised by her rumpled appearance.

Once in the bathroom, Catherine quickly stepped out of her clothes and into the standing bathtub, where she enjoyed the cool water before commencing to wash her tangled hair. Slippery with shampoo, her body felt like a revelation, as though it held secrets she's never before contemplated. She wondered if this heightened sense of her anatomy was pure lust, or if what she was feeling was the natural byproduct of love. Whatever the case, Jimmy's impact on her lingered, and Catherine couldn't imagine how she'd survive until she could be with him again. When her mind turned to their close call at the pond, or their imminent return to separate schools, the thoughts were so painful that she instantly shut them down. Taking slow breaths, she told herself that everything would be fine, that they would find a way to be together, no matter what they might face. Deep down, she believed they were meant to be together. She felt it right down to her bones, and in all the other parts of her body that now yearned for Jimmy so urgently that she knew it simply had to be love.

∽

When Catherine was finally clean, dressed, and ready to face her father and Mama Rae, she emerged from her room to find Mama Rae napping in the living room, and Ben at the kitchen table, doing a crossword puzzle.

"Well, there she is," Ben said, putting down his pen. "I thought you were going to stay in that tub forever." He smiled warmly, and Catherine relaxed, realizing, with great relief, that he was unconcerned about the length of time she'd been away.

"I see you and Jimmy collected a fair amount of litter out of those woods. Good job. Did you have a nice walk around?"

"Yeah, it was great," Catherine said. "I don't know if you remember, but we built a little fort back there when we were kids. We tried to find it, and we did find a few relics, but it's mostly gone now. We also did a little wading in the back side of the pond." Catherine shuddered as she was struck with a flashback of their near disaster.

She crossed the kitchen and grabbed the apron from the hook by the stove. She was just tying it on, thinking about what she needed to do to prepare dinner, when Ben interrupted her thoughts.

"Do you remember Isabel?"

Catherine searched her memory and conjured up a picture of an old woman with thick ankles and a lazy eye who lived in a small house with a screened-in front porch. Her front yard had been a small hill, and Catherine recalled rolling down the hill, then realizing, with horror, that she was covered with ants.

"I vaguely remember her," Catherine said. "I was attacked by ants in her front yard. Do you remember that?"

Ben chuckled. "I do remember that. Although what I mainly remember is an awful lot of screaming. Poor Isabel didn't know what was going on. You about scared her to death."

Catherine laughed. "I was mostly screaming because Mom ripped my clothes off right there on the sidewalk. But who is Isabel exactly? I can't remember. Is she a friend of the family, or an aunt or something?"

"She was Mama Rae's best friend growing up. That little house you remember is in Little Rock. Now that she and Mama Rae are getting older, they don't visit much anymore, but they stay in touch by phone."

Mama Rae shuffled into the kitchen. "Do I hear you two talking about Isabel?" She sat down at the table, looking markedly less chipper than she had earlier in the day. Her face was drawn, and she seemed fragile and unsteady. Her thin hair was down and flattened in the back in a way that reminded Catherine uncomfortably of a nursing home where she'd volunteered briefly as a teenager. Nurses had called the look 'bed head.'

"I was just getting ready to tell Catherine what happened," Ben said.

Catherine read a look of distress on Mama Rae's face. "What happened? Did something happen to Isabel?"

"Well, it seems she had a minor heart attack," Ben said, "so I'm going to take Mama Rae to Little Rock tomorrow to visit her in the hospital."

Catherine experienced a moment of sympathy for her grandmother, then almost instantly recognized the misfortune as an opportunity to be alone with Jimmy. "I hope she's going to be okay," she said, trying to tamp down her excitement.

Mama Rae's words were steadier than her hands. "She's scared me a time or two before, and she's a tough ol' gal, so I think she'll be all right."

Catherine turned to Ben, trying to sound casual. "When were you thinking of leaving?"

"Well, it's a pretty good drive, and it'll be hot, so I'd like to get a reasonably early start. I'd say no later than nine o'clock."

Catherine's brain was spinning. "What about Jimmy?" she asked impulsively. "Do you have something for him to do tomorrow?"

Ben thought for a moment. "No, I think we can let him know he doesn't need to come. I'm sure it'll please Sally to have him home for a change."

He stood up, went to the refrigerator, and pulled out a beer. "What about you? Do you think you can keep yourself out of trouble for a day while we're gone? Or maybe you'd like to come with us."

"No, I'll be fine," Catherine said. "There's stuff I can do around here, and I can call Jimmy if you want me to." She held her breath, and was already formulating a plan.

Ben raised the beer and nodded. "Yeah, okay. Maybe tell him to check back with us on Wednesday. You can get the number from Mama Rae."

Mama Rae took the cue and immediately rattled off Sally's phone number, which introduced a problem. Catherine needed to talk to Jimmy privately, but the phone was in the kitchen, where, at present, she had an audience.

Catherine wrote the phone number on a napkin and put it in her apron pocket, mumbling that she'd call Jimmy later, after first getting dinner started. She then commenced preparing dinner, methodically moving about the kitchen between the refrigerator, sink, and stove. After what felt like an eternity, but was really no more than a few minutes, Ben proclaimed that it was time for the evening news, so he and Mama Rae exited the kitchen, finally giving Catherine the privacy she needed.

She pulled the phone number from her pocket and dialed, praying that Jimmy, and not Sally or one of his sisters, would answer. Much to her relief, Jimmy answered the phone. Catherine spoke in a low tone, hoping not to be overheard over President Eisenhower, whose voice was now emanating from the living room. Luckily, because of Mama Rae's poor hearing, the TV was turned up loud.

"Jimmy," she said, barely above a whisper. "It's me."

Jimmy sounded concerned. "Is everything okay?"

Catherine smiled into the phone. "Everything is perfect. *But, listen,*" she added, hoping to convey that this was serious business. "My father is driving Mama Rae to Little Rock tomorrow, so he says to tell you that there's nothing for you to do here until Wednesday. *But I want you to come tomorrow.* Do you think you can find an excuse to leave the house and come spend the day with me?"

Jimmy didn't hesitate. "Yeah, I'll *definitely* think of something."

His obvious enthusiasm sent a wave of excitement through Catherine. "*Great,*" she whispered. "Try to come around ten o'clock if you can. And if you arrive, and, for some reason, my dad and Mama Rae are still here, have some excuse to explain why you're just dropping by for a minute. But please come, because we'll have the whole place to ourselves all day."

"I'll definitely come," Jimmy said. "The only question is how I'm gonna stand waitin' till tomorrow."

Catherine felt a rush of both affection and lust. Then she whispered a few more words, said good-bye, and resumed making dinner, all the while preoccupied with what it would be like to spend an entire day with Jimmy, safely and deliciously alone.

ೞ

Forty minutes later Catherine called her father and Mama Rae to come eat.

"It sure does smell good in here," Mama Rae commented, entering the kitchen. She had pinned up her hair and now appeared steadier.

Ben followed her in and sat down at the table. "Is that the cake you've been promising me for days that I smell in the oven?"

"Yes it is," Catherine said cheerfully.

Mama Rae took a seat next to Ben. "You put all this together awfully quick. All this food and a cake too?"

"It's the miracle of the modern cake mix," Catherine replied. "But it won't be ready for a while. After it comes out of the oven it'll take some time to cool."

Mama Rae placed her napkin in her lap. "We can eat it later out on the porch. Although I want to turn in early tonight, because we have a big day ahead of us tomorrow."

Catherine experienced a surge of excitement just hearing the word *tomorrow*.

"I hope you like macaroni and cheese," she said, nodding to the plates on the table. "It's a big staple at our house, and one of the only things I know how to cook."

Mama Rae smiled sweetly. "I think I remember it was one of your favorites."

"At least she doesn't eat it with chocolate milk anymore," Ben teased.

Catherine pulled out a chair and sat down. "Hey, don't knock it till you've tried it."

After a quick grace that Ben cracked off for Mama Rae's benefit, they commenced eating, and Catherine tried her best to seem interested in her grandmother's single-minded chatter about Isabel.

"The heartbreak of her life is that she never had kids of her own, much less grandkids," Mama Rae said, glancing warmly at Catherine.

"How long has it been since you've seen her?" Ben asked.

"Well, I saw her at your father's funeral, of course. But that was not a happy visit. Before that, I probably hadn't seen her for maybe a year or so. We don't get around like we used to."

Mama Rae patted Catherine's hand. "Ordinarily, I'd ask you to come with us. I know she'd love to see you if the circumstances were different. But she's not keen on visitors in the hospital. She just barely agreed to see me."

"I'm thinking about maybe getting a motel room in Little Rock," Ben interjected. "That way we won't have to make that long drive twice in one day. And it'll give me a place to stay while Mama Rae's at the hospital."

Catherine tried to keep a straight face.

Ben took a big bite of macaroni and cheese. "Think you'll be all right on your own?"

"I'll be fine," Catherine said, feeling herself blush. She hoped her father wouldn't notice.

After supper, Catherine prepared the pineapple upside down cake, then served it out on the porch, where Mama Rae continued her good-natured stroll down Memory Lane. Over the course of the evening, Catherine and Ben learned of Isabel's near-fatal hysterectomy, her beloved but deceased beagle Barney, her distinguished but mostly-unacknowledged career as an Army nurse, her love of bridge, her distaste for Adlai Stevenson, and more than anyone would ever want to know about her no-account nephew Warren. Mama Rae was just finished recounting an incident involving a nasty neighbor and a hedge clipper when Catherine decided she could take no more, and politely retired to her room, anxious to finally be alone with her thoughts.

CB

Now in her room, and resigned to insomnia, Catherine did her best to block out the nightmare at the pond and worries about the future and focus on the following day. She had no doubts about what she was planning. None. She was still a virgin, but not because she was following anyone else's rules, or morality. She was certain in her desire to make love with Jimmy—so certain that it felt fated, like tomorrow was an entrée to her destiny, whatever it might be.

She was confident they'd be safe in the house, and so filled with love and desire that it was easy to lose herself in thoughts of what was in store. Her mind and body were electric with anticipation, and she imagined that Jimmy was in a similar state. She pictured him in his own bed, having his own fantasies, and her excitement was so great that it was almost impossible to quiet her mind and sleep.

Chapter 6

Catherine was already awake when Ben knocked on her door the next morning to announce that he and Mama Rae were leaving for their journey. She *had* managed to sleep, but not much, and her attempts to limit her thoughts to fantasies about Jimmy had only been partially successful. Worry and fear had constantly battled for her attention. Nevertheless, when the knock came, Catherine was struck with a feeling of exhilaration, determined not to let anything spoil the day that she was anticipating like a honeymoon.

"Knock, knock," Ben called from the hallway.

"Come on in."

Ben opened the door and stood in the doorway. "We're gonna take off. I want to get on the road before it gets too hot."

Mama Rae appeared next to him, looking like she was dressed for church.

"Please deliver my best wishes to Isabel," Catherine said, sitting up in bed.

"We'll give her your best," Ben said, placing his hand on Mama Rae's shoulder as a signal that it was time to leave.

"So, will you be staying in Little Rock overnight?" Catherine asked.

Ben gave Catherine a look that might have signaled a reluctance to leave her alone. "That's the plan, but we'll see."

"Well, you two have a nice trip," Catherine said. "And don't worry about me, I'll be fine."

Ben and Mama Rae turned to go, and Catherine followed them to the front porch, where she watched as they piled into the truck.

"You be good, now!" Ben hollered from the window before starting it up.

"I will," Catherine promised. Then she waved from the porch as the truck came to life and headed towards the road.

ᗡ

Now alone, Catherine sprinted for the bathroom and jumped into the tub. She tried to remain calm, but as always when she was excited or nervous, her heart sped up, and it remained that way as she bathed, as she dressed, as she combed her long hair, as she brushed her teeth in front of the bathroom mirror, all the while visualizing what it would be like when Jimmy arrived.

When she finally heard his car drive up, she thought about running outside to greet him, but decided to wait for his knock. In the meantime she tried to steady herself with deep breathing. Finally the knock came, but at the back door. Jimmy was being cautious.

Catherine walked into the kitchen, took one final deep breath, and opened the door.

"Hello there," Jimmy said, smiling broadly and looking handsome in the morning light. He was wearing a crisp white shirt and pants that were neatly pressed.

"Come on in," Catherine said, beaming back. "But I have to warn you… I'm so nervous that I'm just about ready to have a stroke."

Jimmy walked in and closed the door. "I'm feeling pretty nervous myself," he said, stepping close. He placed his hands on her hips. "I assume we're alone."

"Completely alone," Catherine whispered. "And my father and Mama Rae probably won't be back until tomorrow."

Jimmy exhaled, and it was apparent that he really was nervous. Catherine kissed him sweetly, and then laughed. "Maybe we should sit down for a second before our legs give out on us. Have you had anything to eat?"

"I ate a little bit before I left the house," Jimmy said, "but I don't have much of an appetite. I am pretty shaky, I guess, and I didn't get much sleep last night."

"Me either," Catherine said, kissing him again. This time Jimmy responded, and they kissed deeply, with rising passion. In little more than seconds Catherine's nervousness was overlaid with acute arousal, and it was more than apparent that Jimmy was in a similar state.

"Maybe since we both got so little sleep, we should consider lying down," Catherine suggested with a wry smile.

Jimmy laughed nervously. "You're somethin', you know that?"

"I'm sorry," Catherine said. "Is this too much?"

"No," Jimmy assured. "No. But are you thinking what I think you're thinking?"

"I'm pretty sure I'm thinking what you think I'm thinking. Is that okay?"

"It's fine," Jimmy said. "It's pretty much all I've been thinking about since you called yesterday. But I just wanted to make sure." He paused. "Do you want to talk about it first?"

"I guess we could talk about it."

"We don't have to, if you think it'll spoil the mood or something." Jimmy looked embarrassed. "Sorry. I don't have much experience with this type of thing—or any experience, really."

He smiled and sat down at the kitchen table. "I guess I am a little nervous."

Catherine sat down next to him. "You know that this is new for me too, right?"

"Well, I wasn't quite sure."

"Well it is," Catherine said, blushing. "But I have no doubts whatsoever. None." She took Jimmy's hand. "I've never felt anything like this before. Not even close."

Jimmy wore an expression that Catherine didn't recognize, and she worried that maybe she was coming on too strong. She was wondering what to say next when he stood up and extended his hand. "Come on," he said.

Catherine took his hand and he pulled her gently from her chair. Then the two of them walked out of the kitchen, through the hallway, and back to Catherine's bedroom. As they entered her room, Catherine was swept with waves of emotion that felt totally separate from her physical longing. "I wish there were some way to tell you how I feel right now," she said, turning to face him in the dim light.

"I think I know," Jimmy said. "I feel it too."

They kissed, and their bodies rocked and swayed as if in a slow dance. After some time they separated and looked at one another. Catherine had spent the previous night fantasizing about this moment and what would follow, but now she realized that no fantasy could ever have prepared her for the emotional impact of what was unfolding. "Are you still nervous?" she asked softly.

"A little," Jimmy confessed. "Mainly because I'm scared about how this might change things. I think it could make things a lot harder."

Catherine understood. She had the same fear, but she was willing to risk the pain that would follow for this chance for intimacy that might never come again. She was just about to respond when Jimmy spoke.

"I'm not sayin' I don't want this," he said. "But I guess I do feel like we need to talk about it." He sat down on the bed, and Catherine sat down next to him. "This is going to make it a lot harder for us to say goodbye in a few days. You know that, right?"

Catherine nodded, feeling suddenly sad. "I really do know," she said. "But nothing has ever felt as right to me as this. Being here with you now." She squeezed Jimmy's hand. "I know it sounds melodramatic, or corny or something, but I feel like I need this."

"Okay," Jimmy said, his eyes shining. "I'm definitely not gonna argue with you."

Catherine smiled and lay back. Then Jimmy lay down beside her. Face to face, they shared a look of joy. Then they kissed, and touched, and slowly undressed one another in the dim light.

Despite Catherine's readiness, she was initially shy about removing her clothes and revealing herself completely. But Jimmy was so loving, and so tender, that soon she felt safe, and comfortable, and it made her happy to have his eyes on her, and his hands. When there was finally nothing, no barrier between them, the sensation of skin on skin was so intoxicating that Catherine was struck with a feeling of perfect bliss. She was struck also by the look of their two bodies together, one soft and light, the other sleek and dark. Catherine thought it was the most beautiful thing she'd ever seen.

Their progression towards actual lovemaking was slow and sweet, and Catherine felt completely at ease. There was no awkwardness, or hurry. Only a shared sense of wonder, and an understanding that what they were experiencing was as profound as it was pleasing.

Lying in Jimmy's arms, Catherine was the first to speak in the afterglow of their first fully sexual communion. "I'd do anything if we could stay like this forever," she said, running her fingers across his sweat-slippery chest. "I feel so happy I don't even know what to say."

Jimmy gently caressed the contours of Catherine's body, now glowing in light filtering in through the curtains. "I think I could handle this forever," he said blithely.

Catherine raised her head and they exchanged a sleepy smile, and then a kiss. Neither had slept much the night before, so there was great temptation to sleep, but Catherine chose to stay awake, wanting to savor every moment. Jimmy expressed a similar sentiment, but Catherine encouraged him to nap, assuring him that she would wake him after a few minutes rest, during which time she would enjoy watching him, and listening to the soothing cadence of his breathing.

Catherine was all too aware that this day would eventually end, so she made a conscious effort to commit each detail of their time together to memory. Even as Jimmy slept, she studied the muscles in his arms, the scent of his hair, the contour of his ear, the tiny mole that lived just beneath his left eye. She found him so exquisitely beautiful, so perfectly lovable, that she wondered how she would ever be able to accept the day's passing, much less say good-bye to him in a few days.

She'd known he was right when he'd warned that their intimacy would make parting harder, but contemplating it now, she realized that she'd underestimated just how hard it would be. It would be terrible. She consoled herself with the hope that the pain of separation would solidify their resolve to be together. She knew now with certainty that this is what she wanted, no matter how hard it might be. She prayed Jimmy would feel the same way.

Catherine let Jimmy sleep for twenty or so minutes, then, fearing the loss of any more time, she blew softly into his ear to bring him back to consciousness. He stirred, then opened his eyes with a sleepy smile that Catherine instantly recognized as a vision she'd never forget.

"Hello, beautiful," he whispered, his smile widening as he turned his body to face her. "I hope you didn't let me sleep too long."

"Not long," Catherine said, mirroring back his joyful expression. "But it was nice watching you sleep."

"Well, I can sleep anytime," Jimmy said, yawning. "I don't want to waste a day like today on sleep."

"Don't worry, I won't let you."

They lay together silently for a time, simply caressing one another in a state of shared contentment. Shortly, they resumed kissing, first lightly, then with intensity. Soon they were engaged, once more, in an intimacy of flesh and spirit that was so infused with love that Catherine was eventually brought to tears.

"What is it?" Jimmy asked. "What's making you cry?"

"I'm not even sure," Catherine said, struggling for composure.

They repositioned their bodies so that they were lying face to face. Jimmy wiped a tear from Catherine's cheek. "I just feel so much," she said, her voice trembling.

"I understand," Jimmy said. "If you feel like you need to cry, go ahead and cry." He smiled sweetly, and his voice was tender. "You let me sleep a little, now I can let you cry a little."

Catherine rolled her eyes, then dropped her resistance and was soon crying softly in Jimmy's arms—for happiness, for love, for fate or God or whatever it was that had led them to this day. For feelings so large and so strong that she felt too small to contain them. But she also cried for sorrow, and fear, and for knowing that, apart from all their love and joy, they lived in a world that barely acknowledged Jimmy's humanity, much less his gifts.

"You all right?" Jimmy asked when she'd finally stopped, and was lying quietly in his arms.

"I'm fine," Catherine said. "I'm just overwhelmed, I guess, by so many things." She reached for a tissue on the bedside table and blew her nose. "I'm just so filled up with love, and so happy to be here with you. This is the best day of my life. *Nothing* could ever compare to this, and I will never regret this, no matter how hard it is say good-bye." She touched Jimmy's face, then ran her hand over his shoulder and down the smooth skin of his arm.

"But you look so sad," Jimmy said.

"I guess it's what you said. You know, about saying good-bye. It's going to be terrible." She rubbed his calf with the bottom of her foot, and was struck, once again, by the beauty of their bodies intertwined. "I guess that's not all of it," she continued, trying to put words to her bewilderment. "I just feel so much for you, and it hurts when I think about what could happen to you because of me."

Jimmy stroked Catherine's hair and looked into her eyes. "Nothing is going to happen to me," he whispered.

"I would never forgive myself if it did."

92

"Everything's going to be fine," Jimmy said. "I promise." Then he kissed away her fears, and they were swept, once more, into lovemaking—this time with no tears.

ﻖ

It was one o'clock, and having finally surrendered to the need for food, Catherine and Jimmy were eating sandwiches that Catherine had prepared and brought back to her bedroom.

"This is the most delicious thing I've ever tasted," Jimmy said, now partially dressed and leaning against a pillow propped up against the backboard of the bed. His mouth was full, and he looked so happy that Catherine made another mental note to remember the moment.

"I'm world famous for my bologna sandwiches," she said. "In San Diego, I'm practically a legend." She took a bite of her own sandwich, then commented, "This *is* pretty good." She leaned over to kiss Jimmy on the cheek. "I guess everything seems extra good today."

"You got that right," Jimmy said, pulling her back for a more serious kiss. A moment later he released her to resume eating.

After swallowing his last bite of sandwich, he asked, "What's it like in San Diego?"

"It's great," Catherine said. "The ocean is beautiful, and the town is nice. And you'd like the college." She looked at him hopefully. "You should come see it. I think it's a place where we might be okay. I really do."

Jimmy took his now-empty plate and put it on the table next to the bed. "I have a scholarship for Oberlin. And, honestly, Catherine, I don't like sayin' it, I really don't, but I don't think you realize what life would be like for us no matter where we lived."

"What about Oberlin?" Catherine asked nervously. "Isn't it famous for being a place that's extra open-minded? Maybe I could come there."

Jimmy paused and looked at Catherine sympathetically. "I don't want to spoil this wonderful day. That's the last thing I want. But I'm not sure I want to encourage you in this kind of thinking, either."

Catherine filled up with disappointment.

Reading Catherine's face, Jimmy sighed, then paused for a moment before continuing. "Listen," he said, tenderly, "I love the idea that we could somehow be together. But I don't think there's anywhere we could go where we wouldn't have a really hard time. And I don't want to hurt your feelings, but I don't know if you truly understand what you're asking for."

His voice took on a tenor that touched Catherine at her core. "I didn't choose to be a Negro," he said. "I'm not going to apologize for who I am, or what I am, but it's not something that I chose." He looked at Catherine with eyes filled with sadness. "This is not something you want to sign up for, Catherine. As much as we might feel for one another, the two of us don't make any sense. Not outside of this room."

Catherine persisted. "Do you think your life would be in danger if we tried to live somewhere like California or Ohio?"

"Well, I don't know if I'd need to worry about gettin' lynched, if that's what you're asking. But no matter where we might go, I think we'd have serious problems. Both of us."

Jimmy paused, as if thinking, then went on in a voice that was both sympathetic and firm. "Are you ready for people to despise you, Catherine? Threaten to hurt you? Maybe burn down your house? Are you ready to be barred from living in most neighborhoods? Told there's no room for you in hotels? Told you're trash? Told your children are sub-human?"

Catherine was roiling inside, but remained silent, uncertain how to respond.

"I hate upsetting you," Jimmy continued, "but there's no candy coating this. Your life would be hard. *Really hard.*" His voice softened. "Have you thought about what it would be like to have Negro children?"

Catherine reached across Jimmy, opened the drawer in the table next to the bed, and pulled out the photograph of the two of them. She held it up. "If you're asking me if I could love a child like this," she said, "I think we know the answer."

Jimmy looked at the photo, and it was obvious to Catherine that he was moved by it. He started to say something, then stopped.

"What is it?" Catherine asked. "What were you going to say?"

Jimmy remained quiet for a few moments, then he took the picture from Catherine and studied it. "I remember this day very clearly," he said finally. "When you showed it to me the other day, I didn't let on, but that day was actually one of the most painful days of my life."

He seemed like he might cry, and Catherine's response was to choke up as well. She remained silent and let him collect himself before continuing.

"I guess you could say that this photo captured my last day of innocence," he said. "And the irony of the two of us looking at this photo here, like this..." He exhaled. "Well, it's pretty un-believable."

He looked up from the picture. "You were right the other day when you said that this was the day we were playin' like we were gonna get married. It all happened just like you said, with the popsicles, and Niagara Falls. This was actually the day before you left and never came back." He shook his head. "I remember this like it was yesterday. And the reason I remember it so strongly is because that night I got the whipping of my life. To this day, my mama and I have never really talked about it, because I know she's ashamed. But she whipped me good that night, and I don't think I was ever the same after."

Catherine found it almost impossible to reconcile her image of Sally with the picture Jimmy was painting. "What happened?" she asked, incredulous. "Why on earth would she have whipped you?"

"I understand now why she did it," Jimmy said. "She thought she had to do it to protect me. To teach me how to behave with white people so that I wouldn't get myself killed."

He put the photo down on the bed. "Up to that point, I had a sense that we were different from white people. We obviously looked different, and were poorer than whites, but I hadn't yet really understood that we were considered *less* than white folks, or that we were hated by white folks. When I turned up at home talkin' about marrying you when I grew up—because I took all that play talk seriously—she tried to set me straight, but I wouldn't hear it. I argued with her, so she whipped me, and she tried the best she could to impress upon me that I had no business even thinkin' about marrying a white girl. She told me it had been a big mistake to allow me to play with you, and that from then on, you were off limits."

Catherine tried to remain composed, and she could hear in Jimmy's voice that he was struggling too.

"That night I learned what it *really* meant to be a Negro. And it wasn't just that you were off limits. According to what my mama tried to beat into me that night, my whole concept of life, and of myself, was wrong. Up to that point, I'd thought that I was more or less just like every other human being. But now my own mother was essentially telling me that, because I was a Negro, I had to be careful not to seem too confident around white folks, or too bright, or say things or do things that would call attention to myself, because someone might want to hurt me for it. She told me that night about lynchings, and about how colored folks in our own little town had been beaten or killed for simply acting like they thought they were as good as whites. I remember my brother George trying to stop her, and her tellin' him, no, it was time I learned the truth about being a Negro in a word dominated by the white man."

Jimmy paused to think. "I guess, because I'm stubborn, and 'cause my mama finally did put her fears aside and encourage me to aspire to a better life, I eventually managed to regain most of what I lost that day. But that was a dark day in my life. It took me a long time to recover from that day. The fact that we're looking at this picture together like this...Well, it's ..."

"It's incredible," Catherine whispered.

"Yeah," Jimmy agreed, "it's pretty incredible. But I'm afraid that not too much has changed since this picture was taken. I'm still a fool to be thinking about you like this."

"Well, I don't think you're a fool," Catherine said, "and I'm the one who really matters, right?"

Jimmy cocked his head. "I don't know. As much as I'd like to agree with you, I think the rest of the world really does matter." He stroked Catherine's hair. "How about, for now, we stop worrying about the rest of the world, and the future, and concentrate on today. Today is here now, and it's ticking away as we speak." He pulled her close and she folded herself into his arms.

"Okay," Catherine whispered, feeling a wave of love and a twinge of panic over the time. "We'll concentrate on today."

CB

Catherine was true to her promise to focus on the here and now, and for the next couple of hours the mingling of her flesh and affections with Jimmy's produced a pleasure that was so intoxicating that she felt distant from time and space. While they rested between peaks of exhilaration, it was hard for Catherine to keep her mind from wandering into painful territory, but when she found her thoughts turning dark, she would look at their bodies together, or think about their last act of love, and be pulled, once again, into the splendid universe of the moment, where they were king and queen, and everything made perfect sense.

It was after three o'clock, and, once again, Catherine lay awake as Jimmy napped. She was tempted to sleep herself, but her fear of sleeping too long kept her from succumbing to the temptation to drift off. Finally the urge to doze became so strong that she decided to rouse Jimmy with the proposition of a bath. She rubbed his chest and whispered his name. When he opened his eyes she asked, "How would you like to run through the sprinklers with me?"

Jimmy regarded her with sleepy confusion. "You want to run through the sprinklers?"

"Well, I was thinking of something more like a bath, but I thought it would be a little like old times."

Jimmy pulled her close for a kiss, then released her with a smile. "A bath sounds great."

They got up and headed for the bathroom, where Catherine promptly turned on the water and stepped into the tub. As she ran barely-warm water over her face and body, Jimmy relieved his bladder, and it struck her how utterly comfortable they were together, in their nakedness, and their physical intimacy. After a few moments, Jimmy climbed in, and they carefully arranged their arms and legs as the water rose around them. Once they were comfortably situated, they enjoyed a soapy synergy that was so exquisite that Catherine was surprised she hadn't thought of a bath sooner. "Kind of puts a whole new spin on the sprinklers," she said, rubbing her slippery breasts over Jimmy's chest.

"I don't know if I'll ever be able to enjoy a regular bath again after this experience," Jimmy replied, running his hands over her glistening skin.

Catherine had thought, over the course of the day, that she and Jimmy had experienced about as much pleasure as was possible between a man and a woman, but the addition of soap to the equation opened up a whole new world of sensual wonders.

When they finally returned, refreshed and happy, to Catherine's room, they sat together against the backboard of the bed and began eating an orange that Catherine had peeled and brought in from the kitchen. "Oh, wait a minute," she said suddenly, "I almost forgot." She sprang up and ran for the kitchen. When she returned a moment later, she handed Jimmy a Moon Pie.

"Okay, now my day is complete," he said, removing the wrapper with a broad grin. "I don't know what else could happen that could make this day any better."

"It's the perfect day," Catherine agreed, cuddling up beside him. She closed her eyes and had a vision of possibly her first memory of Jimmy. She opened her eyes. "Do you remember the very first time we saw each other?"

Jimmy thought for a moment. "Well, yeah, I think maybe I do. I'm pretty sure we were around maybe five or six. I remember feelin' kind of scared of you at first. I wasn't used to bein' around white kids."

"You and Sally were the first Negroes I'd ever met up close," Catherine said, "so I was fascinated by you. I remember Sally telling me you were full of beans."

Jimmy laughed. "I guess she had that right."

He took a bite of the Moon Pie. "I remember you and your parents driving up to the house. I was playin' on the front porch, and when I saw you get out of the car, I was both interested and scared. Mama Rae and my mama came outside, and I think I probably hid behind my mama's skirt." He ran his tongue over his front teeth. "I don't remember when we first started runnin' around together. I guess maybe my earliest memory of actually playing with you involves the sprinkler, or maybe the old tortoise that used to live under the front porch."

"Moe!" Catherine exclaimed. "Remember we used to feed him strawberries? I wonder what ever happened to him."

"I asked my mama about him the other day," Jimmy said. "She told me that he died a few years back. Did you know that old tortoise had belonged to your great grandfather?"

"My great grandfather," Catherine mused, rolling her eyes. "I bet he was a prize." She nodded to the Moon Pie and Jimmy gave her a bite. "Speaking of prize, that reminds me," Catherine said. "My dad told me that you won some kind of essay contest, and that's how you got your scholarship. He said there was even a story about it in the newspaper. Is that right?"

"Yeah, that's right. You should have seen my mama's face when she found out I got it. She about jumped through the roof."

Catherine grinned. "I can imagine."

They had been sitting up, and now Jimmy laid down and pulled Catherine down next to him. "I was pretty surprised I got it," he said. "Luckily, the competition was based in New

York, and not here. Otherwise I'd have probably gotten a good horse-whippin' instead of a scholarship."

"Is there any way you can show me the essay?" Catherine asked. "I'd really like to read what you wrote."

"My mama has a copy that I could probably bring over and show you, but it's really not a big deal."

"Well, I think it's a big deal," Catherine said. "Really. I'd like to read it."

"I could probably recite it by heart. It's not that long. They wanted me to read it at my high school graduation, so I memorized it. I practiced it about a million times."

"Oh, please recite it for me. *Please.*"

Jimmy looked embarrassed.

Catherine sat up. "Come on."

"All right. But you're gonna think I'm pretty full of myself."

"I'm not going to think anything like that. Really."

"Okay, give me a second. It's been a while." Jimmy closed his eyes for a few moments, then he put his hands behind his head and opened his eyes. "Okay," he said. "I think I can do it. Are you ready?"

"Ready."

"All right. Here goes. Promise not to laugh?"

"Cross my heart."

Suddenly there was a noise, and both Catherine and Jimmy froze. "*What was that?*" Catherine whispered. Her heart started to race, and they heard it again. This time it was clear that the sound was a knocking at the front door. Without a word, both

Catherine and Jimmy jumped up and began frantically gathering up their clothing. The knocking continued, and soon they could hear a male voice hollering from the front of the house.

Catherine's mind was in a whirl as she and Jimmy strove to dress and make sense of what was happening. They were just getting to their shoes, and were exchanging a look of mutual fear and confusion, when a shadowy shape appeared outside the bedroom window. In an instant, the shape materialized vaguely as two cupped hands, an indiscernible face, and an eye peeking in through a tiny gap in the curtains.

"There's someone inside!" yelled a voice from outside. "And you ain't gonna believe this, but it's the girl and a nigger!"

Catherine was struck with such terror that she had to fight against the impulse to become hysterical. Unable to think straight, she looked to Jimmy, praying that he had the wits to know what to do. He quickly grabbed her hand and pulled her from the room into the dim hallway.

"Think," Jimmy whispered. "I need a weapon." He took a breath to steady his nerves, then started pulling Catherine in the direction of the kitchen. "Show me where you keep the knives."

Catherine resisted. "No," she said, "there's a gun. I saw it when I was going through my grandparents' things." Catherine quickly retrieved a shotgun from the hall closet and handed it to Jimmy.

"Do you see any shells?" he asked.

Catherine began searching, but Jimmy stopped her. "Never mind. It looks like it's loaded."

"*Oh my God!*" Catherine cried, barely able to grasp what was happening.

"This is bad," Jimmy said. "But try to stay calm."

They were starting for the front of the house when suddenly the front door burst open and two young men rushed in. One was JT, and the other Catherine didn't recognize.

"What do you think you're doing breaking into my house?" Catherine shouted. "You get out of my house right now!"

"I came to deliver the things your daddy ordered from the hardware," JT said, "but it looks like, instead, I need to rescue you from this here nigger."

"I don't need rescuing," Catherine shot back, trying to remain calm. "And if you don't get out of here this second, I'm going to have you arrested."

JT looked at Jimmy, who was gripping the gun, but pointing it downward. "Well, I don't know," he said. "This looks like a pretty dangerous nigger to me." He nodded towards the gun. "What you gonna do with that gun, boy?"

Catherine said slowly, "He's protecting me. I gave him the gun. Now get out of here right now or I'm calling the sheriff!"

"Well, why don't you just do that," JT said, "and we'll see who gets arrested—me, or this nigger with the gun."

Jimmy nodded at the shotgun. "I have this because you broke in here. Now it's time for you to leave."

"If you would just please leave," Catherine said, trying to appeal to JT in a friendlier tone, "we can call this a misunderstanding and forget it ever happened."

"We ain't forgettin' nothin'," JT hissed. "Round here, don't no nigger point a gun at a white man and live to talk about it."

"You need to go," Jimmy demanded. He still didn't raise the gun, but his tone was dead serious.

"If we leave," JT's sidekick said in a slow drawl, "we'll be coming back after you with a rope. You know that don't you, boy?"

Jimmy's voice was steady. "All I know is you broke into this house, you've been asked to leave, and you need to go. *Now*."

JT looked straight at Catherine and the expression on his face sent chills down her spine. "Y'all were in the bedroom together."

Jimmy raised the gun. "*I said now*."

"You think I'm scared of you and that rusty piece of shit?" JT sneered. "I got a mind to take you out and lynch you right now. I could probably sell tickets."

The sidekick laughed and Jimmy pointed the gun directly at JT. "I'm not fooling," he said, his voice rising.

JT seemed to be calculating. "We ain't got no more time for this now." He glanced at his partner, then motioned towards the door. "But we ain't finished with y'all. You can count on that. And you," he added, glaring at Catherine. "I'm disappointed in you. I didn't have you figured for a nigger lover."

He turned to leave, and Catherine and Jimmy watched silently as the two boys jumped off the porch stairs and headed for their truck.

JT opened the heavy door, but before he disappeared inside, he gestured towards Jimmy's car and yelled back, "Don't think this is over. Once I give this here license number to my daddy, I'm gonna know where you live." Then he jumped in the truck and roared off in a cloud of dirt and gravel.

Chapter 7

The moment the truck was out of sight the painful reality of what had just happened hit Catherine and Jimmy with full force. "What do we do now?" Catherine cried, once again battling hysteria. "Do we call the sheriff?" She could see by the look on Jimmy's face that he was just as frightened as she was.

"I need a minute to think," he said, putting the shotgun in a corner near the door. He pulled Catherine to him and they held each other silently for a time, trying to calm down.

"I'm not sure what to do," Jimmy said finally, letting Catherine go. "But we might not have much time."

"Do you think they're really coming back?" Catherine asked. "And can they really find out where you live from your license plate? That tall one's father is a deputy sheriff!"

Jimmy was breathing hard and drenched with sweat. It terrified Catherine to see him in such a state of fear, and she felt utterly responsible. "I'm so sorry, Jimmy," she said. "This is all my fault."

"It's not your fault, but we don't have time for all that now," Jimmy said. "We have to think what to do." He sat down in Mama Rae's chair. "I do think they'll come after me. I'd be a fool to think they won't. And if that boy's father really is a deputy, they'll probably go to my house."

"Should we call for help?"

"We can't call the Sheriff's Department. They're just as likely to string me up as those boys are."

Catherine realized in a sudden moment of panic that she had no way to reach her father. She thought about calling her mother, but quickly discounted that instinct as neither practical nor prudent. What could her mother do but worry?

"I think I need to call my house and tell my family to get out of there," Jimmy said finally. "And I hate to say it, but I don't think you're safe here. And I *definitely* can't stay here."

Under an avalanche of guilt and fear, and with her heart pounding harder than ever, Catherine battled to think straight. "Do you think we're safe to drive your car?"

"I was just wonderin' about that," Jimmy said. "I'm not sure, but the license plates are definitely a problem. Do you think that old car in the barn has license plates we can use?"

"I think it might," Catherine said, relieved to have at least a particle of a plan emerging. "Why don't you call home while I run and get the plates."

Catherine experienced a rush of guilt and shame at the thought of the phone call, but she forced herself to put it out of her mind. They were in this situation now whether she liked it or not, and they had to do whatever was necessary, no matter how painful.

She took a deep breath, then ran into the kitchen and grabbed a screwdriver from a drawer. As Jimmy was picking up the telephone to call Sally, she went out the back door and sprinted for the barn. Once inside, she was relieved to see that the old car did, in fact, have plates. But they were rusty, and she soon found that getting them off would not be easy. Even under the most optimal conditions, Catherine was not good with tools, but now, in such a nervous state, and with so much terror and guilt weighing down on her, the simple task of removing a few rusty screws seemed almost impossible. She cursed herself for her incompetency, her selfishness, her lust, and especially for believing that she could love Jimmy without ruining his life.

She was just struggling with the last screw when she heard something and realized, with alarm, that what she was hearing was the sound of cars and voices. She ran out of the barn and was horrified to see JT's truck and two cars, one a sheriff's car, parked in front of the house. Several men, some in uniform, were heading for the porch. In the next instant they were loudly demanding that Jimmy open the door.

Catherine ran for the house. "What are you doing?" she screamed.

"You need to step back," said a tall man in a uniform. "The boy in this house is wanted for armed robbery, and if he doesn't open the door this instant, he's also gonna be charged with resisting arrest."

"What do you mean armed robbery? That's ridiculous, and you know it!" Catherine shouted. "We're the ones who've been the victims of a crime. Just a few minutes ago two boys broke in here and threatened us. You should be protecting us, not terrorizing us with this made-up nonsense!"

She was starting to say more when she was grabbed from behind and pulled back towards the sheriff's car. "You keep quiet, or you'll be arrested too," said a voice filled with hate.

"I want to see your arrest warrant!" Catherine yelled, struggling against her captor.

"We're not showing you nothin'," the tall man in the uniform said. "Now shut your mouth!"

Catherine looked to her left and, for the first time, noticed JT looking on with a malevolent grin. "That's one of the guys who broke in here!" Catherine shouted, pointing to JT. "I want to press charges!"

"You're gonna shut up," the man holding her snarled. He touched her breasts and grabbed her fleetingly between the legs in a gesture that felt like a threat of rape.

"Get your hands off me!" Catherine screamed, straining against his grasp. The bully was just intensifying his grip when suddenly the door to the house flew open and the men on the porch ran in. Catherine prayed that Jimmy would not go for the shotgun this time, because she had no doubt that if he did, he'd be killed on the spot.

In the midst of her terror, Catherine struggled to think. She knew that Jimmy was in great danger of being beaten or even murdered before he ever made it to the sheriff's office, so she decided that the only way to protect him was to try to get herself arrested too. That way, at least he might not be taken off alone.

She elbowed her captor and kicked him with every ounce of her strength, trying as hard as she could to injure him in the groin. "*Let go of me you stupid bastard!*" she screamed.

In response, the man grabbed her by the hair and pulled her head back hard. "You're asking for big trouble you little bitch!" he hissed.

Catherine was just trying to muster up enough saliva to spit in his face when she heard hollering from the house. "He's not here!" called a voice from inside. "It looks like he got away!"

Catherine ceased struggling, and after a moment she was thrust brutally to the ground, where she succumbed to the impulse to cry, partly in fear, and partly for the relief of knowing that Jimmy may somehow have escaped, at least for the moment.

The revelation that Jimmy had apparently fled was followed by a flurry of confusion and harried discussion. As words like *'roadblock'* and *'fugitive'* and especially *'nigger'* spewed forth in an atmosphere of palpable hatred, Catherine made it slowly to the porch, trying to attract as little attention as possible. She was making a move towards entering the house when she was stopped by the tall deputy.

"Just hold on there," the deputy said in a venomous tone. "I have some questions for you." He grabbed her and pushed her onto the porch swing.

"Are you Jesse Taylor?" she asked contemptuously.

"I'm the one asking the questions here," he said. "And you'd better mind your mouth or you're gonna land your tight little ass in jail."

"I have nothing to say except that what you're doing is totally illegal and immoral, and if you don't stop, this town will be crawling with NAACP lawyers, and I know a whole bunch of 'em."

Catherine was bluffing, but she knew that the NAACP was involved in the Emmitt Till case, and she figured it might help to remind him that, because of the NAACP, atrocities against Southern blacks that had previously gone unchallenged were now starting to make headlines.

"You think you're pretty smart, don't you?" spit the deputy. "Well, I knew your daddy, and he thought he was pretty smart too, but he was just a pathetic little shit."

"Well, that pathetic little shit will make sure you don't get away with this," Catherine said. "Besides the NAACP, he has friends in the FBI, so if you hurt my friend, you'll be going to jail."

"Oh, he's your friend is he? Well, I saw some sheets in there that look like y'all are pretty close friends. As a matter of fact,

I'm taking those sheets as evidence, and I may add illegal fornication to the charge of armed robbery. How do you feel about puttin' that one in front of a jury?"

Struck with a renewed sense of terror, Catherine struggled to remain composed. "Look," she said. "You know he didn't commit any robbery. Why don't you just stop this before it goes any further?"

"Oh, it's going further" Jesse Taylor said. "You can count on that. That uppity nigger of yours robbed a hardware store, and I have witnesses to prove it."

Horrified, Catherine turned to where JT had been standing, but now he was gone. She looked back at Jesse Taylor. "No one is going to believe your son. He's the one who broke in here today, and I'll testify to that."

Jesse Taylor spit tobacco juice off the porch. "You got a lot to learn, young lady. As soon as a jury sees you, and finds out what you and that nigger were up to, won't nothing matter except seeing that boy hang, or go to jail if he should be so lucky."

Catherine tried desperately to remain defiant, but inside she was terrified. Things just kept getting worse and worse.

"Now, you listen to me," Jesse Taylor hissed, and there was death in his eyes. "I want that boy. If you know where he is, you'd better tell me right now, because the longer it takes for us to find him, the worse it's gonna be when we finally do catch up with him. And we're gonna find him."

Catherine took a deep breath, then slowly exhaled. "I'm not saying another word. Except if you hurt him, I promise you won't get away with it. You'll be the one sitting in front of a jury."

"We'll just see about that," the deputy said, his face breaking into an ugly grin. Then he spit another mess of tobacco juice, wiped his mouth with the back of his hand, and disappeared back into the house.

Catherine felt as if she were trapped in an extended nightmare. She tried to retain her wits in the midst of the strangers who were milling and raging around her, but as time went on, it became more and more difficult. Finally, after what felt like forever, the men collected themselves back into their cars and sped off, leaving her alone. She was surprised not to have been taken. She'd half-expected to be killed herself, or raped, or at least taken to the sheriff's office and charged with something. She wondered if leaving her behind were an oversight—if any minute they would come racing back for her.

cg

Catherine stood up and went into the house. She was tempted to head for the couch and retreat into the fetal position, but with Jimmy in such great danger, she knew there could be no retreating, no falling apart. The nightmare was only beginning, and she had to pull herself together and figure out what to do. *What on earth was she going to do?*

She sat down on Mama Rae's chair in the living room, then closed her eyes and began taking deep breaths. She needed to calm herself so she could think. After just a few breaths, she opened her eyes with the sudden realization that she needed to call Sally. She had no idea if Jimmy had reached her earlier, but, in any case, she needed to let her know what was happening. She dreaded having to tell her, but she knew she had no choice, so she stood up and headed for the kitchen, praying that her phone number was still in the pocket of the apron.

Catherine grabbed the apron from its hook by the stove and was greatly relieved to find the napkin with Sally's phone number still in the pocket. Staring at the phone, she tried to calm down, but her heart remained stubbornly in high gear.

She cursed herself once again for all her inadequacies, and for causing the catastrophe that was unfolding.

She was just picking up the phone when she heard something—a tapping. She stood still and listened, and soon realized that it was coming from under the house. In an instant she knew that it was Jimmy. His favorite hiding place as a child had been a space under the front porch stairs, and from there it was possible to access a wider area under the house. She ran to where she'd heard the tapping and tapped back. *"Jimmy!"* she cried, trying to keep her voice as low as possible. "Let me look around to make sure no one's here before you come out!"

He tapped again.

Catherine ran to the front door and went outside onto the porch. Then she went around to the back of the house, and all around the perimeter, and saw no one. She returned to the front porch stairs and knelt down. "Everyone is gone," she called, still trying to keep her voice low. "But do you think it's safe to come out? They might come back any time!"

Catherine was just wondering how he could possibly fit through the small space under the steps when Jimmy came walking around the side of the house and almost scared her to death. *"Oh my God!"* Catherine cried, running into his arms. *"Oh my God, Jimmy!"* They hugged one another tightly, then rushed into the house, terrified that the men might come back any second and see them.

Catherine was so overwhelmed by relief and fear that she all but collapsed onto the couch. "How did you get under there?" she asked.

"There's a way in through the back," Jimmy said. "I noticed it the other day when I was in the backyard. When I heard the cars drive up, I knew I didn't have time to run far, so I just figured my best chance was to go out the back door and hide."

"Thank God you're okay. But what are we going to do? Those men are out for blood. Did you hear what they were saying?"

"I heard some, and I heard you, too. You were talking pretty tough. Was all that talk about the NAACP and the FBI true, or were you makin' that up?"

"I made up the part about my dad knowing people, but I'm definitely calling the NAACP, and the FBI, and the newspapers, and I'll call President Eisenhower if I have to."

Sweaty, and stained with dirt from under the house, Jimmy looked depleted. Catherine's instinct was to beg for his forgiveness, but she knew she needed to put all that aside. "Did you reach your mother?" she asked.

"No," Jimmy said. "I tried calling, but no one answered. I guess the first thing we need to do is try again. We have to get everyone out of the house."

Catherine checked outside, and it was still clear, so they headed into the kitchen and Jimmy picked up the phone. After a second he lowered the receiver. "Looks like they cut the phone lines," he said, shaking his head. "The phone's dead."

"Are you kidding?" Catherine cried.

"*Damn!*" Jimmy shouted, slamming the phone in frustration. He went to the sink and splashed cold water on his face and neck, then he gulped down a glass of water.

"We have to hide you until my father gets back," Catherine said. "But there must be a better place than under the house."

"I can't stay here," Jimmy said, sinking into a kitchen chair, drying his face on a dish towel. "I need to get home and warn my family."

"You can't go home! They'll definitely be looking for you there!"

Jimmy looked unconvinced.

"Let me go," Catherine said. "You can hide here, and I'll go to your house."

Jimmy was starting to respond when they heard a car driving up. "Quick!" Catherine reacted, "You need to go back under the house!"

Jimmy sprang up and ran for the back door and Catherine hurried to the kitchen window. Then, shocked by what she saw, she turned around to stop Jimmy. "Wait!" she called. "It's my father!"

Jimmy hesitated at the open door. "What about Mama Rae? Do you think I need to go back and hide?" He seemed panicked. "And what about my family? Can you maybe send your father to my house?" He grimaced in frustration.

Catherine looked back out the window and could see Ben helping Mama Rae out of the car. "We have to hurry!" she said. She handed Jimmy a piece of paper and pencil and told him to write down the address of his house. Then she ran and grabbed a sheet from the hall closet, wrapped an orange and some bread and bologna in the sheet, and handed the bundle to Jimmy. "Take this and go back under the house for now," she said. "I'll tap on the floor when it's safe for you to come out. And I'll send my dad to your house," she added. "I promise."

Jimmy looked doubtful, then went out the back door.

Catherine met Ben and Mama Rae as they were coming up the porch steps. Ben's expression was dead serious, and Mama Rae looked mad. "What is going on?" Ben asked, sounding both angry and fearful. "I got stopped by Jesse Taylor at a police roadblock up on the highway, and I gather they're looking for Jimmy."

"I hope you didn't give them his name," Catherine said.

"Oh, they knew his name," Ben said. "And they seem very serious about finding him."

Catherine's face turned hot and she resisted the urge to cry.

"What the hell happened while we were gone?" Ben demanded, shepherding Mama Rae into the house. "And what's this business about Jimmy robbing a store?"

Mama Rae turned to give Catherine an angry look, then started for the living room. Ben and Catherine went into the kitchen.

"I'm so relieved you're back!" Catherine cried. "I didn't expect you until tomorrow, and I'm so scared. We don't know what to do."

"What happened?" Ben asked impatiently. "And where's Jimmy?"

Catherine took a deep breath, trying to collect herself. "That stupid JT and another guy came here with your stuff from the hardware store. I didn't answer the door, so they peeked through the window and saw Jimmy in the house. Then they just went crazy! They broke in, and threatened us, and they probably would have taken Jimmy off and lynched him except we had Granddaddy's shotgun. The next thing we knew, a big mob was back here with some made-up story about Jimmy robbing the hardware store."

Ben sat down at the kitchen table with a look of extreme worry. "Where is Jimmy now?"

"He's hiding," Catherine said. "But I promised him we'd go warn Sally about all this, because he's scared to death they'll go to his house and terrorize his family."

"Where is he hiding?"

Catherine put her finger to her lips as a signal that she didn't want Mama Rae to hear, then she pointed down at the floor. "There's a way to go under the house from the back-yard," she whispered.

Ben put his head in his hands. "I should never have left the two of you alone," he said. "But you should have known better than to have him in this house when we were gone."

"*I didn't expect people to come peeping in the windows!*" Catherine cried. "How could we have known that would happen? But we don't have time to talk about that now. We have to reach Sally. And, by the way, we have no telephone. Those maniacs cut the phone lines!"

Catherine was not reassured by Ben's expression. He looked as frightened as she was.

"Look, Dad," she said, "We can't let anything happen to Jimmy. *We just can't*. But we have to reach Sally. I promised him." She pulled the address out of her pocket. "Here's where she lives," she said, handing the paper to her father.

"I told you Catherine had no business gettin' involved with that boy!" Mama Rae shouted from the living room. "Y'all didn't listen, and now look what a mess you've made of that boy's life!"

The words stung Catherine to the core, because she knew her grandmother was right.

"Please," Catherine whispered, nodding to the address. She was barely able to breath for the knot in her throat. "If you don't go, Jimmy will, and then they'll get him for sure."

"You know they've probably already been to his house," Ben said. "If they know his name, they probably know where he lives."

"Still, you need to explain to Sally what's happened," Catherine said. "And if she's still in the house, you need to tell her to get out of there. Jimmy doesn't think they're safe."

"Where is she supposed to go?" Ben asked.

"I don't know," Catherine said, "but I assume she must have some friends or relatives they can stay with."

"I saw Sally's car out front," Ben said. "Do we have the key?"

Catherine tried to think, frustrated by yet another variable to consider.

"Because we should probably try to get the car back to her," Ben said. "I don't think it can be of any use to Jimmy. Not with the roadblocks. And if she's going to go somewhere, she may need her car."

Catherine ran to her room and found the key on her dresser, attached to a rabbit's foot key chain. She was struck by the tragic irony of the "good luck" charm, then pictured poor Jimmy, helpless under the house, and was hit with such a rush of guilt and remorse that she almost buckled under its weight. Trying her best to stay strong, she grabbed the key, then returned to the kitchen and placed it on the kitchen table. She could see by the expression on Ben's face that it was not lost on him that she'd retrieved it from her room, but, to her relief, he declined to comment, choosing, instead, to communicate his disappointment with a look and shake of his head.

He picked up the key and took a couple of deep breaths. "For this to make sense, one of us will need to drive Jimmy's car, and one of us will need to follow in the truck. Otherwise I won't be able to get back."

"Will they let us through the roadblock?" Catherine asked.

"I guess we'll find out," Ben said. "They certainly have no legal reason to stop us, but with these guys, I don't think legal really matters. They'll do whatever they want."

"That reminds me," Catherine said. "I told them you have friends in the NAACP and the FBI."

Ben was running his hands through his hair in a gesture of frustration when Mama Rae walked into the kitchen. "I'm coming with y'all," she said. "I know a few things about this town that might be handy at a roadblock, and I feel like I owe it to Sally to try to help out with this mess." She looked at Catherine with a mixture of compassion and scorn. "You know they may kill that boy."

Catherine felt a wave of nausea, and, once again, struggled against hysteria.

"All right," Ben said to Mama Rae. "If we're going to do this, we need to go." He turned to Catherine. "I'll drive Sally's car. You and Mama Rae can follow in the truck." He tossed her his keys, then directed Mama Rae out of the kitchen.

"I'll be right out," Catherine said.

"All right," Ben said. "But hurry up."

As soon as Ben and Mama Rae were out the door, Catherine ran to where she though Jimmy would best be able to hear her through the floor. She fell to her knees. "Jimmy," she said, "Tap twice if you can hear me."

Two taps.

Suddenly Ben appeared next to her. "I think I know a better place to hide," he said. He knelt down. "Jimmy, this is Ben. Come in through the back door as quickly as you can. Do you understand?"

Two taps.

Catherine looked at Ben. "Where are you thinking?" she asked nervously.

"There's a way to get up into the rafters from the closet in my room," he said. "I used to hide girlie magazines up there when I was a teenager. It's not exactly an attic, but part of it was turned into a storage area, and it's got some ventilation, so I think he'll be more comfortable up there than under the house."

They stood up and went to the back door, and in a moment Jimmy appeared with the bundle Catherine had given him. They wasted little time talking, but before they pointed Jimmy to his new hiding place, Ben took him by the shoulders and looked him in the eyes. "We're going to do everything we can to keep you and your family safe," he said. "You just need to sit tight until we get back."

Jimmy reluctantly agreed, then followed Ben and Catherine into Ben's room, where he quickly disappeared through a removable ceiling at the top of a narrow closet.

Chapter 8

It was getting on towards dusk as Catherine started the truck and followed Ben down the long gravel driveway towards the road that led to the highway. At Catherine's suggestion, Ben had quickly replaced the plates on Sally's car with the plates from the car in the barn. They prayed this would help get Ben through the roadblock.

As they headed up the road, Mama Rae was quiet and Catherine was so overwhelmed by fear and shame that she was grateful for the silence. She found it difficult to even look at her grandmother, much less speak to her. Passing the pond, and then the field of grazing horses, Catherine recalled, with excruciating regret, the passion and joy that she and Jimmy had shared earlier in the day. What a terrible price Jimmy was paying for it.

When they finally arrived at the roadblock, Catherine and Mama Rae watched as Ben had a heated exchange with a deputy. After a final flurry of yelling and finger pointing that made Catherine worry that maybe they'd arrest her father, Ben stepped away from the car and waited as the deputy and another man who'd been sitting in a nearby truck searched the car, including the trunk. When they were finished, Ben got back into the car and drove a short distance before pulling over to observe Catherine and Mama Rae's turn at the stop.

Catherine pulled up and rolled the window all the way down. The deputy who approached was not Jesse Taylor, but she recognized him as one of the men who'd been at the house. He was a rough looking man with a large head, pot belly, and dark sweat stains under his arms. When he spoke, his breath was so terrible that Catherine winced and reflexively leaned away.

"Well lookee who we have here," said the ruddy face filling up the window. "It's the little nigger lovin' princess herself." He nodded at Mama Rae. "Who's this? You the little slut's grandma?"

Mama Rae gave the deputy a look of disgust. "You just never mind with that kind of talk and let us through."

The deputy shined a flashlight into the cab, then left to examine the back of the truck. After a moment he returned to the window and asked contemptuously, "Where y'all goin'?"

"That's none of your business," Mama Rae snapped.

Catherine was shocked by Mama Rae, and afraid that her back-talk might make things worse.

"Oh, it's my business," the deputy said. "Especially if it has anything to do with the fugitive nigger we're lookin' for."

He looked straight at Catherine, who was holding her breath. "If we find out that y'all are harboring that boy, you'll be charged with aiding and abetting. And that goes for you too, Grandma," he said, pointing a fat finger at Mama Rae.

"Don't y'all ever get tired of terrorizing innocent people?" Mama Rae cried. "You know perfectly well that boy didn't rob anyone. He's an innocent boy, and y'all are just a bunch of vicious bullies."

"You'd better remember who you're talking to," the deputy spit, his eyes blazing.

"I know exactly who I'm talking to," Mama Rae said. "I know all about you and your mob of thugs, and your hate meetings, and what y'all have been doing to innocent colored folks for as long as I can remember."

The deputy's enormous face was turning purple with rage, but Mama Rae didn't stop.

"I know a lot, and I can name names. And I'm telling you right now that if y'all do one thing to hurt that boy, you will be very sorry. My son has friends in the FBI, and I aim to do a lot of talking to those folks if need be." She straightened her skirt and looked straight ahead. *"Now let us through."*

Smoldering with anger, the deputy glared at Mama Rae. "You'd be wise to watch yourself, old lady," he said. Then he stepped away from the truck and shouted, "Go on and get out of here!"

Astonished by Mama Rae's courageous performance, Catherine started up the truck and waited for Ben to pull out ahead of them. "Wow," she said, when they were back on their way. "Were you bluffing back there, or can you really name names?"

Mama Rae remained silent, so Catherine decided to leave her be, but she had to wonder if her grandfather had been involved with the *'mob of thugs'* Mama Rae referred to, and if the mob she was talking about was the KKK. The thought made her feel sick to her stomach.

Soon they were on Main Street, heading towards the far side of town, and Catherine was growing more and more uncomfortable with the gulf between herself and Mama Rae. She wanted to tell her grandmother that she was sorry, but no words seemed sufficient to express the magnitude of remorse she was feeling for the nightmare she'd created. She was just struggling to think of *something* she could say when Mama Rae spoke up.

"Catherine," she said, "I know you're upset and frightened, but I just don't know what I can say that can help."

"I understand," Catherine said, struggling to contain her emotions.

Mama Rae sighed. "I know you think I'm angry with you, but more than anything, I'm ashamed of this terrible town." She placed her hand on Catherine's back. "No matter how you might feel about your part in all this, try to remember that you're not the real villain here. The villains are the *grown men* who have nothing better to do than to torture an innocent boy."

Catherine was both surprised and touched by her grandmother's words. "Thank you, Mama Rae," she said. "But because of me, Jimmy's life is probably ruined. If they don't kill him, he'll probably end up in jail."

"Well, we're going to do everything we can to make sure none of that happens," Mama Rae said. "I was serious back there when I was talking to that fat deputy. Did you see the look on his face? That was the fear of God."

"I noticed you borrowed my line about the FBI."

"Yeah, well that was a good one, so I figured I'd use it."

Catherine followed Ben through some twists and turns, and soon they were driving down an unpaved street of small homes that were little better than shacks. Ordinarily, Catherine would have been fascinated by the children playing in the street, and the dogs and chickens that seemed to roam freely, but with her mind focused on Jimmy, all she could see was the meager life he had miraculously escaped, only to have everything destroyed by her reckless affections. She remembered her grandmother's words about the "real villains," but they did little to assuage her guilt or fear. She pictured poor Jimmy in the boiling rafters of her grandmother's house, and her heart literally ached with regret.

Towards the end of a long street, Ben pulled up in front of a small neatly-kept home under the shade of a large tree. Catherine parked behind him, and though she didn't think she could be more nervous, she suddenly became so shaky that she wasn't sure she could stand. She was terrified of facing Sally.

Ben walked over to the truck and was just telling Catherine it was fine for her to stay outside when Sally came running out of the house. There was no doubt that she knew something was wrong, because she looked frantic, and it was evident from her swollen face that she'd been crying. *"What is happening? Where's my son?"* she exclaimed as she approached the truck.

She veered to look into her car, obviously searching for Jimmy, then jagged back and confronted Ben. "What are you doing with my car? And where is Jimmy? I don't understand what's happening. The sheriff was here talking about arresting him for robbing a store!" She looked at Catherine and Mama Rae, then back to Ben, and was so distraught that she seemed in danger of collapsing.

"Let's go inside," Ben said, "and I'll do my best to explain everything."

Catherine would sooner have walked into hell than follow Sally into her house, but she knew she had to face the situation squarely, no matter how painful, so she opened the door to the truck and was ushered into a tidy living room. Sally sat down in an old cloth chair, and Ben, Mama Rae, and Catherine settled across from her on a large, low couch.

Sally looked straight at Catherine. "This has something to do with the two of you, doesn't it?" Her voice was bitter. "Jimmy said he was gonna spend the day with his old teacher, Mr. Harris, but I'm guessing he was off somewhere with you. Is that right?"

Catherine wanted to answer, but she was so nervous and fearful, she was unable to speak.

Ben jumped in. "Here's what we know," he said. "Jimmy and Catherine were at the house today, and while they were inside, a boy showed up to deliver some things I ordered from the hardware store. He'd seen Catherine at the store, and also at the pond, and I think she's the reason he really came to the house, because we weren't expecting a delivery."

He sighed heavily. "When no one answered, he looked through a window and saw Jimmy with Catherine, and then kind of went crazy, I guess. He and another boy broke into the house and were making threats, and later he concocted the story about Jimmy robbing the hardware store."

Sally's face was the picture of pain. She began shaking her head, and issuing a low, anguished moan. "Oh Lord," she cried. "Lord, please don't let this be happening to my sweet Jimmy. Not Jimmy."

Watching Sally, Catherine experienced a whole new level of grief. She could feel Sally's pain as if it were flowing straight into her heart, and the agony was almost unbearable. She turned away and was suddenly looking at a wall filled with family photographs. One was of Sally with a handsome man that Catherine assumed was Jimmy's father. Others were of Jimmy and his siblings at various ages. On the far left, the newspaper story about Jimmy's college scholarship was framed. Catherine stared at the newspaper photo of Jimmy, smiling his trademark smile, and had the searing realization that he might never return to college. Next to the newspaper story was a blank space where it was plain something was missing. Catherine wondered what had hung there, then turned her attention back to Ben, who was still explaining the situation to Sally.

"Unfortunately," he was saying, "the boy's father is a deputy sheriff. I knew him in school, and I'm afraid he's a pretty terrible character. I don't like saying this, but I think he may harm Jimmy if he catches up with him."

"But where is he?" Sally demanded.

"For the moment we have him hidden back at the house," Ben said. "But I'm not sure how long he'll be safe there. I'm guessing they may go back there again looking for him."

"So what do we do? Where can he go?"

"Well, they have roadblocks set up on the highway, so he can't go anywhere by car. I'm thinking that maybe we need to find him a lawyer. A lawyer might at least be able to keep him safe until we get the whole mess sorted out."

Sally was shaking her head again.

"Don't worry about the lawyer," Ben said. "I'll help out with that. But first we promised Jimmy we'd make sure you and your daughters are safe. Where are your girls?"

Sally ignored the question. "No lawyer can save Jimmy if they find him. If there's a trial, they'll put him in prison as sure as I'm sitting here. That's if they don't kill him. No white jury in this town is gonna side up with my boy against a white boy. It's just that simple."

She wiped tears from her eyes and blew her nose in a handkerchief she'd been clutching. "This is what they do to 'uppity' Negroes around here," she said, trembling. "If they don't take 'em out in the woods and hang 'em, they arrest 'em on some made-up charge." She nodded at Catherine with scorn. "If they connect Jimmy with this one here..."

She put her head in her hands. "I should have listened to Mama Rae and *never* brought Jimmy around. You didn't need to be messing with Jimmy! He was going to college! He was gonna make something of himself!"

Mama Rae took Catherine's hand and squeezed it, but Catherine was so tuned in to Sally's pain that she was beyond comforting.

Ben interrupted. "I'm sorry, but we don't have time for all this. We need to get back home, but I need to get you out of this house first, Sally. Where are your daughters?"

Sally blew her nose again, then took a deep breath and slowly exhaled. "I sent 'em to my sister Mary's house when the sheriff was here. They'll be safe over there."

"Well, we need to get you over there too," Ben said. "With some of these characters riled up like they are, you might be in danger here."

"So I'm supposed to just let 'em drive me out of my own house?" she asked defiantly. "No. Uh-uh. I'm staying right here. I got my son George on his way. He's on a train from Chicago right now, and he should be here by tomorrow."

Mama Rae leaned forward. "Let us take you to your sister's house until George arrives," she said. "We don't feel comfortable leaving you here alone."

Sally's posture turned angry, and it was evident that, on top of everything else, she didn't like being told what to do.

"Please, Sally," Ben said. "We need to make sure you're safe before we can get back to Jimmy."

"I promised him," Catherine pleaded.

Sally looked at Catherine with stifled rage.

"Why don't you let me take you over in your car," Ben said. "Catherine and Mama Rae can follow us in the truck. Once we see you're settled, we'll go back and see about Jimmy. But we need to hurry."

After some more argument, Sally finally agreed, then disappeared into her bedroom to get some things together. In the meantime, Catherine walked over to the wall of photographs and was surprised to find Jimmy's essay near the newspaper story she'd noticed earlier. Catherine beckoned Ben over and they read it together.

Why I Want a College Scholarship
By James Emerson

My name is James Emerson. I read Shakespeare, Joyce, Hemingway. I study calculus, history, philosophy. I write poetry. I enjoy debate. I dream of studying law. I dream of a life with purpose. My teachers call me bright. Others call me "inferior," call me "nigger."

Because I am a Negro, I am considered "uppity." Because I am a Negro, I am told to behave in a manner befitting my low station, or fear the consequences. I must move off the sidewalk when a white man approaches. I must avert my eyes in the presence of white women. I must not swim in the white man's pool, eat at the white man's table, or study at the white man's schools.

I am barred from libraries, barred from businesses, barred from juries. I am turned away by white doctors. I am forced to use separate entrances, to use separate bathrooms, to stand in separate lines, lest I disturb white sensibilities. I am told to keep my head down, to know my place, to hold my tongue while my people are humiliated, persecuted, and punished for the crime of having dark skin. I am told to do these things or risk injury or death at the hands of angry white men.

Because I am a Negro, I have heard from my people what it was like to be property. What it was like to be sold like horses and pigs; to be torn from family with no recourse; to endure beatings and rape as a matter of normal life; to be owned, like dogs, by cruel masters. I have heard from my people of "free" men, falsely accused and convicted, condemned to years of chain gang labor. I have heard of poor sharecroppers, enslaved by unreasonable debt to dishonest land owners. I have heard of men all over the South, even in my own town, tortured and lynched for sport.

I have listened to stories told with bitter tears by people who have been released from bondage, but for whom freedom is a lie—because there is no freedom without dignity, without opportunity, without justice. There is no freedom for people who are forced to live in fear of arbitrary violence, who are denied equal access to education, who are denied equal treatment under the law, who are denied even the most basic human rights.

My name is James Emerson, and I am applying for a college scholarship because I want to devote my life to the cause of making this country fulfill the promise of freedom for Negro citizens, especially those in the South who suffer under the tyranny of laws that are antithetical to the values on which this county was founded.

As a first step, I will enroll in a four year college and study history and literature. Afterwards, I will pursue a degree in law. Then, in the tradition of men like W.E.B. Du Bois, Charles Hamilton Houston, and Thurgood Marshall, I will use my status as a lawyer to fight against legal and social injustices with the goal of remaking this country into one in which all people are granted the dignity, freedom, and opportunity they deserve.

After Catherine finished reading, she looked at Ben, and there were tears in his eyes. "He's going to be a great man, isn't he?" Catherine asked, her voice trembling.

"This is pretty powerful," Ben said. "I think, given the chance, he might really do great things."

129

"James Emerson," Catherine whispered, turning back to his words. Ben put his arms around her and held her tight. "We need to have faith," he said.

ᐊ

A short time later they were on their way to Sally's sister's house, which was several blocks away on the edge of town. As Catherine and Mama Rae drove slowly past homes, churches, and small businesses alive with the sights and sounds of Southern Negro life, Catherine could tell from the looks and stares of those they passed that their presence was a curiosity. Ordinarily, she would have met each face turned their way with a friendly look or gesture, but in her anguished state, all she could manage was an expression of quiet despair.

When they pulled up in front of Mary's house, they were met by the barking of a large yellow dog that was tethered to a tree in the front yard. Sally's sister emerged from inside, and moments later a whole new pandemonium broke out as Sally learned that Dee and Martha had never arrived. With this new discovery, and the very real possibility that the girls had been taken, Catherine wondered how she would find the strength to cope with the terrible reality that seemed to be getting worse by the moment. Then her thoughts turned to Sally and Jimmy, and to his innocent sisters who might be enduring God-only-knows-what horrors, and she hated herself anew for even considering her own misery.

Catherine and Mama Rae stayed in the truck, but Ben was now with Sally and her sister in the front yard of Mary's house. Soon they were joined by Mary's husband Will, and several men and women who had noticed the commotion and walked over from nearby houses. Sally was near collapse with fear and panic, so Mary helped her inside while Will and some of the neighbors had a highly-charged discussion. There was tough talk and rage about the missing girls, and it quickly became plain that they were uninformed as to the situation with Jimmy. Ben stepped up to explain, and when the group learned about Jimmy, they became so distraught and panicked that Catherine had to look away. Will, in particular, was so affected, that when Catherine finally found the courage to look back, she was met with the sight of him sobbing into his hands. Catherine could tell by his, and all the other terrified faces, that underlying all their rage and grief was a sense of helplessness and frustration, it being understood by everyone that they were up against men who could do whatever they pleased with virtual impunity.

Before disappearing into the house, Sally had pleaded with Ben to *please go check on Jimmy*, so Ben wasted no time before joining Catherine and Mama Rae back in the truck. As they drove off, Will and his neighbors were in a heated discussion about the possibility of enlisting the aid of local church leaders, since it was agreed by all that calling for the help of law enforcement was not an option.

Catherine was drowning with despair and worry. Now, on top of her fears for Jimmy, she was frantic about the welfare of his sisters, whom she still pictured as tiny girls playing sweetly on her grandparents' porch. She found it beyond belief that there could be no appealing to the law on their behalf, and her feeling of responsibility for their predicament added yet another laceration to her already stinging conscience. Sandwiched now between her father and Mama Rae, and finally on her way back to Jimmy, Catherine struggled to maintain her composure. She looked at her father and tried to imagine what he must be feeling. He was supposed to be the strong one—the big, fearless dad who would know what to do to make everything okay. And yet, what was he supposed to do? What could he do? She had no doubt that the weight he felt was crushing.

Catherine wondered how many times nightmares like this had been inflicted on Southern blacks. How many fathers had felt this kind of weight, and been helpless? How many mothers had suffered the agony of watching their innocent children made victims? How many young men had been killed, tortured, or imprisoned for having the temerity to assert their humanity? How many young girls had been taken by hostile white men? She didn't know the answers to these questions, but she was certain the numbers were staggering, especially when you counted two hundred years of slavery. She wondered how many horrific crimes might be playing out right now, all over the South.

Catherine had contemplated the violence and injustices suffered by Negroes many times before, from the perspective of a compassionate outsider, but now, in the midst of this horror, she realized how impossible it was for any outsider to truly appreciate the impact of the twisted Jim Crow ethos on people's lives. And though Catherine was involved in this particular nightmare, she was aware that her position was still just a ringside seat. How must Jimmy feel? Or Sally? Or Sally's daughters? Catherine found these questions excruciating.

When they arrived back at the highway roadblock it was dark, but Catherine could see, as they waited behind a car stopped in front of them, that the deputy stopping people had a photograph of Jimmy, no doubt accounting for the blank spot on Sally's wall. Through the open window of the truck, she heard the deputy call Jimmy a '*nigger*.' She visualized screaming at him, and, judging by the look on Ben's face, he was having a similar fantasy.

Mama Rae was the one who spoke up. "Can you believe I've seen that man singing in church? Singing and praising the Lord right up to the rafters." She shook her head in disgust, then leaned forward and craned her head around Catherine to look at Ben. "It pains me to tell you this, but your father was in cahoots with some of these characters." She seemed on the verge of crying. "I hope he was never involved with anything this terrible. I tried not to think about it then, and it makes me sick wonderin' about it now."

As Catherine processed her grandmother's words, Mama Rae leaned back and Ben pulled up for their turn at the stop. This time they weren't recognized by the deputy, who was not the same one who'd met them on the way in.

"I'm sorry to inconvenience y' all," he said, "but we got a local nigger on the run, so we need to do a quick search of your vehicle." He examined the back of the truck, then returned to the window to shine a flashlight in the cab. "Y'all can go on through in just a second, but first I'd like you to take a look at this picture."

He held up the photo, and Catherine nearly broke down when she saw Jimmy's smiling face. "If any of y'all see this boy," he said, "be advised that he's armed and dangerous, and please contact the Sheriff's Department immediately."

Mama Rae called out, "What exactly did he do?"

The deputy peered into the cab. "He held up a store in town, and he's also suspected of raping a white girl."

Mama Rae grabbed Catherine's hand and leaned across her towards the window. "Deputy," she said, "I've know this boy since he was a baby. He's the son of my housekeeper. Now, I know what you've been *told* he did, but *I'm* telling you that it's a damn lie."

The deputy started to say something, but Mama Rae interrupted him. "*Let me finish!* Now, maybe you're one of them that just wants to hurt innocent people because you get some kind of sick pleasure out of it. I don't know. But if you're not, and if you want the truth, I'm telling you that this boy didn't commit any crime. The whole thing was just made up because he and my granddaughter here, who's visiting from California, are old friends from when they were kids, and some boy in town doesn't like it."

Once again, the deputy tried to interrupt, but Mama Rae wouldn't have it. "Just hold on!" she shouted. "Now, we've just come from the boy's family, and there are two little girls missing. His sisters. It looks like someone may have taken those girls, but the family's afraid to call the sheriff, because they believe the sheriff and some of y'all may be involved."

She pointed a bony finger at the deputy. "If you're a Christian, which I know you are, because I've seen you in church, I just ask you to think about those little girls, and that innocent boy and his family. No good Christian would be involved in harming those people, or going along with folks who take pleasure in hurtin' others. And I know you know what I'm talking about. There's been too much of this kind of nonsense in this town, and I think it's high time that good white Christians stood up and stopped it. And I'll just leave you with that thought."

There was silence, and the deputy seemed to be waiting to make sure Mama Rae was finished. When she said no more, he simply said, "Yes ma'am." Then he surprised them all by tipping his hat and waving them through.

An instant later, they were finally headed back to Jimmy. As they neared the turnoff to their road, Catherine's heart started up again, and soon it was beating so hard that she wondered if she might actually die of fear. She had heard of such a thing, and now understood the physical impact that fear could have on a body. Her heart was literally pounding in her chest. It occurred to her that if something were to happen to Jimmy or his sisters, she would probably welcome death, but, for the moment, she began a campaign of deep breathing in an attempt to calm herself down.

She looked at her father, and his expression was one of extreme distress. "What are you thinking?" Catherine asked, afraid of what he might say.

"That business about rape does not bode well for Jimmy," he said. "If that's what they're telling people on the road, I imagine their goal is to try to get folks worked up into a frenzy."

"Well, if that happens," Mama Rae said, "I suggest we try to whip up a frenzy of our own. I meant what I said back there. It's way past time people in this town start standing up for decency. The Klan and their thugs have ruled the roost around here for too long."

This was Mama Rae's first actual mention of the KKK, and it confirmed Catherine's worst fears. She was just going to respond to her grandmother's remark when she was struck mute by the appearance of lights as they turned into their driveway.

"This is not good," Ben pronounced, as they all realized, with horror, that several sheriff's cars and a large gray sedan were parked in front of the house. Men with flashlights were milling around the porch and barn, and lights were visible in the nearby woods as well.

Ben parked, then took a deep breath and got out of the truck. Catherine and Mama Rae, now holding hands, were frozen in place. Catherine pictured Jimmy, terror-struck in the rafters of the house, and prayed they wouldn't find him. *"Please God, please God, please God, please God..."*

She'd murmured these same words at the pond, and now asked herself why, after that close call, she and Jimmy had so recklessly persisted in their dangerous behavior. She contemplated the answer, then became enraged by the thought that love was a crime punishable by death. In an instant, she was struck by a feeling of hatred so powerful that she wanted to scream with all her strength. She looked out at the men circling the house like sharks, and it took every ounce of self-control she could muster to stay in the truck and keep quiet.

She had been squeezing Mama Rae's hand, and suddenly realized that she was in danger of breaking her grandmother's small bones. "I'm sorry," she said to Mama Rae, letting up on the pressure.

"It's all right," Mama Rae said. "I understand just how you feel."

They turned their attention to Ben, whom they could hear through the open window.

"What's going on?" he asked one of the men in uniform.

Catherine was relieved to see that it wasn't Jesse Taylor or the first deputy who'd stopped them at the roadblock.

"I'm Sheriff White," the man said to Ben. "Is this your house?"

"It's my mother's house," Ben said. "What's this all about?"

"I think you know what it's about," the sheriff said. "We have reason to believe you may be harboring a suspect in a crime, and we have a warrant to search the premises."

"Sheriff White," Ben said coolly, "I hired the boy you're looking for to do some work around the place. He's a fine boy, the son of my mother's housekeeper, home from college for the summer. My family has known him since he was a youngster, and I can guarantee that he hasn't committed any crime. This is all just something that was cooked up by a young man who didn't like seeing him talking to my daughter—which, to my knowledge, is not a crime."

"It's my understanding that there was a lot more going on than just talking," the sheriff said icily. "But on the question of whether or not a crime has been committed, I'm afraid that'll be for a jury to decide. Right now it's my job to exercise this warrant, and that's what we're doing. We only got here a few minutes ago, but we've already entered the house. My men are inside now. And I have to warn you; if we find the boy in the house, we'll be charging you with harboring a fugitive."

"You won't find him in the house," Ben stated. "I don't know where he is. But I do know that if any harm comes to him as a result of this campaign of racial hatred—which is what this is—no one'll be sweeping this one under the rug. You can count on it."

While Ben was talking, Jesse Taylor walked up and was listening with an air of amusement. "Well, look who we have here," he said to Ben. He looked at the sheriff. "Old Ben and I were friends back in high school, weren't we Ben?"

Ben gave him a look of contempt, then turned back to the sheriff. "Your deputy here was a menace in high school, and his son is no different." He kicked some gravel and seemed to be trying to collect his thoughts and contain his emotions. "That boy is lying about what happened, and I'm betting you suspect it, if you don't know it."

"You'd better watch yourself," Jesse Taylor hissed. "I don't think you know who you're dealing with here. This ain't high school no more. You're talkin' to the law." He put his hand on his gun in a not-too-subtle threat.

"It's time to break this up," Sheriff White said. He nodded to Jesse to back off, then turned to Ben. "We need to finish our search, so I'd like you to go wait in your truck. But don't go anywhere. I'll be getting back to y'all later."

Jesse Taylor reluctantly retreated. The sheriff was starting to walk off when Ben waved him back. "I don't know if any money was really taken from the hardware store," Ben said, "but if it was, that deputy's son would be the prime suspect. I suggest you search his place."

"I'll thank you to keep your suggestions to yourself," the sheriff snapped. "We have our suspect, and I'm confident we'll be bringing him to justice real soon."

As Sheriff White disappeared into the house, Ben rejoined Catherine and Mama Rae in the truck. "Try to behave as calmly as you can," he said after closing the door. "We have to look like we don't think he's in the house."

"Do you think it's possible they won't find him?" Catherine asked, her voice trembling.

"I don't know," Ben said. "I suppose it's possible, but I just don't know."

Mama Rae took Catherine's hand and squeezed it. "All we can do now is pray."

慔

They remained mostly silent for the next few minutes, with their eyes glued to the front of the house. As Mama Rae mouthed silent prayers, Ben worked the heel of his foot and Catherine focused on deep breathing. Soon, they began hearing thunder off in the distance and it started to sprinkle. Not long after, it began to rain, then pour. Some of the men who had been searching away from the house came running to the front porch for cover. Others retreated to their cars. Then, in an instant, the sky lit up and thunder boomed so loudly overhead that Catherine screamed and fell sobbing into her father's arms.

After several more dramatic strikes of lightning and thunder, and with rain now coming down in sheets, there were some sharp knocks on Ben's foggy window, causing Catherine to sit up at attention. Ben rolled down the window to see the sheriff standing in the deluge, water dripping from his hat. "The house and property appear to be clear," he said "so we'll be leaving now. But I want to warn you that if we come back and find the suspect on the premises, I'll personally make sure you pay the full penalty." Then, before there could be any response, he turned and sprinted for his car.

Ben rolled up the window, then looked at Catherine and Mama Rae, who were wide-eyed. "Let's wait until the cars are all gone before we react to this," he said. Catherine didn't move, but experienced such a sense of relief that she was once more reduced to tears.

"Our prayers have been answered," Mama Rae whispered.

Ben exhaled. "We'll see. But we have a long way to go before this thing's over."

The three of them watched as each of the cars turned on their headlights, then drove back down the driveway and disappeared onto the road. When the cars were all gone, they hugged one another and shared their relief. Then Ben drove the truck as close as possible to the house before they all exited, anxious to check on Jimmy, and unconcerned about the rain, which was still pouring down in buckets. It was just starting to hail as Ben helped Mama Rae out of the truck and Catherine ran for the door.

Once inside, Catherine was shocked by what she saw. It looked as if the interior of the house had been struck by a tornado. Furniture was turned over, articles had been pulled from drawers and shelves, and clothes and linens were strewn everywhere. She peeked into the kitchen and found it so littered with items pulled from cabinets, drawers, and the refrigerator, that she could barely see the floor. The sheriff had claimed they were looking for Jimmy, but it was obvious that a major part of his agenda was to do as much damage to their house as possible. Stepping over and around debris, Catherine headed cautiously to her father's room and opened the closet door. "Jimmy," she called to the ceiling. "Jimmy, we're back and all the men are gone!"

"Oh you think so, do ya?"

Catherine shrieked with alarm, then turned and was thunderstruck to see Jesse Taylor standing in the doorway.

An instant later, Ben was behind him in the hallway, vigorously shaking his head. "I should have *known* they'd try something like this!"

"Yeah, well you were always stupid," Jesse Taylor gloated. "We knew y'all were hiding the nigger. It was just a matter of lettin' you lead us to him. Now we got him wrapped up in a bow, thanks to you."

Stunned, and overcome with terror, Catherine staggered to the dresser for support. After feeling such great relief, she simply couldn't believe this was happening.

Mama Rae was now standing next to Ben, her eyes blazing. "You are an evil man!" she yelled at the deputy. "One day you'll be punished for this. You can be sure of that."

Jesse Taylor was gleeful. "The only thing I'm sure of is we got our nigger. And now I'm takin' him in." He marched into the closet and used a long flashlight to push the false ceiling aside. Noise from the rain and hail beating down on the roof added to Catherine's terror.

The deputy looked up and began to holler, "Come on out now! We got you!"

Catherine held her breath, but there was no sound or movement from above.

He shouted again, "If you make me come up there after you, you're gonna be sorry. Now come on down from there!"

Still nothing.

"Go get me a chair," Jesse ordered Ben.

"Get your own damn chair!" Ben spat.

The deputy muscled Ben and Mama Rae aside, then disappeared down the hall. After a few moments, he returned with a kitchen chair and slammed it down in the closet. With one hand on the gun at his hip, he stepped onto the chair and shined his flashlight up above the ceiling and looked around. "Come on down from there you lousy nigger!" he bellowed. "If I have to come up there after you, you'll be comin' down with a bullet in your head!"

"He's gone," Ben said. "If he were up there, you'd see him."

"He ain't gone, now shut your mouth!"

Catherine locked eyes with her father, and she could see that he had hope.

In a frenzy of frustration, Jesse Taylor jumped down from the chair and ran to the kitchen to phone for assistance. He returned shortly, seething with anger.

"Guess someone cut the phone line," Catherine said.

"Well, I got someone comin' back for me real soon," Jesse spat back. "We'll get that boy outta there if I have to burn the place down to do it. And that's a promise."

He went back to the closet and, once again, stood on the chair and shined the flashlight around the interior of the roof. "I'm giving you one more chance to come down from there!" Jesse screamed, his voice mixing with the roar of rain and hail reverberating in the rafters. "If you don't come down right now, I swear to God I'm gonna kill you!"

"I'm telling you, he's gone," Ben said.

As Jesse Taylor stepped down from the chair, Catherine exchanged another look with her father and prayed that what he was saying was true.

Mama Rae was loudly demanding that Jesse Taylor get out of her house when a wet and skinny deputy barged past her and entered Ben's room. He took off his hat and shook it. "What have we got?"

"Nigger's up in the roof and won't come down," Jesse said. "The entrance is in there." He nodded at the closet.

"We'll get him out of there," the deputy said. He smoothed back his hair, placed his hat back on, then moved into the closet and stepped up onto the chair. "Hand me your flashlight."

Catherine silently prayed as the deputy took the flashlight and shined it up into the rafters in all directions. "Are you sure he's up there?" he asked. "It don't look to me like there's much space up there to hide. Have you heard anything?"

"I ain't heard shit with this goddamn storm," Jesse said, "but he's up there all right. The girl made a beeline for the closet the moment she entered the house."

The skinny deputy looked down at Catherine with disdain. "Your boyfriend up there?"

Catherine was vibrating with contempt. "Your people are a disgrace."

"Oh, we're a disgrace?" he shot back. "I'll show you a disgrace. Look in the mirror."

Ben stepped up close to Jesse. "I want you two out of this house. There's no one up there. You've seen for yourself."

The deputy looked at Ben with stone hatred. "I guess you think you're pretty superior, don't ya?" He smirked. "Well, Mr. Superior, how do you feel about your daughter here screwin' a nigger? If she were my daughter, I'd kill her."

142

At that Mama Rae shrieked, *"That's it! Get your ass out of my house this instant!"*

"We'll leave when we're good and ready!" he roared back.

The other deputy called from the closet, "Hoist me up, Jesse."

Jesse Taylor boosted the deputy up through the ceiling and Catherine held her breath as she watched him disappear. After just a few seconds, he called down, "Ain't nothing up here but a few moldy boxes and a whole lot of rat shit!"

When he jumped down a few moments later, his uniform was soiled with dirt and feces, which he began flicking with exaggerated disgust. "Let's get out of here!" he spat. He kicked over the chair. "Ain't nothin' here but rat shit and white trash."

Purple with rage, Jesse Taylor glared at Ben. "We're gonna find that boy," he snarled. Then he followed the other deputy down the hall and back out into the storm.

Chapter 9

Catherine felt shell shocked, and she could see that her father and Mama Rae were in the same condition. As she contemplated the disaster in which they were embedded, she had no words—only relief that Jimmy might be safe, and a shrieking desire for the nightmare to go away.

Mama Rae was the first to speak. "I don't know about anyone else, but if I don't get some food in me, I'm gonna fall apart completely."

Relieved to be presented with a task that seemed manageable, Catherine took a deep breath, then responded, "I'll see if I can find you something to eat."

"I'll fix up a place in the living room for you to sit down," Ben said.

Dazed and weary, they all began slowly moving about the house, carefully stepping over the debris that was strewn everywhere. None of them yet had the energy or will to begin putting things back together. Catherine was at the threshold of the kitchen when she had a thought that stopped her in her tracks. *Suppose Jimmy had gone back under the house?* She went to where she'd heard him knocking earlier in the day and fell to her knees. She looked around, afraid of being surprised once again, and was aware only of Ben, who saw her and instantly understood what she was doing. Catherine closed her eyes and knocked three times on the floor.

Nothing.

She knocked again, and there was still no response. She looked up at Ben. "Where do you think he is?" she asked. "Where did he go?"

"I don't know," Ben said.

Catherine suddenly had a terrible thought. "You don't suppose they took him, do you? What if they took him, but just don't want us to know?"

Ben placed his hand on Catherine's back. "I don't think they found him. I can't imagine Jesse being that good an actor. Did you see the veins busting out of his neck? His head all but exploded towards the end there." He helped Catherine to her feet. "I'm sure Jimmy just felt trapped and decided to make a run for it."

Ben began picking up items strewn on the kitchen floor. "If you think about it," he said, "we didn't ask him what he wanted to do. We just shoved him up through a hole in the ceiling and left him alone."

Catherine realized, with remorse, that what Ben was saying was true. "But where do you think he might have gone? Do you think maybe he went to Sally's sister's house?"

"I don't know, maybe," Ben said, picking up pieces of a broken plate. "But he could be anywhere."

"Sally mentioned a teacher," Catherine said. "Maybe that's where he's gone." She thought about the possibility and it gave her hope that Jimmy might be somewhere safe.

"For now," Ben said, "I agree with Mama Rae. We're not going to be any good to anyone if we don't get some food in us."

Ben and Catherine surveyed the disaster in the kitchen and soon realized that they had very little that was fit to eat. The food that had been in the refrigerator was part of the trampled mess on the floor, and most of the items in the pantry had been savaged as well.

"What do you say we leave this chaos and go over to the diner on Main Street?" Ben suggested. "That might be the quickest solution under the circumstances."

Catherine hated the prospect of facing the roadblock again, but she knew her father was right. They needed food. She looked out the window and saw that the rain was starting to let up.

Mama Rae limped into the kitchen. "Will you look at this mess," she said. She sounded both bitter and exhausted. Ben offered her a chair and she sat down at the table. "Did I hear you say you were going out again?" she asked.

"They ruined most of our food," Ben explained, "so I think we're going to have to."

Mama Rae looked deflated.

Ben sighed. "I suppose we could bring something back for you, but my instinct tells me it's probably not wise to leave you alone. I think you'd better come with us."

Mama Rae reluctantly agreed, and a few minutes later they were back in the truck. When they arrived at the roadblock, Ben rolled down the window and the same deputy that had stopped them the last time looked surprised to see them again.

"The sheriff and his goons tore up our house," Ben reported bitterly, "so we're going to town for some food."

"Well, I'm sorry to hear about your house," the deputy said, "but I'm afraid I'll need to do another search before I can let you through."

The deputy did a quick search, then signaled them to go on. As he did, he met Catherine's eyes with a look that smacked of regret. "Hold on," Catherine said, just as Ben was stepping on the gas. "Stop."

Ben stopped the truck and Catherine waved the deputy over. "What's your name?" she asked as he returned to the window.

He hesitated.

"Please," Catherine said, "What's your name?"

He glanced down at a small black and white name tag pinned to his shirt. "I'm Dan Tucker," he said.

"Okay. Thank you, Deputy Tucker," Catherine replied, giving him a look that she hoped would stir his sympathy. He responded by once again tipping his hat, then he stepped back and waved them on.

Back on the road, Ben commented on the interaction. "I know what you're thinking about the deputy back there," he said, "but I wouldn't get your hopes too high on his account."

"Well, it can't hurt to have at least one friend in the department," Catherine said.

"What-all were you up to in the house with Jimmy?" Mama Rae asked out of the blue.

Catherine had been expecting the question, and she was prepared with the answer. "We weren't doing anything," she said with conviction. "We were just eating sandwiches and talking at the kitchen table."

"Well, that's what I thought," Mama Rae said. "Those men have sick minds. But y'all still should have known better."

Catherine glanced at Ben, who was staring straight ahead with a blank look on his face. She wondered what he was thinking, but was not anxious to find out.

 beginning

Catherine and Ben and Mama Rae were in the diner, nervously eating pot roast and chicken fried steak, when they looked up and were surprised to see JT's friend Teddy standing next to their table, his ducktail hidden beneath a blue baseball cap.

"Hey," he said to Catherine and Ben, who were sitting on one side of a red Naugahyde booth. "I recognized your truck out front."

He nodded to Mama Rae. "Ma'am."

"Do y'all remember me?" he asked, looking back to Catherine and Ben.

"I remember you," Catherine said. She had a vision of their close call at the pond and felt a chill. "Your name is Teddy."

"Yeah, that's right," he said.

"What can we do for you, Teddy?" Ben asked coolly.

Teddy seemed apprehensive, then said in a low voice, "Well, I saw your truck, and I just wanted to tell y'all that I don't go along with what JT and them are up to."

Ben locked eyes with the boy. "What, exactly, is it they're up to, Teddy?"

Teddy was sweating. "Look," he said, barely audible, "I don't want to get in the middle of this, but I think y'all should know that they're trying to get up a mob to go after the boy they're lookin' for. And if they find him, I think they may be plannin' something pretty bad."

Just then, a truck filled with raucous men whizzed past the window in the direction of the highway.

"That's probably some of 'em now," Teddy said, moving away from the window. "They're having a meeting in the clearing up past the high school."

148

"Are we talking about what I think we're talking about?" Ben asked, his face flushing red.

Teddy was now visibly shaking. He looked around the diner. There were no other customers, and the waitress was in the kitchen. "If you mean, you know, *the Klan*," he whispered, "then yeah. The sheriff and JT's daddy are ringleaders. Everyone in town pretty much knows it."

Another truck roared past the window, and Catherine felt like she was going to be sick. Mama Rae took her hand across the table.

"Listen to me, Teddy," Ben said. "Is there anything else you can tell us? Anything you might have heard that could be important for us to know?"

"All's I know is this ain't the first time they've had this particular boy in their sights," he said. "There was a story about him in the newspaper a couple of years back, and they were thinking about goin' after him then." He looked around again to double-check he wasn't being overheard. "They don't like his type," he whispered. "You know, Negroes that try to go above their station."

He focused in on Catherine. "I don't go along with that kind of thinkin'. I'm gettin' out of this town just as soon as I can. But JT and them, they're crazy. They might even come after y'all." He adjusted his cap. "I wouldn't put nothin' past 'em."

Ben and Catherine thanked Teddy, and moments later he headed nervously out the door. Feeling suddenly sick, Catherine rushed to the ladies room and threw up what little potroast she'd managed eat. She was in the process of splashing cold water on her face when Mama Rae appeared beside her.

"I'm so sorry, Sweetheart," she said, brushing back a strand of Catherine's hair. "I don't know what to tell you, except some of the people in this town are just plain vile." Her blue eyes were rimmed with red and filled with anguish. "I don't know what makes 'em behave the way they do."

Catherine dried her face with a paper towel, then hugged her grandmother, whose tiny frame felt fragile in her arms. "I'm so scared," she said, now leaning against the sink. "I feel like I'm trapped in a nightmare and can't wake up." She suddenly felt like she might be sick again and took some deep breaths to steady herself. "What are we going to do? What if they find Jimmy? And what about his poor sisters! Do you think they're going to hurt his sisters?"

"I don't know," Mama Rae said. "I just don't know." She put her hand on Catherine's back. "Let's go back out and talk to your father."

Catherine and Mama Rae left the bathroom and rejoined Ben at the table. "What do we do now?" Catherine asked, sinking back into the booth.

Ben wiped his mouth with a napkin, then tossed it on his plate. "I've ordered some food to go, so we'll have something to eat tomorrow morning. After we get that, I'm thinking we should drive back to Sally's sister's house and see if they've found the girls. We also need to warn them about what we just learned."

Catherine's eyes filled up with tears. The thought of facing Sally's family again terrified her, but she knew her father was right.

"Try to hold on," Ben said, seeing how much she was struggling. "I know you feel responsible for all this, but you're not. You could never have imagined something like this."

"You're wrong," Catherine said bitterly. "I could have imagined. I knew about things like this. What have you been telling me all these years? I've heard stories; I've seen pictures—

of men who were tortured, and lynched. I've read about things like this. *I could have imagined this.* I just didn't want to. I didn't want to believe that anything like this could really happen. And look what's happened! *Look what I've done!"*

"That's enough of that kind of talk," Mama Rae scolded. "The people to blame here are the hate mongers who are pretending to be the law when they're nothing more than vicious thugs. Don't you take the blame on yourself. I don't care what you and Jimmy were up to in the house. That's between you and Jimmy and it's none of their goddamned business."

Ben shot Mama Rae a look of astonished gratitude, then turned to Catherine. "Listen to your grandmother," he said.

ભ

When they were back in the truck, Ben was careful to make sure they weren't being followed. "I'd like you to stay in the truck when we get there," he told Catherine. "There's no need for you to put yourself through any more stress." He looked past Catherine to Mama Rae. "You can stay with her. I'll just run in and tell everyone what we know and find out if they have anything new."

When they got to Mary's long street, most of the tiny houses were quiet, but some had people out front enjoying the relative cool of the evening. Catherine noticed faces turn to follow their truck as it passed, and she was relieved by the knowledge that, in the darkness, they couldn't see her white skin, which felt to her like a mantle of shame.

When they got to Mary's house, people were still in the yard, and this time the crowd was bigger. Ben parked, and Mary's husband Will stepped up to greet them. "Any news about Jimmy?" he asked anxiously.

"When we got back to the house he was gone," Ben said. "But that's a blessing, because the sheriff and his goons arrived just before we did, and they took the place apart looking for him."

Just as her father was finishing his sentence, Catherine caught sight of something that made her sit up and hold her breath. It was two teenage girls that she hoped were Jimmy's sisters.

"Daddy!" she gasped, pulling on Ben's arm. She pointed to the girls, then looked at Will expectantly, unable to speak.

He glanced to where she was pointing. "We got 'em back about a half hour ago," he said. "They weren't physically harmed, praise God, but they were scared pretty bad."

"What happened?" Ben asked. "Where were they?"

"Well, from what we've been able to put together, it seems they were grabbed by a couple of sheriff's deputies right up the road from Sally's house. They told the girls they were taking 'em in for questioning, but they took 'em out on the highway first—you know, like they were gonna take 'em off somewhere—so it's clear they mainly wanted to put the fear of God in 'em."

He took a red bandana out of his back pocket and wiped his face. "When they finally did take the girls to the station, they told 'em a lot of lies about Jimmy, and threatened 'em. They wouldn't let 'em call home, wouldn't let 'em use the toilet. Poor Martha was so fearful she soiled herself." He shook his head and put the bandana back in his pocket. "When they'd finally had enough fun, they dumped the girls back at Sally's house and took off."

Will turned and looked to where Catherine had seen the girls, but they'd gone back in the house. "They're pretty shook up," he said, "but they're mainly worried about Jimmy." He nodded towards the people in the yard. "We're all worried."

Suddenly Sally was at the truck window, accompanied by Mary. "Have you seen Jimmy?" she asked, sounding desperate.

"I'm afraid not," Ben said. "He wasn't at the house when we got there, so we don't know where he is. We were thinking he may have gone to the teacher you mentioned earlier. Do you think that's somewhere he might go for help?"

Sally looked at Catherine and her eyes were filled with blame. Catherine wanted to say something, but she had no words. The force of Sally's anger was shattering.

Sally looked back at Ben. "We called Mr. Harris, Jimmy's teacher. He hasn't seen Jimmy in over a year."

She turned once more to Catherine, and was plainly thinking about the lie Jimmy had told her that morning when he'd left the house. Catherine wished so desperately that he hadn't lied, that he *had* visited the teacher that morning.

"Do you think he might go back to your house?" Mama Rae asked. Her voice was motherly and sympathetic.

Will was listening. "We have someone there in case he does," he said. "If we can just find him, our church has arranged to keep him safe until we can figure out a way to get him out of town."

"I don't like telling you this," Ben said, "but it looks like there may be people putting together some kind of a..." He faltered, seeming unable to bring himself to say what he was thinking.

"A lynch mob?" Sally asked bitterly. She looked straight at Catherine. "They're putting together a lynch mob?"

Catherine tried to think of something to say. *Something* that would communicate the depth of her regret, but when she opened her mouth all that came out was the whisper of two feeble words. *"I'm sorry."*

Unmoved, Sally looked past Catherine at Mama Rae. "Mama Rae," she said, with blazing eyes, "just as soon as we find Jimmy, I'm takin' my family to Chicago, and we won't never be comin' back."

Chapter 10

When they finally arrived back home, Catherine and Ben and Mama Rae were so exhausted that they decided to keep ignoring the disastrous state of the house and retreat to their separate rooms. There were no more words to be spoken, and nothing they could do but pray that things would somehow look up in the morning.

As Catherine entered her room, she saw that, true to his word, Jesse Taylor had taken one of the sheets from her bed. She cried when she realized that he'd left her the top sheet, still fragrant with the scent of love. *How many times had she cried today?* she wondered. *Starting with the tears she'd shed in Jimmy's arms.* She found it impossible to fathom that, just hours before, she'd been engaged in the most loving experience of her life. And now... *Now...*

Catherine wrapped herself in the sheet, trying to lose herself in Jimmy's scent and find comfort in recalling scenes from earlier in the day. But there was no comfort. Only stinging, unrelenting regret.

She was lying in the dark, wrapped in the sheet, when she suddenly remembered her picture and was struck with a fear of such magnitude that her heart, once again, began racing. In a panic, she jumped up, turned on the light, and began searching the room, praying that, in their destructive rampage, the men had not taken or destroyed what might be the only thing she had left of Jimmy. In the midst of her frenzied searching, she felt like she was becoming unhinged, but she didn't care.

All she cared about was finding the picture, which, in her fragile state, seemed more important than her own life. She was just reaching around desperately under the bed when she heard a knock on the door.

"Catherine," Ben called. "Catherine, can I come in?"

Not waiting for her to answer, he opened the door and stepped into her room. "What are you doing?" he asked. "What are you looking for?"

Catherine collapsed into a heap of delirium, and Ben picked her up and held her, sobbing, in his arms.

"What'll they do to Jimmy if they find him?" she asked, when she was calm enough to talk. *Are they going to kill him?"*

"I don't think they're going to find him," Ben said soothingly. "Jimmy is smart. That's why he left here. He knew they'd come looking for him." He smoothed Catherine's tousled hair and handed her his handkerchief. "My guess is he's gotten himself somewhere safe, and he'll be fine. We just need to have faith in him."

Catherine pondered her father's words and realized that he had a point. Jimmy *was* smart. "You're right," she said, snuggling into his shoulder. "We need to have faith in him."

She decided to cling to this thought. This would be the thing that would get her through the night.

Ben reached for something that was stuck between the mattress and wall and pulled out the photograph of Catherine and Jimmy on the horse. "Would this, by any chance, be what you were looking for?" he asked, holding the picture so she could see it.

Catherine saw the photo and began crying all over again. This time for relief, and also for hope.

༄

It was well past midnight, and Catherine had finally managed to get some sleep. But it was a fitful sleep, and between periods of unconsciousness, she experienced states of near delirium as her faith inevitably devolved into panic. She had just awakened into one of these panicked states when she became conscious of her father's voice and then, seconds later, smelled smoke. As she bolted up in alarm, Mama Rae appeared in her room with the horrifying announcement, "The barn's on fire!"

"*Oh my God!*" Catherine screamed, rushing out of bed.

She and Mama Rae joined Ben on the front porch, and there, they watched helplessly as the barn was consumed in a torrent of flames that lit up the night sky. "It could just as easily have been the house," Ben said, putting his arms around both Catherine and Mama Rae.

Catherine felt strangely numb as she stood watching the fire shoot sparks into the heavens in vivid eruptions of light and sound. It was as though she were already so filled up with fear and dread that she had no more room to process this new horror. Instead, she became almost mesmerized by the flames, whose destructive beauty seemed a cruel but fitting symbol of the terrible consequences of her passions. Catherine wondered if she would ever again be able to think of the barn, with all its magic and memories, without searing pain. How brutally appropriate, she thought, that it should go up in a blaze of light.

"Do you think we're safe to stay here?" Mama Rae asked.

"I don't know," Ben said, sounding defeated. "But I wouldn't count on it."

Once again Catherine felt sympathy for her father's powerlessness. There was little he could do at the moment but be grateful that they'd only burned the barn. He had no phone that he could use to call for help—assuming there were anyone to call, or anything that could be done—and he had no means to protect them should the men decide to come back to inflict more damage. The sheriff had taken their shotgun.

With her thoughts turning towards escape, Catherine glanced at the truck, which was parked near the side of the house. "Oh my God!" she exclaimed suddenly. "Look!" She pointed to the truck, and Ben cursed when he saw, by the light of the fire, why Catherine was alarmed. The truck's tires had been slashed.

Ben tried his best to hide it, and appear strong, but Catherine could see by the color in his face that he was monumentally frustrated, and burning with anger.

"I've said it before," Mama Rae commented, limping to the porch swing and carefully planting herself. "Those men are pure evil."

Catherine looked back at the barn, which was rapidly being reduced to a pile of flaming rubble. "Do you think they'll burn Jimmy's house?" she asked Ben, trying to subdue a rising feeling of panic. "Or Mary's?" She was suddenly struck with the terrifying image of Mary's house, filled with all Jimmy's loved ones, going up in flames.

"I don't know," Ben said, joining Mama Rae on the swing. "These are terrible people. I imagine they're capable of just about anything."

Catherine looked in the direction of the farm with the rooster, and wondered aloud why no one had come running over to see about the fire. Surely they'd smelled the smoke.

"Well, I don't like having to tell you this," Mama Rae said, "but when the family with all the wild kids moved off the place, one of the biggest haters in town bought it. I know for sure he's part of the mob on this one, because I saw him here when they were wrecking the house." She shook her head in disgust. "It wouldn't surprise me to find out he was the one started the fire."

"Mama Rae," Ben said. "I don't know how you managed to live so many years in this hell hole."

"I don't know either," Mama Rae said, gazing over at the last flaming vestiges of the barn. "You'd think I was blind, deaf, and dumb."

આ

It was after three in the morning, and Ben insisted that Catherine and Mama Rae go back and try to get some more sleep. "I'll stay out here until the fire dies down," he said. "Then I'll camp out in the living room. If anyone comes back and tries anything with the house, I'll know it and make sure everyone gets out safe."

Catherine was too tired to do anything but obey, so she went back to her room and passed out from sheer exhaustion—though, once again, her sleep was intermixed with bouts of bleary panic and despair. When she finally awoke to daylight, the smell of smoke was still strong, and she wondered how she would possibly find the strength to face another day of terror and uncertainty.

She remained in a state of half-consciousness for some time, not anxious to trade the relative comfort of bed for the reality of whatever awaited her. As she lay in a state of fearful languor, she felt mocked by the rooster, whose incessant crowing seemed to suggest that this was just another day. She knew that this was no ordinary day, and she wondered if she would ever again experience anything as ordinary. She felt as if life itself had shattered, and she knew, as she made the first painful motions towards dragging herself into the day, that there was a strong chance it would never be repaired.

When Catherine finally stumbled into the kitchen she was amazed to find both Ben and Mama Rae sitting at the kitchen table, drinking coffee and eating toast. They looked tired, and the kitchen was still in a state of some disrepair, but the scene was markedly less chaotic than she'd expected. "Wow," she remarked, surveying the scene.

"Your father is a marvel," Mama Rae said. "I've been telling him to go get some sleep, but he won't listen to me."

Catherine hugged and kissed Mama Rae, then did the same to her father. "Did you stay up all night?" she asked, reaching for the coffee on the stove.

"Well, I may have dozed for an hour or so, but I was too worked up to sleep, so I used my energy to put things back together as best I could. We still have a ways to go before it's done."

"Tell her the best part," Mama Rae prodded, looking at Ben with pride.

"Well, I went out and repaired the phone line," Ben said.

"You can do that?" Catherine asked with surprise. She was both impressed by her father and relieved to see progress in the right direction for a change.

"It turns out it wasn't that big a deal," Ben said. "It was just a matter of twisting the wires back together and taping them up. I tried the phone, and it's working again. As a matter of fact, I just called someone to come fix the truck. He should be here later this morning."

Catherine poured herself a cup of coffee and sat down at the table. She looked at Ben and almost managed a smile. "I was afraid to get out of bed," she said. "But the way the morning is starting off, I almost have hope that things will turn around." She leaned over and kissed her father. "Thanks, Dad."

Mama Rae patted Ben's hand. "Like I said, he's a marvel."

"I think you're pretty marvelous too," Catherine said, now turning her affections towards her grandmother. "Yesterday you were downright heroic at those roadblocks."

"Well, I wouldn't say heroic."

"No, you were heroic," Catherine insisted. "You should have seen her at the first roadblock, Dad. By the time she was done chewing out that deputy, his big fat head was ready to explode."

"Yeah, well I might 'a done more harm than good," Mama Rae countered. "For all we know, he's the one came back here and lit up the barn."

"In any case," Ben injected, "Catherine and I are impressed by the way you've been stepping up."

"Well, thank you," Mama Rae said. "But it's the least I can do. I feel like all of this is my fault."

Catherine looked at her grandmother with puzzlement. "What on earth makes you say it's your fault?"

Mama Rae put down her coffee cup and folded her hands in front of her. "Catherine," she said, "I've lived among these people and seen the terrible way they treat the Negroes all my life. I knew better, but I kept still."

She turned to Ben. "Your father was one of these monsters. You saw it, and you got out. But I stayed and turned a blind eye, and now look at this mess. Poor Jimmy's running for his life, Sally's life may be ruined, Catherine may never be the same, and it's all because of people like me who are too weak and cowardly to stand up for what's right."

"Well, you're hardly responsible," Ben said. "But we appreciate that you're standing up now, and just as soon as we get this nightmare straightened out, we're taking you back to San Diego with us."

Mama Rae wiped her eyes behind her glasses. "I just pray we get it straightened out, because, right now, I'm pretty fearful for that boy."

With her elbows on the table, Catherine put her head in her hands and closed her eyes, willing herself to remain calm.

"Remember what I told you," Ben said, seeing Catherine's distress. "Jimmy is smart. He'll figure out where to go to keep himself safe."

"I hope you're right," Catherine said, looking up at her father. Then she stood up and began slowly putting the rest of the kitchen back together, grateful to be starting the day with a modicum of hope.

Cʒ

Catherine was standing on the front porch watching smoke rise from the glowing heap of charcoal that used to be the barn when Mama Rae came out and sat down on the porch swing. Off to the side of the house, Ben was supervising as the tires on the truck were being replaced by a skinny man in faded green coveralls. The sun was bright, and the day was turning out to be uncharacteristically cool. Birds rising from the trees at the edge of the pasture caught Catherine's attention, reminding her that she and Jimmy had never searched out the tree that they'd climbed as children.

Her thoughts turned to how she and Jimmy had laughed in the barn, and how their laughter had led to their first kisses. How quickly those kisses had brought them passion, and then love. She'd felt so certain that their love was fated, that they could find a place where they could live, and be happy, no matter what the obstacles. She'd never believed that something like this could really happen. Now, staring at the smoldering barn and the shell of the old car, which was the only thing recognizable in the wreckage, Catherine wondered if she would ever see Jimmy again, and how she would be able to live with herself if anything were to happen to him.

Catherine turned to Mama Rae on the swing. "Can I ask you a question about Granddaddy?"

Mama Rae had a blank look on her face. "Ask away," she said.

Catherine was hesitant.

"It's all right, go on," Mama Rae said, seeming to come back to life.

"Was he in the KKK?"

Mama Rae started to respond, but Catherine stopped her. "I'm sorry," she said. "I shouldn't have asked that."

"No, you have every right to ask," Mama Rae said. "I'm just ashamed of the answer."

"So he was?"

"Well, I was never quite sure," Mama Rae said. "I'm embarrassed to tell you that I didn't really want to know. But I think he probably was. He'd go out from time to time, and say he was bowling, or playing cards, but I had an idea what he was up to, because I'd hear talk in town, and at church. I didn't like to think about what he might have done, but I'd hear about things—boys who were beaten, homes that were burned, men who were..." Mama Rae began to cry.

Catherine sat down next to her grandmother and took her hand as she wept. When Mama Rae had collected herself enough to speak, she continued as best she could.

"There was a colored man who started a little car repair business," she said. "He built up a reputation as being good, and honest, and he became so successful he eventually moved

163

into a bigger place, and hired a few people, including a couple of white men." She paused and took some deep breaths. "Some of the white men in town, including your grandfather, got hot and bothered when they saw this man making money. They didn't like seeing a colored man doing well. So they got some girl at the high school to cry rape, and he was arrested. Then, sure as rain, he was convicted."

Mama Rae shook her head, and her eyes were angry. "Everyone knew it was utter nonsense. He had a nice family, and he was also supposed to be some kind of war hero—which, of course, rubbed some people the wrong way. But when the jury said 'Guilty,' that was that. Case closed."

Mama Rae looked tortured. Catherine wanted to comfort her, but she didn't know what to say. She leaned in for a hug, but was rebuffed.

"I'm not finished," Mama Rae said. "That's not the end of the story." She pulled a handkerchief from a pocket in her dress and blew her nose. "They were supposedly moving him—his name was Walter Brown. They were supposedly moving him to another jail after he was convicted, and the car he was riding in was stopped by a truck full of hooded men and he was taken out in the woods and lynched. It happened right out behind the high school."

Once again, Mama Rae broke down, and it took her some time to continue. "I don't know if your grandfather had anything to do with that one, but I suspect he might have. I remember him laughing about it. It made me ill."

Catherine was horrified by the story, and at a loss for how to respond. Finally, she asked, "Why did you stay with him?"

Mama Rae sighed and looked at Catherine through tear-filled eyes. "That's a very good question, and the answer is *I don't know*. Looking back now, I just really don't know. I guess

I was afraid, and I was weak. I felt trapped, I guess. But there's no excuse for turning a blind eye to such terrible things. I'd have been better off selling pencils on the street corner than living with that monster."

"You could have come live with us," Catherine said.

"Well, I thought about it, but I didn't want to be a burden, and I was so ashamed of the way things broke up."

Catherine's thoughts turned to her father's story about her grandfather and Jimmy at the pond. "Do you remember my dad accusing Granddaddy of trying to drown Jimmy at the pond?" she asked.

"I remember the argument," Mama Rae said. "It was a bad one."

"Do you think what my dad said was true?"

Mama Rae sighed and thought about it for a few moments. "If you'd asked me then, I'd have probably said your grandfather was innocent on that one. But, at the time, I don't think I wanted to believe it." She twisted the handkerchief in her lap, then looked Catherine in the eye. "I was pretty attached to Sally. If I'd thought your grandfather had really tried to kill her son, how could I have kept her on? I'd have had to let her go."

She shook her head. "No, I think I believed what I wanted to believe. But now...now I don't know. If you were to ask me if he were capable of doing such a terrible thing, I guess I'd have to say yes." She looked down at her hands, then back up at Catherine. "As much as I hate to say it, I think it was more in his character to try to kill that little boy than teach him how to swim."

cs

Catherine was back in the kitchen when she heard knocking on the back door. Her heart skipped a beat at the thought it might be Jimmy, but it turned out to be Ben. Catherine unlocked the door and opened it for her father.

"The truck's all set," Ben said, wiping his feet on the mat outside the door. He stepped inside. "I'm gonna run over and check on Sally and see if Jimmy's turned up."

"Do you think I should come?" Catherine asked. She was frantic for information on Jimmy, but also reticent about facing Sally again.

Ben looked uncertain. "I've been thinking about it, and I'm not sure how I feel about leaving you and Mama Rae alone. What do you think?" He glanced to his right and said, "What's F.A.?"

Catherine turned to where he was looking and saw that someone had written F.A. and circled it on the small blackboard that was hanging on the wall by the door. "I have no idea what that is," she said.

Ben passed through the kitchen and found Mama Rae in the living room. "Did you write F.A. on the blackboard?"

"Did I what?" Mama Rae asked.

"Someone wrote F.A. on the chalkboard by the back door. Was that you?"

"Not me. Maybe it was Sally. It's probably something she needs from the store."

"It doesn't look like her handwriting," Ben said.

"Maybe those goons put it there," Mama Rae offered. "I can think of some choice words those letters might stand for."

"I think if they were going to write choice words, they'd probably just write the words," Ben said. "They don't strike me as the types to be cryptic."

"What are you thinking?" Catherine asked from the doorway. "Do you think it might be some kind of message from Jimmy?"

"Well, I don't know," Ben said, "but someone put that there. Can you think of what *F.A.* might mean?"

In an instant Catherine had it. "Oh my gosh," she exclaimed, *"Fort Apache!"*

"What's Fort Apache?" Mama Rae asked.

"It's a fort Jimmy and I built when we were kids."

"I thought you said you looked for it and it was gone," Ben said.

"Well, it is," Catherine said, now wondering if she'd really solved the mystery. She thought about it for a moment. "Maybe he wants us to go to where it was. Maybe he's up in a tree or something. That might be it. Maybe he's hiding in a tree!"

Catherine started to get excited. "We used to climb trees back in that area all the time! We even talked about one special tree that was our favorite. Maybe that's it. Maybe that's where we'll find him!"

"Well, if he's back there, we need to be really careful not to lead anyone to him," Ben said. "I don't want a repeat of the closet debacle."

"Can we go now?" Catherine pleaded.

"We'll go take a look," Ben said, "But we need to think about what to do if we find him. We can't bring him back to the house."

Catherine started feeling panicked. Her father was right. Just finding him didn't solve the problem.

"What do you think we should do?" she asked, her emotions vibrating somewhere between excitement and fear.

"I'll tell you what," Ben said. "Let's go take a look, but let's not go in from this side, just in case they might be watching from the neighbor's house. For all we know, they're over there watching us with binoculars."

After a morning of relative calm, Catherine felt the night-mare coming back to life, and she prayed that somehow, some way, everything could be made right again.

Ben seemed to be thinking. "How about this?" he said. "We can take a walk up the road a ways, then we'll slip into the trees in a spot where we're sure no one will see us go in."

"That sound's good," Catherine said. "Can we go now?"

"Yeah, we can go," Ben said.

"Do you think it's too risky to take some food and water with us?" Catherine asked. "He's bound to be hungry and thirsty if he's been up a tree all night."

Ben pondered. "If we're caught on the road with food and water, they'll know what we're up to and comb the woods. I think, for now, we'd better just see if we can find him. We can worry about the rest later."

Five minutes later Catherine and Ben were on the road, waiting for the right place and time to slip into the woods. Catherine had a large apple with a bite out of it in her hand, figuring it would be safe to have in the event that they were stopped on the road.

"I never realized you were so sneaky," Ben said, nodding to the apple.

"You have no idea."

"Well, I'm sure I'm happier not knowing."

Catherine was hit with a sudden rush of emotion, remembering how she and Jimmy had laughed about some of the crazy things they'd done when they were children.

"Dad," she said, feeling once again like she was going to cry. "If this thing turns out bad, I'll never be able to forgive myself. Mama Rae was right. I'll never be the same."

"Try to hold on," Ben said. "Let's just take everything a step at a time. We'll go check out Fort Apache, then we'll see where to go from there."

Ben looked up and down the road, then pointed. "Let's go in here," he said, stepping off the road and into the trees. Catherine followed him, and soon she was running in the direction of where she and Jimmy had found the ruins of their old fort, with her eyes in the treetops.

It wasn't long before she found the spot where they'd had their fort, but there was no sign of Jimmy in any of the trees. Nearby, she was pretty sure she identified the tree that had been their favorite, but he wasn't there either.

"He might have been here, but then left," Catherine said. "That would make sense, right? He couldn't stay up in a tree forever."

Ben stooped down to pick up a soggy piece of paper that was poking out from beneath one of the two-by-fours that had been part of the fort.

"What's that?" Catherine asked.

"I was thinking it was litter," Ben said, examining the paper, "but now I think it might be a letter."

"It's gotta be from Jimmy," Catherine said, her pulse quickening. "It must be why he wanted us to come here. He couldn't risk leaving it at the house, because he didn't know who might find it!"

"Unfortunately, because of the rain, I'm not sure we're going to be able to read it," Ben said, carefully opening the wet and fragile paper, which was folded twice.

Catherine held her breath as her father slowly unfolded the paper to reveal a page full of writing that was so blurred and stained with ink and mud that it was impossible to decipher.

"Why did it have to rain?" Catherine cried in frustration, as she tried, but was unable to read even a few of the precious words.

"Let's get this home," Ben said. "Maybe once it dries out we'll be able to make some sense out of it."

Catherine looked at the letter, and was so filled with anguish and longing that she was tempted to throw herself on the ground and wail.

"I know this is hard," Ben said, seeing her agony. "But just try to hang on."

He cautiously folded the letter in half, then put his hand on Catherine's back and ushered her back in the direction of the road. "We might be able to read some of it when we get home," he said once again, trying to comfort her. But Catherine was beyond comfort. Though she was trying to remain calm on the outside, inside she was frantic, desperate to know what Jimmy had written.

CR

Back at the house, Ben carefully spread Jimmy's letter onto the kitchen table. Neither he nor Catherine were optimistic about reading most of it; the rain and mud had rendered it almost completely unintelligible. But they hoped that if they were able to pick out enough words, they'd be able to figure out what Jimmy had wanted to tell them, and where he'd gone.

"I'm pretty sure this is my name," Catherine said, pointing to the top of the letter. "And right here," she said, pointing farther down on the page, "this looks like *'try to'...something.'"

Ben pointed to a blurry line at the top. "Do you think this might be something about being sorry?"

"I think you're right," Catherine said, peering at the line, but nothing that came after was legible.

They scoured the paper for anything else that could be deciphered. "Maybe when it's completely dry, it'll be a little better," Ben said.

Catherine felt a surge of emotion upon recognizing the word *love* towards the bottom of the page. She stared silently at the smeary line in which it was embedded, but the rest of the words were gone. Giving up, she plopped down in a chair. "This is hopeless," she said in despair.

Mama Rae had been in her room when they first arrived back. Now she entered the kitchen. "What's this?" she asked, looking at the paper on the table.

"Jimmy left a message out where the kids built their fort, but it got ruined in the storm," Ben said. "He must have used my fountain pen, which I think I left on the kitchen table yesterday, because the ink is a mess. "We've been trying to read it, but so far we've only been able to pick out a word or two."

"Let me take a look," Mama Rae said. She walked up to the table and studied the page.

"Well, this word here is *love*," Mama Rae said. She turned to Catherine. "I guess we know what that's about."

Catherine blushed, and glanced at her father, who gave her a knowing look.

"What about this here?" Ben said. "This looks like *jump*, or maybe *just.*"

"Have you tried turning it over?" Mama Rae asked. "Maybe if you rub the back with a pencil the words'll magically appear. I saw that once on *Martin Kane, Private Eye.*"

"It's worth a try," Ben said. "But we'll need to wait until it's completely dry. It's still pretty soggy."

"What about this?" Mama Rae said, pointing to the last line. "Could this be *barn*?"

Ben took a look. "I don't know, possibly, but I can't make out any of the rest of it."

Catherine was flooded with bittersweet memories of the barn, but then was seized by a horrifying thought. *"Oh my God!"* she cried, jumping up from her chair. *"You don't think Jimmy could have gone back to hide in the barn, do you? You don't suppose that's why they burned the barn?"*

Catherine could tell by the look on Ben's face that he was having the same thought.

"Oh my God, Dad, do you think he might have been in the barn?"

"Don't panic," Ben said. "We aren't even sure that's what he wrote."

Catherine re-examined the paper and wasn't sure, but it was definitely possible. Jimmy may have written *barn*.

∛

Catherine was engaged in deep breathing when she was interrupted by the sound of a car driving up to the house. She froze, terrified that it might be the sheriff, back to wreak more havoc—or maybe Jesse Taylor, or the KKK. Catherine's imagination was in the process of running wild when Ben announced from the window that it was Will, accompanied by another Negro man whom he didn't recognize.

"Maybe they're coming to tell us they've found him!" Catherine said, her spirit soaring at the prospect.

"Sweet Jesus, let it be true," Mama Rae said.

Ben walked out into the yard to greet the men, and Catherine followed him as far as the screen door. When she realized she wasn't able to hear most of what they were saying, she moved quietly onto the porch and sat down on the swing, trying to attract as little attention as possible. Both Will and the other man looked over and nervously acknowledged her, and Catherine nodded back a subdued greeting. As Catherine strained to hear the conversation, she couldn't help but glance at the site of the fire, telling herself that Jimmy was not there. *Please let him not be there...*

Focusing back on the men, Catherine was crushed to learn that there was still no word on Jimmy's whereabouts.

"I see you had some trouble over yonder," Will said, motioning towards to the remains of the barn. He appeared highly distressed, as was the man next to him, whom Catherine recognized as Jimmy's brother George.

They all turned towards the remains, and Catherine could hear Ben talking about the letter. "We don't believe he was in the barn," he said, "but we'll need to take a look to make sure."

Will and George looked at one another, and Catherine could see the fear in their faces. A moment later, George glanced at Catherine, and she knew by his expression that he understood her part in everything. She wanted so desperately to communicate to him the depth of her sorrow and regret, but she knew that there was nothing she could ever do or say that would be adequate. Nevertheless, she met his gaze with as much sympathy as she could muster, and prayed that he at least understood that her feelings for Jimmy were sincere.

Overcome with grief and remorse, Catherine closed her eyes and tried to calm herself. When she opened them, she was shaken by the sight of George approaching the house.

"You're Catherine," he said when he arrived at the porch. He took off his fedora. "I'm George. Jimmy's brother."

Catherine detected a kindness in his eyes that belied the stifled anger in his voice. He resembled Jimmy, but was broader, and looked much older.

She nodded and tried to speak, but was unable. She took a deep breath and met George's gaze, struggling to maintain some semblance of compose. "I'm so sorry..." she said finally, her voice quavering. "I know this is my fault."

George's face was filled with pain, and he seemed as uncertain as Catherine what to say.

Catherine attempted once again to find words, but none would come. All she could offer were tears of remorse.

George pulled a handkerchief from his pocket and handed it to her. "I have an idea you and Jimmy have feelings for one another," he said, his face solemn. "I remember he was sweet on you when you were kids."

Catherine nodded and trembled with emotion.

"If we find him, and figure a way of gettin' him out a here," George said, "I think it's best you let it go." His tone made it clear that he was telling and not asking.

Catherine wanted so much to beg for George's forgiveness, to tell him what was in her heart, but she knew that nothing mattered except finding Jimmy safe, so her only response was a meager nod. She wiped her face with the handkerchief, then took a deep breath and exhaled. "How's Sally?"

"Her sister's lookin' after her," George said, "but God help her if they hurt that boy." He fiddled with the hat in his hands. "God help us all if they hurt that boy."

He looked over his shoulder and noticed that Ben and Will were headed over to the site of the fire. "I best be gettin' back," he said. He nodded at the handkerchief. "You can keep that." Then he put his hat back on and loped off to join Ben and Will, leaving Catherine in a state of broken silence.

Mama Rae was opening the screen door to join Catherine on the porch when a sheriff's car turned into the driveway and came rumbling up towards the house. "Oh for God's sake, what's next?" she said. She looked at Catherine, who was frozen in terror. "Go on back inside and let your father and me handle this."

Catherine reluctantly obeyed, then watched through the screen door as the car stopped and Jesse Taylor emerged like a venomous snake. In another moment, the big-headed deputy from the first roadblock materialized from the passenger's side.

"Well now, what have we here?" Jesse Taylor said, noticing Will and George, both of whom were looking back at him with dismay.

"What we have here," Mama Rae said boldly, "is someone set fire to our barn last night."

Ben was briskly walking over, but Will and George held back, clearly fearful of approaching the deputies.

"What now?" Ben asked angrily. "Have you come back to burn down our house?"

"We're just here to have another look around. But first we're gonna need to question those niggers over yonder. I'm thinking maybe we got lucky and one of them's the one we're lookin' for."

"The innocent boy you're looking for is missing," Ben said, "and those are members of his family who are rightly afraid for his safety."

"Roy," Jesse Taylor said to the other deputy, "Go on in the car and get the photo of the suspect. We'll just see who we have here."

While the deputy retrieved the picture of Jimmy, Jesse Taylor waved and shouted over to Will and George, who were still standing next to the site of the fire. "You niggers come on over here!" he hollered, shooting a sideways look of satisfaction at Ben.

With no choice but to obey, Will and George headed over as Ben, Mama Rae, and Catherine looked helplessly on, worrying what might happen next.

Standing at the screen door with her adrenaline racing, Catherine had the urge to run out and unleash all her pent up rage at the deputies. She felt such a desire to scream and rage that it was all she could do to contain herself. She looked at her father, and she could see that he was also struggling with violent emotions, but he was locked into submission. Because Jesse Taylor and his sidekick had guns and badges, he was powerless. They were all powerless—especially poor Will and George, who knew, as they approached, that anything might happen.

"I'm gonna need you two to raise your hands above your heads," Jesse Taylor instructed as Will and George cautiously stepped up. Even from inside the house, Catherine could see the anger smoldering on their faces as Will and George had no choice but to raise their hands and allow the deputies to roughly search them.

"I think maybe we got him, Jesse," Roy said when they were finished. He'd retrieved the photo of Jimmy from the hood of their car, and was examining it. He pointed to George. "This one here looks like a match to me."

Will and George looked at each other with expressions of suppressed fury, but it was plain to Catherine that they knew the danger in talking back.

"This is ridiculous," Ben said. "I already told you that these men are family members. This is the boy's brother."

"Well, that remains to be seen," Jesse Taylor said with relish. "For all I know, this here nigger is the real perpetrator, and all along this has been a case of mistaken identity." He spit tobacco juice and looked at Ben as though he'd just scored a point in some perverse game. "We're gonna need to take him in and let JT have a look at him."

Now Will and George were shaking their heads, and the fear on their faces was palpable. Both Ben and Mama Rae began loudly protesting, but the deputies only grinned in response, seeming to enjoy their anger.

The whole scene was so painful to watch that Catherine's frustration and bitterness felt like something physically burning inside of her. Jesse Taylor was just starting to put handcuffs on a very distressed looking George when something in her gave way, and she went running out onto the porch in a state that felt like madness.

"YOU MEN ARE EVIL!" she screamed with every ounce of her strength and pent up hatred. *"YOU ARE DISGUSTING, EVIL MONSTERS WHO BELONG IN HELL!"*

She continued to scream and rage until her voice finally ran out, and she collapsed onto the swing, physically and emotionally depleted.

Jesse Taylor appeared more pleased than angry over her outburst. "You'd better teach you daughter to mind her manners," he said to Ben with a smirk. Then he looked over at Roy and they shared a look of amusement.

Ben was seething. "She's just expressing the truth."

"Well the truth," Jesse Taylor said, "is I'm taking this nigger in, and there's not a damn thing you can do about it." Then he marched George over to his car and pushed him roughly into the back seat.

Ben and Will looked at one another in a joint state of panic and frustration. They both knew that anything might happen to George now.

"You look after Catherine," Ben said to Mama Rae, who was now comforting Catherine on the swing. "I'm going to follow them into town."

Ben and Will exchanged some frenzied words, then jumped into their respective vehicles and followed as George, helpless and frightened, disappeared onto the road with the two triumphant deputies.

CзахЗ

Ben had been gone for more than an hour, and Catherine was lying down in her room, trying to calm her nerves, when she heard the phone ring. A few minutes later, Mama Rae was at her door with the news that her mother was on the phone.

"Does she know about everything?" Catherine asked fearfully, wondering how she could ever explain to her mother all that had happened in the last couple of days.

"Your father called her early this morning, and I just told her the latest," Mama Rae said. "She's understandably worried, and anxious to talk to you."

Catherine's emotions began to rise, and she knew she'd have difficulty talking, but she reluctantly got out of bed and headed for the phone.

"*Catherine!*" came her mother's voice when she picked up the phone. "*Are you all right?*"

Catherine tried to answer, but her voice was so constricted with emotion that she was virtually unable to speak. She finally managed to tell her mother that she would only be all right once Jimmy and George were safe.

"I'm coming to get you," her mother announced. "Your father and I have agreed that you and Mama Rae need to come back to San Diego as soon as possible, so I'm coming in the station wagon. It's all arranged. My brother's going to come with me so that we can take turns driving, and drive all night. I'll be arriving sometime late tomorrow afternoon, and we'll drive back the next morning. Your father will stay behind as long as necessary to take care of things there."

"I can't possibly leave until I know Jimmy and George are safe!" Catherine responded in a panic. She then proceeded to stubbornly argue until they finally gave up in a stalemate, agreeing to talk about it when her mother arrived.

ॐ

It was late afternoon and Catherine was lying on her bed when Ben returned. When she heard his voice, she rushed to the living room and found him talking to Mama Rae, whose disheveled hair was an indication that she'd also been resting.

"What happened with George?" Catherine cried anxiously.

"Well," Ben said, collapsing onto the couch, "they have him over in the jail, and I hated to leave him there, but the good news is we found him a lawyer who seems decent. His name is Abe Stone. Will and I had a chance to talk to him a little bit, and I think he's a good man."

Ben leaned over and began untying his shoes. "They're denying George bail, but Abe thinks they'll have to release him soon, because the railroad will be able to provide him with a clear alibi for the so-called robbery."

"Do you think he'll be all right?" Catherine asked. She hated to think of poor George hidden in a jail, totally at the mercy of his captors.

Ben looked exhausted. "I hope so, but I just don't know." He stretched his neck backwards, then around in a circle. "The feeling I got from Abe is he'll probably be all right. They know they're gonna have to let him go, and they probably also know that if they hurt George in custody, they might not get away with it. Sally's family has done a good job of rallying the Negro community around what's going on. There was a large group, including several Negro ministers, over at the jail calling for George to be released."

Ben yawned. "Abe says that the sheriff and Jesse and some of the other local troublemakers are starting to lose favor with important people in town, including one of the local judges. He thinks the Emmitt Till thing is also having an impact. So he feels good about George's chances of having the whole thing dropped by sometime early tomorrow."

Relieved, Catherine sat down next to her father. "Have you heard anything about Jimmy?"

"Well," Ben said. "I drove by Will's house before I came back here, and I didn't see Sally, but I talked to Mary, and she says they still don't know anything. I guess Sally's in pretty bad shape."

Ben sighed. "I don't know what to think about Jimmy." He paused, then shook his head. "I hate to say it, but we're gonna need to take a look at the remains of the barn."

"I've been thinking about that," Catherine said. "Jimmy and I used to play hide and seek, and I'm pretty sure he wouldn't hide in the barn. There's nowhere to really hide in there. Most of it's just open space."

"Well, nevertheless," Ben said, "I promised Will I'd take a look. We need to make sure. But I may wait until tomorrow. I'm dead tired. I'm also pretty hungry."

"Your dad brought home some groceries," Mama Rae said. "How about we let him rest and you and I go rustle up something for all of us to eat."

"All right," Catherine said wearily. She turned to her father. "Thank you for taking care of everything." She sat down next to him on the couch and embraced him in a long tight hug. When she finally let go, his eyes were closed, and she knew that, in no time, he'd be asleep.

ℜ

Catherine entered the kitchen to find her grandmother standing at the sink, rinsing potatoes. "You sit down, Mama Rae," she said. "I'll take care of dinner."

"Nonsense," Mama Rae said. "I might be old, but I'm not an invalid." She turned from the sink and looked at Catherine. "You go ahead and sit down. I'll put you to work in a minute."

Catherine obeyed, planting herself at the kitchen table. "My mom says she's coming to take both of us back to San Diego, but I can't leave until we find Jimmy and get George out of jail."

"I understand how you feel," Mama Rae said, drying her hands on her apron, "but your parents are worried about you. I know you want to look out for Jimmy and George. We all do. But we want to look out for you too. This is a lot to handle."

Catherine put her head down on the table, overcome once again with the urge to cry. She knew she needed to pull herself together before her mother arrived, but she didn't know how to calm herself. She looked up at Mama Rae. "How do you do it?" she asked. "How do you keep going when things just keep getting worse and worse?"

Mama Rae sat down at the kitchen table. "Catherine," she said, "I wouldn't know how to begin to tell you about all the things that have been goin' on inside me over the last few days. But my way has always been to push things off to the side, and not deal with 'em head on. I suppose you could say that when things are too painful, I just wall 'em off into some corner of my brain and avoid thinking about 'em. It may not be the best thing to do, but it's what I've always done, I guess."

She patted Catherine's hand. "I don't want you to think I don't feel things. I'm worried sick about Jimmy and his brother. And poor Sally. I'm heartsick over all she's goin' through. But I've discovered over the years that there's no use in keeping myself stirred up over things I can't change. So I put 'em in the attic, you might say, so that I can function. I guess I learned to do it when your father was a boy, because I had to. If I'd fallen apart then, what would have become of him?"

Catherine tried to picture Mama Rae as a young mother, doing her best to raise her son in a house with a husband she hated and probably feared. She'd obviously done something right for her father to have turned out to be such a good man. Catherine brought to mind a photograph that was framed on her parents' living room mantle. It was her father at around ten or eleven, sitting on the steps of the front porch in knickers and a wool cap.

"What was my dad like when he was a boy?" Catherine asked.

Mama Rae thought for a moment. "I guess he was always a bit of a loner," she said. "He had a few friends over the years, but he was never one to be part of a group." She got a faraway look in her eyes. "He was smart. Always got good grades, always did well in his studies. More than anything, I'd say he was kind, which is pretty surprising, I guess, considering what his father was like. He was always a sensitive boy, and that rubbed your grandfather the wrong way, of course. He considered your dad a sissy. But he wasn't a sissy. He just wasn't a roughneck, or a bully. He used to stand up for other kids who got bullied, and that got him in trouble more than a few times."

"Do you remember any times in particular?" Catherine asked. "I'd love to hear any stories you can remember."

Mama Rae pursed her lips and thought. "Well, here's something he may already have told you about," she said. She folded her hands on the table. "Has he ever told you about the school bus?"

Catherine had heard many stories about the school bus, but she shook her head because she wanted to hear what Mama Rae would say.

"Well," Mama Rae began, "there used to be a school bus that would take him back and forth to school every day. All the white kids who lived out in the country like we did had a school bus. The colored children, they didn't have a bus. Those children had to walk to school. And some of them had to walk a good long ways, too—several miles each way. And, of course, they went to a different school. The whites and Negroes always had separate schools.

"Anyway, sometimes the kids on Ben's school bus would throw things or spit on the colored children when they'd see 'em walking on the road. And they'd yell ugly things, and call 'em names. I'm sure you can imagine some of the names they called those children." Mama Rae shook her head in disgust. "According to your father, the bus driver used to laugh, and encourage 'em. He'd actually slow down so the kids could throw things, and yell."

Catherine had once found her father's stories about the bus hard to imagine. Now she could picture such things with crystal clarity.

"That sort of behavior really bothered your father," Mama Rae continued. "When he was small, he was too frightened to say anything, because most of the boys doing it were a lot bigger than Ben. But as he got older, he started speaking up, and then he became a target for those boys. He got himself bruised up a few times over it, and then he finally just refused to take the bus anymore. I wanted to drive him to school, but your grandfather wouldn't have it. He made him walk. But Ben didn't seem to mind. I think he enjoyed doing it on principle." Mama Rae smiled, and her haggard face took on a look of pride.

"Anyhow," she went on, "for the last couple of years of school, your dad walked three miles each way, rain or shine, rather than ride that bus and be party to those boys misbehavin' like that. And, of course, the boys threw stuff and hollered at him when they'd see him on the road, but Ben didn't care. He preferred walking and being a target himself to being part of that nonsense on the bus."

Mama Rae took off her glasses and rubbed her eyes. "I guess that was when things started really heatin' up between your father and your grandfather, but I was proud of Ben. He was against that kind of behavior, and he stuck to his guns, even though it meant he was asking for trouble himself."

"I wonder if Jesse Taylor was on that school bus," Catherine said.

Mama Rae put her glasses back on. "I bet he was," she said. "Now that I think about it, I just bet he was."

♋

Dinner was finished, the dishes were washed and dried, and Ben had gone off to his room to sleep. Dinner had been oddly silent, as if there were some unspoken agreement to take a break from reality. It was all Ben could do to stay awake long enough to eat a pork chop and a few mouthfuls of potatoes, and Catherine could see that he needed some quiet time to replenish before facing whatever curve balls or horrors might come next.

Before turning in, Mama Rae called Isabel and received the good news that she was now home and feeling back to normal. Mama Rae made no mention of what *she'd* returned home to, and Catherine was amazed by her grandmother's ability to feign cheeriness and engage in happy chit-chat. When she hung up, Catherine gave her a look of surprise.

She was quick to respond. "Well, you don't want me to give her another heart attack, do you?"

"No," Catherine said, with admiration for her grandmother's fortitude. Then she hugged her and said good night before Mama Rae went off to her room and Catherine went out to sit on the front porch.

Now, sitting on the swing, Catherine resolved to take a lesson from her grandmother and somehow find a way to become stronger. She prayed that things would turn around for the better, but no matter what, she had to find a way to cope, if only to avoid being hauled off by her mother against her will.

She thought about Mama Rae's method of walling things off, and wondered if she would have to resort to the same strategy. Would she have to live the rest of her life with Jimmy bricked off into some dark corner of her brain? And where was Jimmy? Was he even alive? The last question was so terrible that she bricked *that* off, then tried as hard as she could to concentrate on the stars, and the frogs chirping at the pond.

Eventually she closed her eyes and entered a state of quiet equilibrium, focusing only on the sensation of the breeze in the air and the rhythmic singing of the frogs. It was the first time in days that she'd felt anything resembling calm, and she savored the feeling. She might have stayed in that state for hours, but she was finally driven inside by mosquitoes, and the need for sleep.

She was just entering the kitchen to turn out the light when she remembered Jimmy's letter, and noticed it peeking out from under a book on the kitchen sideboard. She knew that looking at it might set her back in her effort to remain calm, but she was unable to resist. Now that it was completely dry, maybe more of it would be legible. She retrieved the paper, flattened it on the table, then sat down in front of it.

Unfortunately, no magical difference was apparent. Her eyes were pulled to the bottom of the page, where the indisputable '*love*' stood as a painful reminder of the crime for which they were being punished. *Had Jimmy told her he loved her?* She strained to make sense of the blur surrounding the word. Most everything was still unreadable, but a word starting with an '*f*' had materialized nearby. She thought it could be '*forget*,' but wasn't sure. It was just before the word that looked like '*barn*.' Maybe he'd told her he'd never forget the barn.

She struggled to find anything else they'd missed before, but there was nothing. She went to a drawer, found a pencil, and ran the side of the lead lightly over the back of the paper. Unfortunately, Mama Rae's TV solution didn't work. Nothing appeared, so she returned the letter to the sideboard, switched off the kitchen light, and went to her room for another night of tortured half sleep.

Chapter 11

It was now morning, and Catherine was awakened by the sound of the phone ringing. She heard only two rings, so she assumed that either Ben or Mama Rae had answered it. She looked at the clock by the bed. It was early. Only 6:15. She wondered who would be calling this early, and was surprised that anyone was awake to answer. *It must be her father*, she thought. He was normally a fairly early riser.

She listened carefully, but could hear nothing of the conversation. Maybe it was her mother calling from the road, or some news about Jimmy or George. She was anxious to know who was calling, but she was also fearful. Any news might be bad news, and she did not want to hear bad news. She pulled the covers over her head and closed her eyes, telling herself that, whatever came, she needed to try to be strong. A moment later there was a knock at her door.

"Catherine," Ben called from the hallway. "Can I come in?"

She knew now that the phone call had produced some kind of news. She pulled the covers from her head and answered back. "Come on in, Dad. I'm awake."

The instant she saw Ben's face she knew that whatever the phone call had been about, it was not good. "What is it? What's happened?"

Ben sat down on the bed. "I just got a call from Will. Last night there was a fire at Sally's house."

Catherine sat up and was terrified by the look on her father's face. She'd never seen him look so distressed.

"I need to take the truck and go out for a while," Ben said.

"But wait," Catherine pressed. "Did the whole house burn down? There wasn't anyone in the house was there?"

Ben hesitated.

"Please, Dad. I need to know."

Ben looked shaken, and Catherine knew that whatever he was going to say, it was terrible. Despite her best efforts to contain her emotions, she began to cry. "Please tell me no one was hurt in the fire," she pleaded.

"Here's what I know," Ben said, trying to steady his voice. "Sometime late last night—or early this morning, I guess—a truck full of men wearing hoods set fire to Sally's house."

Catherine clutched her father's arm.

"According to Will, it's a total loss," Ben continued. "They burned it to the ground." He paused, seeming not to want to say any more.

Catherine searched his face, waiting for him to continue. She could tell by his expression that there was more. "Sally's family is still at Mary's house," he added finally. "She and the girls are fine. But according to some of the neighbors, there may have been someone in the house."

Catherine's heart took off like a racehorse. "What makes them think someone was in the house?" she cried. "And are you saying that there may have been someone in the house who didn't get out? Who was killed in the fire?"

Ben seemed to be wondering at the wisdom of telling her more.

"Please," Catherine pleaded. "You need to tell me."

"Let's just wait and see what they find," Ben said. "It may be that no one was there."

Catherine was horrified to imagine that, because of her, someone might have been killed. And what if it was Jimmy? *What if Jimmy had been killed?*

"Why do they think someone was in the house?" she cried. "Please! What did Will say?"

"I shouldn't have mentioned it until we're sure," Ben said. "Will just said that some of the neighbors thought there might have been someone there. He didn't know any more than that, so for the moment it's just a rumor. We need to wait and see what they find before we start panicking."

Mama Rae walked into the room looking frail in her pink housecoat and slippers. "What's happened? Why are we panicking?" she asked.

"We're not panicking," Ben said.

Catherine couldn't contain herself. "They burned down Sally's house!" she cried. "The KKK burned down Sally's house, and someone may have been killed in the fire!"

Mama Rae staggered and looked like she might faint, and Ben jumped up to steady her.

"Now let's all calm down," Ben said, holding on to Mama Rae. "There's been a fire, but there's no good reason to believe that anyone was hurt. Sally and her girls are fine. They're still at Mary's house."

Mama Rae, who still looked faint, was shaking her head as Ben steered her back out of Catherine's room.

Passing through the doorway, Ben shot Catherine a look as if to say, *I'm frightened too, but please let's try to stay calm.*

ᘓ

Catherine and Ben were attending to Mama Rae in the living room when the phone rang again. "Let me get that," Ben said, seeing Catherine's anxious look. "You stay here with Mama Rae."

Ben disappeared into the kitchen, and soon it was apparent from what Catherine could overhear that the caller was Abe Stone. "Absolutely," she heard Ben say. "Sure. I can be there; I can do that. Absolutely. Sure. No, I agree. I think that's best. Sure."

There was a long silence while Ben was listening. Then he was talking again, and Catherine surmised that he was discussing the fire. "Yeah, we're pretty worried over here, too," he said. "Hopefully, they'll be able to tell us something definitive soon." Ben listened some more, then said, "Okay, will do. Thanks for calling, Abe. I'll see you soon."

When he returned to the living room he was met by two sets of nervous eyes.

"Well?" Mama Rae asked expectantly.

"What did he say?" Catherine asked. "Was that Abe?"

"Yeah," Ben said. "It seems there's a lot of commotion over at the jail. Because of the fire and all, Sally's family and the whole Negro community, really, are very concerned about George's well-being. There are a lot of people over there now, and I gather things are pretty tense."

Ben sat down on the couch. "Abe and George will be meeting with a judge this morning, and Abe wants me to come too. He thinks I might be able to help give the judge an understanding of what's going on here. I think I told you before, a lot of people in town are concerned about the sheriff and Jesse and the KKK. People have had enough. Abe says the charges against George will probably be dropped. He thinks that they arrested George because they were hoping it would make Jimmy give himself up—you know, to get George out of hot water—but they may be forced to give up on that idea once the railroad chimes in with his alibi. And if it can be shown that Sheriff White or Jesse Taylor or anyone in the Sheriff's Department had anything to do with the fire at Sally's, they may be in pretty serious trouble. At least, that's the hope."

"What about me?" Catherine asked. "Can I come with you? I can tell the judge about JT breaking in here."

"No." Ben shook his head emphatically. "You need to stay out of sight. We all agree that the less said about you and Jimmy the better. People might be tired of the KKK, but they will not be happy if they think there was something going on between you and Jimmy. You can only do harm by being involved in this, so you need to just sit tight and let me handle things."

"What about the fire?" Catherine asked. "Did Abe say anything about that? Are they looking to see if anyone was in the house?"

"They'll let us know as soon as they know anything," Ben said. "And that reminds me. I don't have to be at the courthouse for another couple of hours, so before I go over there I need to take a look around the barn. I don't expect I'll find anything, but I promised Will I'd take a look and make sure."

ೞ

Catherine worked on breakfast while Ben went out to sift through the remains of the barn. She was confident that he'd come back with good news, but she was worried sick about Sally's house, and she had a terrible feeling that her father was keeping something from her.

Mama Rae was just entering the kitchen when the phone rang. Catherine and Mama Rae shared a fearful look. They both knew that it could be news about the fire. Catherine picked up the phone. "Hello," she said, her eyes locked on Mama Rae.

"You're going to get yours, nigger lover," said a male voice in a low tone.

Before the caller could say more, Catherine hung up in alarm.

"Who was that?" Mama Rae demanded. "What did they say?"

Catherine shook her head. "You don't want to know."

Mama Rae sat down at the kitchen table. A moment later, Ben came in through the back door. "The barn's clear," he declared. "I didn't see anything out there to be concerned about, and I poked around pretty good."

"We just got an ugly call," Mama Rae said. "Catherine answered."

Ben sighed and was giving Catherine a sympathetic look when the phone rang again. This time Ben picked it up. He listened for a moment, then slammed down the receiver.

He looked back and forth between Catherine and Mama Rae. "Unfortunately, we need to answer the phone when it rings, because it could be Will or Abe. But if you pick it up again and it's another call like that, just hang up immediately. We don't want to give whoever this is the satisfaction of listening to a single word. Do you understand?"

Both Catherine and Mama Rae nodded.

"What if they come here?" Catherine asked. She was at the stove, scrambling eggs. "Do you think they might come here while you're at the courthouse?"

"Well, that's a concern," Ben said. He shook his head and gave a sigh of exasperation, then sat down at the table. Catherine put a cup of coffee in front of him, then went back to the stove.

"Maybe there's some place I can drop you and Mama Rae while I'm out," Ben said. "I'll feel better about things if I know you two are somewhere safe. These guys have shown they're capable of anything." He looked at Mama Rae. "Can you think of anywhere I can take you? Maybe to a friend's house, or the church?"

"What about the diner?" Catherine asked. She put a plate of eggs and ham in front of Mama Rae, then returned a moment later with a plate for herself and her father. She sat down at the table. "How far is the diner on Main Street from the courthouse?"

"Catherine, I don't want you anywhere near the courthouse," Ben said, taking a bite of eggs.

"If I were to just take a walk over there, no one would know who I am."

"Well, that's not entirely true," Ben said. "All the men who were here when they came looking for Jimmy would probably recognize you, and there's JT."

"I can make myself inconspicuous," Catherine said. "And I promise I won't go inside. But I'd like to see what's going on outside. You know, the commotion. What exactly did Abe say about that, anyway?"

"Well, I guess there are a lot of people stepping up to try to protect George," Ben said. "Several of the Negro churches in town have been rallying people. But, unfortunately, there are also some people on the other side of things who've come out of the woodwork, so things could be pretty volatile."

"Is the jail by the courthouse?" Catherine asked.

"Yes, but you're not listening to what I'm telling you, Catherine," Ben said. "*I want you to stay out of it!* The whole point of my taking you somewhere is so that I don't have to worry about you. I don't want you out in the fray. Like I said, it's not just the Negros who are exercised over this thing. It's the whites, too. And some of these characters, as soon as they have the least excuse to spout their hatred, they take it. And I gather that's what's going on over there. Both sides are getting worked up, and I don't want you mixed up in it. And I don't want to argue with you about it, Catherine. For once in your life, you need to just please do what you're told!"

Before Catherine could say more than a couple of words back, Mama Rae jumped in. "Catherine," she said angrily. "We've been more than sympathetic about your role in all this. We know you're feeling terrible about everything, so we've held our tongues. But you need to listen to your father and not do any more damage. If he says stay away, you need to stay away!"

Stung by her father's and grandmother's words, Catherine stood up and took her plate to the sink. A moment later the phone rang. Ben picked it up, then slammed down the receiver and stormed out of the kitchen.

As Mama Rae finished her breakfast and Catherine washed dishes and pans at the sink, a strained silence floated between them. Catherine stared out the window, feeling both fearful and ashamed. She was trying to think of what to say to ease the tension when the phone rang again. Catherine turned around to look at Mama Rae just as Ben entered the kitchen and abruptly picked it up, obviously anticipating another belligerent call. But he didn't slam the phone this time. Instead, he listened intently for what seemed to Catherine like an unbearably long time, then he simply said, "Okay. Thanks for calling, Abe."

The look on Ben's face made it plain that something terrible had happened. "What is it?" Catherine cried. "What did he say?"

Ben was rendered momentarily speechless by whatever it was, and Catherine felt her legs weaken. She sat down at the table and linked eyes with Mama Rae, who appeared just as frightened as she was by Ben's expression.

Ben lowered himself into the chair next to Catherine. His jaw was trembling, and his forehead was furrowed, and beaded with sweat.

Catherine was terror-stricken. *"What is it? What happened?"*

Ben seemed unable speak. He glanced quickly at Mama Rae, then looked down at his hands, which were clenched tightly in front of him.

"Please, Dad," Catherine cried, "Tell me! Is it about the fire? Did they find Jimmy in the fire, is that it?"

Ben took a long deep breath, then slowly exhaled. "Well, there are a couple of things," he said finally, trying to appear steady. "First, they've let George go and won't be charging him with anything. It seems the railroad came through with his alibi, and the county prosecutor and the judge I mentioned before are both pretty unhappy about the whole mess. There's been a pretty big ruckus over at the jail and the courthouse, and I gather there's a local reporter—the same one who wrote the story about Jimmy's scholarship—who is asking a lot of embarrassing questions. Abe warned me that he'd probably be showing up here, trying to talk to us for a story."

Catherine held her breath, because she knew there was more. "What else?" she demanded. "I know there's something else." Her heart was racing and her face was burning up.

Ben flushed red, and then he began to cry, igniting Catherine's worst fears. She couldn't remember ever seeing her father outright cry.

"Please tell me they haven't found Jimmy in the fire," Catherine pleaded, barely able to speak. "Please, Dad. Please tell me that's not it."

Tears flowed from Ben's eyes, and he began to shake his head. "I'm sorry, Catherine," he said, visibly straining to contain his emotions. "I'm sorry, but it seems as if they may have found him."

"At Sally's? *At the fire?*"

Ben slowly nodded. "I'm sorry..."

Chapter 12

Three hours later Catherine emerged from her room and entered the kitchen in need of a drink of water. She felt raw and hollow from non-stop crying, and she was relieved to find the kitchen deserted. Mama Rae was asleep in her chair in the living room, and Ben was nowhere in sight. Since Catherine had received the news about Jimmy, she'd stayed in her room and refused to talk. Both Ben and Mama Rae had tried to console her, but she'd sent them away, wanting to be alone, believing she was not deserving of consolation. There was no denying her role in Jimmy's death, no use pretending she was not to blame. She hated herself, and she hated the monsters who'd killed Jimmy with a fury so violent that she felt it coursing through her body like a living thing.

While in her room, she'd heard the phone ring several more times, and assumed they'd received more vicious calls. Now, as she entered the kitchen, the phone rang again. Not wanting the ringing to summon her father or grandmother, she quickly picked up the receiver, fully expecting to hang up immediately.

"Hello," she said blankly.

"Hello," came a voice on the other end. "Is this Catherine?" The voice sounded kind.

"Who is this?" Catherine asked.

"My name is David Ross. I'm a friend of Jimmy's."

Catherine froze.

"Are you there?"

"It's not a good time," Catherine managed.

It occurred to her now that the caller was probably the reporter that her father had mentioned. "I'm sorry, but I can't talk," she said. "I'm going to hang up."

"Please," the voice said. "Can you listen for a moment before you hang up? I'm a friend, and I only want to help. I promise."

Catherine was reluctant, but there was something about his tone that made her agree. "Okay," she said. "But are you a reporter?"

"Well, I guess you could say that, but that's not really why I'm calling," he said.

"I'm sorry, Mr. Ross," Catherine said, "but I really don't want to talk to a reporter right now, not even as a friend."

"Call me David. And please just hear me out."

Catherine was uncertain, but agreed.

"It's true that I may write a story about what's happened," David said, "but only because I care about Jimmy and his family. He really was my friend. I saw him just a few days ago, and he talked to me about you. That's what I want to talk to you about. I know what you must be going through right now, and I thought it might help you to talk to me." He paused, waiting for Catherine to respond, but she didn't. "I think Jimmy would want us to talk," he added. "Really."

Catherine was confused about what to do. Her better judgment told her that this man might be trying to trick her into talking to him for a newspaper story, and she wasn't in any condition to talk lucidly about what had happened. But if he really had spoken to Jimmy about her, she wanted to hear what he had to say.

"I don't know," Catherine said.

"He told me that you and he had been friends when you were children, and that, seeing you again, it felt like you'd never been separated. Does that help?"

Catherine choked up and now felt unable to talk.

"Catherine," David said. "Would it be okay if I were to come see you? I can come right away, and I promise it won't be as a reporter. Only as a friend."

"Okay," Catherine whispered. Then she gave him directions and hung up, praying she hadn't agreed to something she'd regret.

CB

Catherine was in front of the bathroom mirror staring at a face she didn't recognize. Ben knocked on the door. "Catherine. Are you okay?"

She opened the door. "I'm not in here slitting my wrists, if that's what you're worried about."

Ben let the comment go. "Who was that on the phone?"

"Someone named David Ross," Catherine said. "I think he's the reporter you mentioned. He says he was a friend of Jimmy's, and he wants to talk to me."

"I don't know if it's wise to talk to him," Ben said.

"He says he talked to Jimmy a few days ago, and I'd like to hear what he has to say."

"Well, I know better than to argue with you, but please be careful," Ben said. "Anything you say could end up in the newspaper."

"I know," Catherine mumbled. "I'll be careful."

"Is he coming over here now?"

"He should be here any minute."

Catherine looked back at the mirror. Her face was red and swollen from crying, and her tangled hair was pulled back into a crooked ponytail, but she didn't care. She felt like an empty shell.

She turned back to her father, who was still standing in the doorway. He looked as depleted as she did. "I love you, Dad," she said.

"I love you, too, Sweetie."

They hugged, then Catherine left the bathroom and walked back to her bedroom.

Ben followed her. "You know, you and I have never really talked about you and Jimmy," he said. "I have an idea that you thought you were in love. Is that right, or am I imagining something that's not true?"

Catherine sat down on the bed, and it was all she could do not to break down again. She had cried so much over the last few days, sometimes she felt like she might spend the rest of her life in tears.

She looked up at her father. "I know it might seem crazy, since I've only been here a few days, but I do love him. And I think he loved me too, although he was more realistic about things than I was. I was the one pushing to try to find a way to be together. I was the one who invited him to come to the house when you were gone."

"Well, I don't imagine you had to try too hard to convince him," Ben said.

"We really did think we'd be safe in the house," Catherine explained. "I thought it might be my only chance to be safely alone with him. I never thought something like this would happen if we stayed in the house."

Ben sat down next to her and took her in his arms. "I know," he said, holding her tight.

"I don't know how I'm going to live with this, Dad," Catherine cried. "This is just too terrible. And Sally. *Oh my God,* what she and her family must be going through right now. I can't stand to even think about it."

"I don't know what to tell you," Ben said, "but I don't think Jimmy would want you to blame yourself. Instead of turning on yourself, direct your anger towards the people who really did this."

"Do you think they're going to get away with it?"

"I don't know," Ben said, shaking his head. "I hope not. I've talked to Abe about it, and he's going to contact the FBI, but because of the local Sheriff's Department, and their involvement in everything, it may be tricky."

"Do you think that if I tell the reporter why this all happened it might help?" Catherine asked. "Maybe instead of being afraid to talk to him, I should want to talk to him."

"It's something to think about," Ben said. "If Jimmy had been arrested and put on trial for robbery, it would have made sense to keep you out of it because of the impact your relationship with Jimmy would have had on a jury. *But now...*"

Ben stopped, and Catherine knew what he was afraid to say. *But now your relationship with Jimmy was the motive for his murder.*

They were interrupted by Mama Rae calling from the front of the house. *"Are y'all expecting someone?"*

Catherine looked at her father with confusion in her eyes.

"For now," Ben said, "just be careful what you say. If he were to write anything too inflammatory about you and

Jimmy, it might put you in danger, and I'm hoping to get you out of here in one piece."

Catherine hugged her father, then left her room to find Mama Rae and David Ross staring at one another through the screen door.

"This young man says that you're expecting him," Mama Rae said when Catherine appeared. "Is that right?"

Catherine nodded. "It's fine. I'll take it from here."

She greeted the surprisingly young face on the other side of the screen, then opened the door and stepped out onto the porch. Ben started to follow, but she put her hand on him as a gesture to stay inside. "It's okay, Dad," she whispered.

oz

"Would it be all right if we walked?" Catherine asked. "It might help me pull myself together if I can move around a little."

"Whatever you want is fine," David said, his blue eyes filled with compassion. "I understand how you must be feeling. Believe me. I knew Jimmy."

Catherine stepped off the porch and began walking in the direction of the pasture. "You and Jimmy were friends?"

"Yeah, we became friends after I wrote a story about him a couple of years ago. I was thinking of going to law school, and he was also interested in maybe going to law school someday, so we had that in common. And we had other things in common too, so we hit it off." He paused, obviously struggling with strong feelings. "I still can't really believe this has happened."

Catherine suddenly regretted agreeing to meet with the man walking beside her. She was physically and emotionally

202

spent, and could barely think straight. There was an uncomfortable silence between them now, and she blurted out a question that seemed too casual under the circumstances. But, for the moment, she was incapable of talking about Jimmy. "So are you still a local reporter?"

"Well, not really. I'm not actually working for any particular paper right now. I'm what's called a *stringer* for a couple of papers, which really just means I'm a freelancer. I sell a story every now and then, just to keep my hand in, but I don't have the time to do much writing these days. I'm in Law School now, so that keeps me pretty busy. But to answer your question, I don't write for the local paper here anymore. I only did that for a brief period the summer after I graduated from college."

Catherine looked at him quizzically. "How old are you? You don't look old enough to have already graduated from college and be in law school."

"I get that a lot," he said. "I skipped a grade, and I was on the young side of my class to begin with, so I actually started college when I was sixteen. I'm twenty-three."

"What are you doing in town now?" Catherine asked. "Are you here for the summer?"

"No," he said, "I'm just here to visit my family for a week. Kind of like you, I guess. I got to town the day before I saw Jimmy, which was right before all this happened, and now I'm just kind of using my old status as a local reporter to try to figure out what the hell's going on. He told me a little bit about you, so I've kind of put two and two together. I'm guessing that maybe someone saw the two of you together?"

Catherine dodged the question for the moment. "Are you really thinking about writing something about it?" she asked.

"I don't know. Maybe. I think it's an important story, and, more importantly, I want to make sure Jimmy's murder isn't swept under the rug." He frowned. "The people who did this can't be allowed to get away with it. And Jimmy, of all people, wouldn't want them to. I'm sure you know that the reason he wanted to go into law was to help put a stop to this kind of thing."

David stopped walking. "Jimmy and I talked about things like this a lot. It's kind of the reason we became friends. We even talked about maybe practicing law together someday."

Catherine suddenly pictured a law office with *Emerson & Ross* stenciled on a frosted glass door, and was struck by a sense of regret so terrible that she actually closed her eyes and shook her head, as if trying to banish the painful image.

She was trying to think of what to say when David went on. "I don't want you to think that I came here today because I'm writing a story," he said. "I mainly wanted to come because I know how you must be feeling, and I thought you'd be interested in the conversation I had with Jimmy when I saw him."

"On the phone you said he talked to you about me."

"Yeah, he did. And I felt honored that he felt he could confide in me."

Catherine could tell by the look on David's face that he was genuinely in pain.

"When we first became friends," he said, "we used to walk together down by the railroad tracks." He paused to collect himself. "When we ran into each other in town the other day, we went down to the tracks like old times, and he talked about a lot of things, including you."

"What did he say?" Catherine asked, trying not to break down.

"Well, he told me you were an *Abolitionist*, which is what he called white people who believe passionately in equality for Negroes. He said your father was too. He thought a lot of your father."

He squinted in the sun and ran a hand through his curly hair. "It was clear to me that the two of you were falling in love. He said he felt like you belonged together."

"He said that?"

"Yes he did. But, of course, he understood the dangers, and it worried him. He asked me what I thought he should do."

Catherine's face turned hot. "What did you tell him?"

"I told him that if he really loved you, and you loved him, that you should follow your hearts. I said it would be a revolutionary act, and might be hard, but that someone had to start breaking down barriers, and why not the two of you?"

Catherine's eyes filled with tears. "And what did he say?"

"He agreed that unless people had the courage to step out of the boundaries, things would never change. But he was uncertain—mostly because of what it would mean for you. And he was also worried about what things might be like if you had children."

Catherine thought about the impact that she'd had on *his* life. *On ending his life.* "And what did you say about those worries?"

"I told him that it should be your choice. That if you truly loved him, you might embrace the opportunity to stand up for your beliefs."

Catherine looked off towards the trail that led to the pond. "I know it sounds crazy," she said, "but it really did feel like we belonged together. It felt that way from almost the first second we saw each other." She looked back at David. "You some-times hear about '*chemistry*,' and now I know what that means. Ours was so strong that there was just no denying it. And now, after only having been with him for just a few days, I feel like I can't live without him. And I do feel responsible for what hap-pened. How can I not feel that way? *He lost his life!*"

"I understand why you feel that way," David said, "but I don't think you *should* feel that way. Jimmy wouldn't blame you. And, for what it's worth, I don't. You and Jimmy had every right to love one another. That's what the two of you be-lieved, right?"

Catherine nodded as tears ran down her face. "Can I ask you a question?"

"Sure, anything."

"What was it like for you living here? Seeing all the horrors that go on here?"

"Well, I mostly grew up in California," David said. "I lived in San Francisco until I was almost thirteen. Then my dad died, and my mom had a hard time supporting our family, so we moved here to live with my grandparents."

"It must have been a pretty big shock moving here from San Francisco."

David made a face. "That's putting it mildly. I hated it here for all the reasons you can imagine. But now I think it was the best thing that could have happened to me. Seeing so many terrible things here is what made me want to make a difference. It's why I write, and why I'm studying law. It's why Jimmy and I became such good friends." His face flushed. "*No one* had the right to interfere with you and Jimmy, Catherine, and I want to make sure that the people who did this to him are held accountable. But I don't hold you accountable, and you shouldn't either. And I damn sure know Jimmy wouldn't."

"What are you planning to do?" Catherine asked. "I'm sure you know that the Sheriff's Department is involved."

"Yeah, well everyone in town knows about the sheriff and the KKK. The investigation is going to have to involve the FBI. I talked to a lawyer over at the courthouse who is already looking into getting them involved."

"That would be Abe."

"That's right. I talked to him this morning. He seems like a good guy, and he told me he's been talking to your father."

David nodded over to the remains of the barn. "It looks like you had a fire here, too. When did that happen?"

"That was our barn," Catherine said. "They burned it down two nights ago. We've also been getting some pretty scary phone calls."

Suddenly they heard a car approaching, and Catherine and David turned to see a sheriff's car driving up. When Catherine realized who it was, she looked at David with fear in her eyes. "That's Jesse Taylor," she said. "He's one of the KKK ringleaders. He and his son JT are the ones who made the robbery accusations against Jimmy. JT and some other guy came around and were peeking inside the house, looking for me I guess, and that's when they saw Jimmy and me together. It was after that that JT made up the story about the robbery."

Catherine and David began to walk slowly back in the direction of the house. When they were near enough to see and hear what was going to happen, they stopped. Jesse Taylor was just getting out of the car. He looked over at Catherine and David, but didn't acknowledge them. He was approaching the house when Ben opened the screen door and stepped out onto the front porch.

"What do you want, Jesse?" Ben called with contempt. "Have you come looking for someone else to murder?"

"You'd better watch your mouth," Jesse hissed. "I've come to tie up some loose ends."

"*You've come to gloat!*" Mama Rae yelled, emerging from the house and joining Ben on the porch. "*And I want you to get the hell off my property!*" She was armed with a double-barreled shotgun, which she raised and aimed at the deputy. Catherine wondered where she'd gotten the gun.

Jesse Taylor slowly placed his right hand on his sidearm. "You'd better put that down, or there may just be another killing yet."

"Put your hands in the air," Mama Rae demanded, "or the person killed is gonna be you." She brandished the gun with an authority that made it clear she knew what she was doing.

Catherine shared an astonished look with David, then turned back to Mama Rae, who appeared dead serious. Standing next to her, Ben looked equally stunned. He made a motion as if he were going to take the gun, but Mama Rae moved out of his reach and demanded, "Leave me be."

Jesse Taylor showed no intention of raising his hands. "I don't know what you think you're doing you crazy old bitch," he hollered, "but you'll be going to jail for this. I'm an officer of the law, and..."

"*Shut up and put your hands in the air!*" Mama Rae yelled. Then the shotgun went off with a blast that made Catherine and David jump and sent gravel flying up around the deputy's feet.

"*You almost hit me!*" Jesse Taylor screamed, his sweaty face turning purple with rage. His right hand was now midway between up and his revolver, and he seemed to be thinking of his chances of drawing on Mama Rae before she could shoot him.

"If I'd wanted to hit you, you'd be dead," Mama Rae hollered. "And it'd be a pleasure to shoot you, so go ahead and try for your gun, or don't raise your hands, and we'll see." She wore an expression that seemed to say she was enjoying herself.

Ben appeared both shocked and afraid. "Mama Rae, I don't know what..."

"Hush!" she snapped. "I aim to tell this shit pile what I think of him, and no one is going to stop me, not even you." She turned back to Jesse Taylor. "Now get your hands up before I shoot you for real!" She held up the shotgun and took aim.

Jesse Taylor glared at Mama Rae with loathing, and his right hand was twitching, as though ready to go for his gun. "Y'all are going to pay for this, and that's a promise."

Mama Rae made a motion as if she were going to shoot again, and Jesse Taylor jumped and raised his hands in alarm. Catherine shared a stunned look with David, then looked at Ben, who seemed uncertain what to do.

"That's better," Mama Rae proclaimed when the deputy's hands were up. "Now you're going to listen to me, and then I may just shoot you anyway for the sheer pleasure of watching you get what you deserve. And just so you know, I've been told by my doctor that I don't have long to live. Maybe a month or two. So I don't care a whit what happens to me over this. I aim to say my piece, and if I have to shoot you to get you to cooperate, so much the better."

Mama Rae looked at Ben, then Catherine. "I'm sorry to tell you this way, but, to be honest, the freedom I feel right now is worth everything. I have it in my mind to tell this sorry excuse for a human being what I think of him and his mob of murdering half-wits, and I'm going to enjoy every second of it."

Jesse Taylor looked at Ben with a silent appeal to intervene, but Ben ignored him, seeming to be resigned to the situation as it was unfolding. He sat down on the porch swing and crossed his arms, then looked at Mama Rae, as if to cue her to continue.

"First of all," Mama Rae spat, staring at the deputy with scorn, "that handsome boy you killed—you are not fit to shine his shoes. He had more intelligence in his pinky finger than you and all your hooded pea brains have put together."

She shifted the gun, signaling that she was ready to use it at any time. "You and your kind pretend you're superior to the Negroes, but nothing could be farther from the truth. The reason you're so filled with hatred for them, and try so hard to keep them poor, and separate, is y'all are terrified that if you give colored people an even chance, they'll take something away from you—or compete with you, and maybe be better than you, which is your deepest darkest fear. Y'all are just a bunch of ignorant, pathetic cowards who want to stack the deck in your favor, and you can be sure that you'll burn in hell for the things you've done to decent people like our friend Jimmy."

"You're crazy!" Jesse Taylor shouted. "And as far as that uppity nigger is concerned, he got what was coming to him. No one points a gun at my boy and gets away with it. And you're not going to get away with this, neither, and that's a promise. All of y'all are going to be *very* sorry for this."

"Well, I may just have to shoot you then," Mama Rae yelled back. "As long as I'm going out, maybe I'll do the world a favor and take you out with me. It's what you deserve for all the innocent blood you've spilled in your lifetime, and all of us here know it."

Jesse Taylor was sweating profusely. "Do you also know that your little slut granddaughter here was having sex with that nigger when my boy came to your house? What do you think about that?"

"What my granddaughter did or did not do is of no concern to you or anyone else," Mama Rae shouted.

"Well, I think your husband would have been concerned," Jesse Taylor sneered. "I knew him, and now, seeing you, I can understand why he was such a mean old cuss." His face took on a look of satisfaction. "He used to enjoy a good lynching, you know. He hated niggers as much as anyone."

Mama Rae shifted the shotgun and her face turned an alarming shade of red.

"As a matter of fact," Jesse added with glee, "if he were still alive, he'd have been the first to light the match on that smooth-talkin' college nigger of yours. I'll bet he's dancing in his grave at the thought of it right now."

Suddenly the gun in Mama Rae's hands exploded.

Jesse Taylor flew back and landed, face up, in the dirt. His chest was a mess of blood, and his face was frozen in an expression of wide-eyed horror.

There was a moment of stunned silence, then Ben abruptly stood up and jumped from the porch to crouch over the deputy's bleeding body. "You killed him, Mama Rae," he said, stating what was already obvious to everyone. "I can't believe you did that."

Mama Rae looked as stunned as anyone. "Well, I guess I did," she said. "But he had it comin'."

Catherine looked at David, who appeared frozen in disbelief. Then she walked over to Ben, trying not to look at the grisly remains of the deputy. "What do we do now?"

"I don't think we have much choice," Ben said. "I think we have to call the sheriff. But first we'd better call Abe."

"I'm sorry if this is gonna cause a lot of worry and trouble for y'all," Mama Rae said, "but for the moment at least, I can't honestly say I'm sorry I shot him."

"Well, you may be sorry before the day is over," Ben replied. His shirt was drenched with perspiration, and he was visibly frightened. "This is serious, Mama Rae. I don't see any way of keeping you out of jail over this."

"Well, maybe I'm a fool," Mama Rae said, her voice surprisingly calm, "but I just really don't care. And I mean that."

Ben headed back up to the porch and directed Mama Rae to the swing. "You sit tight, Mama Rae," he said. "I'm gonna try to reach Abe and have him come over if he can. I'll probably have him call the sheriff, too. That's not a call I'm anxious to make. In the meantime, I don't know what to say except hang on, everyone. It looks like we might be in for a wild ride." He shook his head in exasperation, then disappeared inside.

When Ben entered the house, Catherine was left struggling to reconcile so many traumatic events and emotions that she felt immobilized. She looked at her grandmother, who was sitting on the porch swing in a state of seeming serenity, then turned to David. She was comforted by his presence, and he appeared to understand this, because he returned her look with eyes filled with kindness.

"I'm glad you're here," Catherine said.

"I'll stay as long as you want me to."

Catherine took a deep breath, then began heading towards Mama Rae with the intention of saying something to her about her health, but before she arrived Mama Rae stood up and declared, "I'm gonna go in and rest. Y'all can let me know when things start happening."

Catherine gave her a look of concern, but Mama Rae waved her off. "I'll be all right," she said. "I made this bed, and I'm prepared to lie in it." Then she limped into the house, making it clear that she neither wanted nor needed anyone to make a fuss over her.

ᗥ

Twenty minutes later Abe arrived, followed just a few minutes later by Sheriff White, who, predictably, was not pleased. Catherine was relieved to see that the sheriff was accompanied by Dan Tucker, whom they'd met at the highway roadblock. She'd half-expected JT and a truckload of Klansmen to arrive too, and she was terrified by the thought of what their reaction would be to Jesse's death. Ben had a similar fear, so they already had a plan for evacuating their house. Until Catherine's mother arrived, they would stay in a motel somewhere outside of town. Then, as soon as possible, Catherine would go back to San Diego with her mother, and Ben would remain to see Mama Rae through whatever was in store. Catherine had argued to remain as well, but Ben was clear, and there was no budging him: Catherine had to leave as soon as possible. If she needed to return for a trial, fine, but Ben believed she was not safe to stay in town, and she had to grudgingly agree that he was probably right. David, who'd been allowed to listen to their discussion, agreed. Catherine needed to get out of town as quickly as she could.

"What exactly happened here?" the sheriff asked angrily upon stepping out of his car. Jesse Taylor's body was just ten feet from where he'd parked. His shirt was blood-soaked, and both his mouth and eyes were open, his face having the fierce look of a warrior struck down on the battlefield. Catherine found it difficult to look at him, and she prayed that someone would come take his body before JT or any other hostile parties arrived to see it.

"This shooting was a clear case of temporary insanity," Abe said to the sheriff, his voice solid with conviction. "The deputy arrived here shortly after these folks heard the terrible news that the beloved son of the family's housekeeper was murdered in a fire set by the Ku Klux Klan, who, as we all know, has a strong association with members of your department, including, but not restricted to, the deceased."

He looked Sheriff White straight in the eye, then nodded to Jesse's body. "That man came here to rub these folks' noses in it."

The sheriff's face flushed red. "You'd better be very careful what you say, Mr. Stone." His tone was low and threatening.

"According to witnesses," Abe continued defiantly, "the deputy here was shouting inflammatory remarks regarding the murder of the young Negro victim. Mrs. Bennett, who is currently resting in the house, shot Deputy Taylor in a state of extreme psychological distress."

It was the first time Catherine had heard her grandmother called anything but Mama Rae, and it made the situation seem all the more surreal, as if everything were happening to strangers, and not her own family. She was still having a hard time processing all the events of the last few days. She felt like she'd fallen into some kind of deranged, alternate reality, and she wondered if she would ever find her way back.

Mama Rae stepped out onto the porch. Her hair was neatly arranged, and she was clutching her purse as if she were ready for a short trip to the market.

"Don't you say anything now, Mrs. Bennett," Abe instructed. "You have the right to keep quiet and not incriminate yourself, and I want you to exercise that right until you and I have a chance to have a discussion. Do you understand?"

"I understand," Mama Rae said. "But when the time comes, I'm gonna say plenty." Her words sounded like a threat, and she looked straight at the sheriff when she delivered them.

Ben went to her side and held her arm as she walked carefully down the steps and then over to the sheriff, where she held up her hands as if to say, *Go ahead and cuff me.*

"That won't be necessary," the Sheriff said stiffly. He looked over at David with suspicion. "Who the hell are you?"

"I'm David Ross," David answered with an air of confidence. "I'm a stringer for the New York Times."

℅

It was late-afternoon, Mama Rae was in custody, and the County Coroner had long since collected Jesse Taylor's body. The news of Jesse's death had been delivered to his family, and filtered through town, and the expected backlash was starting to materialize. As Catherine and Ben and David were preparing to leave the Sheriff's office—having finished making their statements and commiserating with Abe about the well-being of Mama Rae, who was now in jail pending arraignment—they were aware of shouting and a great ruckus taking place outside the building, where a ferocious mob was demanding justice for Jesse Taylor. Catherine wasn't certain, but she thought she heard JT's voice screaming for vengeance at a high pitch. It sent shivers down her spine.

"I think the three of you had better try to sneak out the back," instructed Abe, who, in his rumpled linen suit, reminded Catherine of Spencer Tracy. He had found a place for Ben and Catherine to stay outside of town, and offered to take Catherine to his house until Ben could collect Catherine's mother, who was expected to arrive that evening. Ben had no way of reaching her on the road, and he was worried for her safety should she and her brother arrive at the farm while they were gone. He and Catherine dreaded telling her the latest chapter of their drama, which they were still having a hard time fathoming themselves.

Since arriving at the Sheriff's office, they'd learned that Jimmy's body had been positively identified. They'd been told that it was impossible to determine the cause of death, since he'd been so badly burned, but that his dentist had identified his teeth. It was a detail that devastated Catherine, forever tainting her memory of his singular smile.

Mama Rae was expected to be charged with first degree murder, and she was scheduled for arraignment the next morning. There were still no charges against anyone for the fire at Sally's house, much less Jimmy's murder, but Abe assured Ben and Catherine that the FBI would soon be called in to investigate.

David, who had not lied about his association with the New York Times, was talking about possibly taking a leave of absence from law school to write a series of articles for the paper, which was anxious to piggy-back on the national interest generated by the Emmitt Till case. The Times wanted to follow not only Mama Rae's trial, but the circumstances surrounding Jimmy's death, and the possible involvement of the KKK.

Mama Rae, who was continuing to express no remorse for killing Jesse Taylor, *was* expressing a desire to, as she'd threatened, *name names*, and it looked like she might, as Abe put it, blow the lid off decades of local KKK violence, encouraged if not facilitated by the Sheriff's Department. According to David, the time was right to shine a spotlight on the suffering of Negroes in the Jim Crow South, and Mama Rae was poised to become a champion in the cause. It only remained to be seen if she would live long enough to see the fruits of her determination.

Following Abe's advice, Catherine, Ben, and David left the Sheriff's office through the back door, where Abe was waiting in a large black Oldsmobile. But their exit did not go unnoticed. Persons stationed by the door called around front, and soon the car was surrounded by an angry group of men that included a crazed JT, his face misshapen with rage. Catherine might have felt sympathy for a son grieving his father, but she was terrified by the force of his ravings, and she knew, as she turned away from his enraged visage, that even if JT and his father had not been the ones who actually murdered Jimmy, they had gotten the ball rolling. They were ultimately to blame for Jimmy's death, and it was right that both father and son should pay for it.

Chapter 13

San Diego, 1955

For Catherine, the next few days and weeks were a blur. True to her word, Catherine's mother had arrived on schedule. Within forty-eight hours, Catherine was packed into her car and on the road back to San Diego, having promised both Abe and the County Prosecutor that she would return to testify in court, if needed.

Ben remained in town to be close to Mama Rae. He might have stayed at the farm, but two days after Catherine left town, their house, too, was burned to the ground. There were no witnesses, but it was plain to everyone that it was probably more handiwork of the KKK, or possibly JT.

Sally kept her promise to take her family to Chicago. Within days of Mama Rae's arrest, she was gone without a trace.

After several weeks, it became clear that no charges would ever be filed against anyone for Jimmy's murder, or for the torching of Sally's house, despite the FBI's promise to investigate the matter. An FBI agent had come to town briefly and poked around, but there was no indication that the case was taken seriously, despite the best efforts of Ben, Abe, and David to demand justice for Jimmy and his family.

Against Abe's advice, Mama Rae pled guilty to first degree murder, insisting she had no interest in spending her last days in a "kangaroo court." She hadn't been lying about her medical condition. She had lung cancer—no doubt from her husband's fifty-some-odd years of chain smoking—and her condition deteriorated rapidly after her arrest. Nevertheless, she was determined, before she died, on spilling everything she'd ever known or suspected about crimes committed against innocent Negroes in town, up to and including the murder of Jimmy Emerson—and David Ross, in particular, was intent on listening.

Once it became clear that there would be no trial, the New York Times and other national newspapers that had originally covered the story lost interest. But David did not lose interest. On the contrary, he was so devoted to calling attention to Jimmy's murder, and uncovering the town's ugly history, that he put law school on hold to do research for a book that he hoped would one day make the town famous, not only for its racially-inspired violence, but also—with Catherine's permission—for the love story that resulted in its now most infamous murders.

⊗

Catherine had been home in San Diego for little more than a month when she first realized she might be pregnant. Since returning home, she'd mostly slept, or watched TV in a bleary state of grief. Her mother had made periodic attempts to console her, but Catherine had little interest in consolation or discussion of any kind, preferring to be left alone. Since the start of her extended nightmare, she'd mostly blocked memories of her sexual experience with Jimmy, finding them too painful, so the possibility of pregnancy had never occurred to her. But tenderness and a noticeable plumping of her breasts eventually brought the question: *Wasn't she overdue for her period?*

When the thought first struck her, she was in such a diminished state that she experienced little emotion. But her detached reaction was short lived. All too soon she was hit with emotions that were as confusing as they were strong. She felt no small measure of panic at the thought of a child growing inside of her, but she also experienced a hint of elation. *Maybe this was not a terrible thing. Maybe this was a miracle that would, in a sense, bring Jimmy back to life.* Though she was not yet even certain she was pregnant, she decided to live with the idea for a time before determining if having a child would be a disaster, or an unexpected blessing.

By the time that her pregnancy was confirmed, she'd decided that the baby was a blessing. It was this miracle, she believed, that would help her find the strength to move on with her life—which she would now devote to Jimmy's child. It was also this baby who would ultimately bring another great blessing into her life. And that was David, who became a semi-regular visitor to San Diego upon learning that Catherine was pregnant.

Initially David's interest was not expressed as a romantic one. Having known and cared about Jimmy, he felt a sense of protectiveness towards Catherine and her child. But his feelings almost inevitably transformed into affection, devotion, and then love, and soon he found it difficult to pretend his feelings were otherwise.

α

Catherine was breastfeeding Hannah, who was now three months old, when she first had an inkling that David's feelings were deepening. She felt no inhibitions about nursing Hannah in his presence. She'd done so many times. But this time, with him watching her from across her parent's living room, things felt somehow different. As she placed Hannah, moist with perspiration, and now asleep, into a small wicker bassinet on the dining room table, she felt his eyes on her in a way that seemed noticeably tender, and loving. Catherine was standing next to her sleeping baby, whose tiny red lips were still in motion, when David joined her and placed his hand on her back. "She's the most beautiful thing I've ever seen," he whispered. "The two of you together are almost too much for me."

Catherine understood at that moment that David's interest in her was more than platonic, but she was still so emotionally bound to Jimmy, and so focused on Hannah—who's beautiful little face was just like her father's—that she was unable to entertain the possibility of a relationship with another man, even one as wonderful as David.

"You probably know that I love you," David said, his eyes fixed on the sleeping child. "Both of you."

Catherine was uncertain what to say.

"I know it's too soon," David said. "And if time goes by, and you decide that I'm not the one for you, I'll be satisfied to be Uncle David. I promise. But if the day comes when you feel like you want me in your life as more than a friend, I'll be here. And if the day ever comes when you can love me, I'll be the luckiest man in the world."

Over the next several months, David was patient, Catherine slowly began to heal, and both found solace in the beautiful child that had begun to feel like *their* daughter. Finally, almost a year after Hannah was born—the same week that David found a publisher for his book—Catherine and David were married. A year later, David's book was released, later to become a widely known and respected part of the history of Southern racial violence. Published under a pseudonym, it was titled, *Arkansas Summer: Malice and Murder in a Small Arkansas Town.*

Chapter 14

Los Angeles, 1986

The sun was hanging low over the ocean when Catherine finally stopped talking. Hannah, who had listened raptly and made few interruptions, now sat in silence, looking at her mother through eyes that felt brand new. The story she'd just heard bore no resemblance to the fiction she'd been told as a child about her natural father, and she was having a hard time recalibrating.

She was familiar with the story of the young white woman and bright Negro college student whose love affair in a 1950's Arkansas town had culminated in two murders, then sparked an investigation that uncovered decades of violence and lynchings associated with the KKK and local sheriff. She'd read the book in an African American Studies class in college.

She thought about some of the names in the book—Kathleen, Rachel, and Richard Bennett. She'd never suspected that the people who shared her mother's maiden name were actually her own family. The discovery that this well-known story was actually her parents' story—her own birth story—and that it had been written by her father, was so far out of left field that Hannah was stunned.

"It's all pretty unbelievable," Hannah said. "You're Kathleen, and Rachel and Richard Bennett are Mama Rae and Ben."

Catherine nodded. "My father's real name is Richard. Ben was a nickname he got in school. And Mama Rae's name was Rachel. He got away with changing my name because it was never in the newspapers."

"But why have you never told me this before?" Hannah asked. "Why the big lie?"

"Well, initially we didn't want to tell you because it was just too terrible. How do you tell a child that her father was murdered? That he was burned to death? We didn't want to burden you with that." She shook her head. "Trust me, these are terrible images to live with."

"Then why are you telling me now, Mom? Why today?"

Catherine was silent.

"Really, Mom. Why today, and not a month from now, or a year? Or why tell me at all?"

"I don't know," Catherine said. "It's complicated. I can maybe try to explain it to you later, but, at the moment, I'm exhausted." She turned and gazed out over the ocean, which was now lit up by the setting sun.

Hannah pulled her mother into a long embrace. She felt no anger towards her parents for the secret they'd kept from her. What she mostly felt was a terrible sadness. She thought about the tragedy of Jimmy, whom she'd read about, and even discussed in a college course. He was her father—it was almost impossible to believe. And her poor mother. It hurt Hannah to think about the pain and guilt she'd had to keep buried for so many years.

Catherine started to say something, then stopped.

"What were you going to say?" Hannah asked.

Catherine looked hesitant.

"Really, Mom. What?"

"You're probably going to think I'm crazy," Catherine said.

"Try me," Hannah said. "After everything you've just told me, I doubt you could say anything that would surprise me."

"I'm sure it was just my imagination playing tricks on me."

"What?"

"Well, I know it sounds ridiculous, but I could swear I saw Jimmy at your father's memorial."

Hannah was confused. "But that's impossible, right? You said his body was absolutely identified."

"That's what we were told," Catherine said. "But there was a man standing in the back of your father's memorial service that looked so much like Jimmy that I thought I was going to faint when I saw him. I only saw him for a moment, and just that once, but I haven't been able to stop thinking about it. I guess I kind of took it as a sign that it was time to tell you the truth."

"But you don't really think it was him, right?"

"I'm sure it was probably just someone who looked like him," Catherine said. "But it was a pretty big shock seeing that face in the middle of your dad's memorial."

"I've seen the picture, you know," Hannah said. "The one of you and Jimmy on the horse."

"How is that possible?" Catherine asked. "I'm sure I've never shown you that picture."

"Well, I guess after the confession you just laid on me, it's okay to confess to you that when I was little, I used to look through your jewelry box, not to mention all your bedroom drawers."

Catherine gave Hannah a look of surprise.

"I never took anything, but I did find the photo hidden at the bottom of your jewelry box, and I remember wondering about it. I would have asked you about it, but then you would have known I was rummaging through your things when you weren't looking." She chuckled. "Now that I think about it, that adorable little boy did look a little bit like me."

"He was definitely adorable," Catherine said. "And he looked a lot like you. You inherited his beautiful smile, and you have his eyes."

Catherine's face took on a sad, faraway look. "It still hurts me every day to think about what happened to him. If it hadn't been for you, I don't know what would have happened to me. It's been a lot to live with all these years."

"Do you think, if he'd lived, you would have ended up together?" Hannah asked.

"I think so," Catherine said. "I was certainly motivated, and I'm sure that once he realized I was pregnant with you, he'd have wanted to raise you. Of course now, looking back, it doesn't seem like it would have been that hard. But it was such a different time. It's amazing, really, to think about how much things have changed since then."

After pausing for a few quiet moments to watch the sun go down, Catherine and Hannah headed back in the direction of the car.

"I have so many questions about everything that I don't even know where to start," Hannah said, stepping around a large pile of seaweed.

"Well, how about for now we go back to thinking about your father," Catherine said. "I know I've opened up a can of worms here, and I understand you have questions, but, for the moment, let's let it rest. We'll have plenty of time to talk, and I'll be happy to answer any questions you have. I promise. But later."

"Okay, I understand," Hannah agreed.

"In the meantime, I'd appreciate it if you would keep all this to yourself," Catherine said. "If it were to get out, it would probably draw attention, and I'm, frankly, not anxious for that kind of attention. Especially not while I'm grieving your father."

Hannah hadn't even considered that her newfound identity might be newsworthy. But she realized now that her mother was right. The history surrounding her parents made no mention of a baby, so her existence might be considered news. She wasn't sure how she felt about that, but, in any case, she was fine with keeping the secret, at least for the present.

೮೩

"What you told me today puts a whole new light on Grandpa Ben," Hannah said. She and her mother had gone back to Catherine's house and cooked dinner together, and they were just sitting down to eat. She'd kept her promise to hold her questions about her mother's story, but was now succumbing to the temptation to reintroduce the subject. She hoped her mother wouldn't mind, and was holding her breath, waiting to see what would come back.

"Your grandfather was pretty wonderful," Catherine said. She put down her fork and picked up her wine glass.

"Is it okay if I tell him that I know about everything the next time I see him?" Hannah asked.

"Yeah. I'll talk to him first and let him know I told you."

"One of the things I find the most incredible is Mama Rae killing the deputy," Hannah said.

Catherine was silent.

"I'm sorry," Hannah said. "I know I told you I'd hold my questions for a while."

"It's fine," Catherine said. "I can't expect to drop a bomb like this on you, and then be unwilling to answer your questions. I'm actually pretty impressed that you've been able to hold out this long." She smiled and took a sip of her wine.

"What was it like seeing Mama Rae shoot Jesse Taylor?" Hannah asked. "Were you shocked that she did it?"

"It was pretty shocking. I think she was as shocked as anyone. But once she did it, she seemed just fine about it. As far as I know, she never expressed a speck of remorse."

"Did you ever see her again before she died?"

"No," Catherine said, shaking her head. "My father spent a lot of time with her once they moved her to a hospital, but I never went back. I wanted to, but everyone thought it would be too dangerous." She raised an eyebrow. "It was one of the few times I wasn't able to wear my parents down. I did talk to her a few times on the phone, but that was another battle, because at first they wouldn't let her have a phone. Abe went to bat on that one and finally won."

Catherine looked wistful. "Your dad spent a lot of time with her before she died. A lot of the things he uncovered started with conversations he had with her in the hospital."

"It's all so unbelievable," Hannah said. "So how much did Mama Rae actually know?"

"She didn't know a lot of specifics, but she told your dad about all kinds of terrible things she'd heard about over the years. Then he went to people in the black community, and they were the ones who really filled in the details."

Catherine's face took on a pained look. "None of us could believe how many horrific crimes had gone unpunished over the years. But it was par for the course in those days, I guess. And, of course, because the Sheriff's Department was essentially an arm of the KKK, it was all the worse." She reached for the wine bottle and poured more wine into both their glasses. "Unfortunately, I don't think anyone was ever prosecuted for any of the crimes your father wrote about, but at least they were brought to light." She looked at Hannah with regret. "I'm glad you're finally finding out that it was your father who wrote the book."

"Why didn't he publish it under his own name?" Hannah asked.

"Well, it's like I said. He wanted to protect you from the story, which we thought was just too terrible for a child to deal with. And, also, I think he thought it might offer us a little bit of protection against a backlash. He always feared retaliation— because his book did *not* go over well with a lot of people when it first came out. *To say the least.*"

"But you could have told me the truth eventually," Hannah said. "Why not tell me?"

"Well, that's where I kind of have to point to your father," Catherine said. "And I don't like blaming him, because he's not here to defend himself, but the honest truth is that I really did want to tell you, but he didn't want me to, and I could never convince him to agree to it. Although I guess I didn't really push that hard."

"But what was he afraid of?"

"I'm not really sure," Catherine said. "I could never get a satisfactory answer out of him. He used to mainly give the *'why rock the boat?'* response. But I always suspected that, deep down, he was afraid that if you were to find out that Jimmy and I were your parents, you'd romanticize your birth story to an extent that would somehow diminish his role as your father." Catherine reached for her daughter's hand and squeezed. "Being your father meant more to him than anything in the world."

Chapter 15

Catherine was walking down a busy city street. Her clothes were unaccountably wet, and she was wearing no shoes. She was late for an appointment, but she couldn't remember where she was supposed to go, or who she was meeting. Panicked, she searched her purse for a slip of paper that might contain the address, or some indication of where she was supposed to be. She found a paper, but when she tried to read it, she couldn't understand the words. She continued down the street, increasingly alarmed and confused. She did not know where she was. The city and its buildings were unfamiliar, and the people all around her seemed threatening.

She became aware of someone behind her. She turned around and saw a man who frightened her. He was wearing a uniform and had a snarling look on his face. He reached for her, and she began to run, but her legs were heavy, as though she were trying to run through water.

Up ahead she saw a face that looked familiar. It was Jimmy. He was on the other side of a busy street. She tried to cross the street, but was stopped by a thin clear film that seemed to divide her world from his. She touched the film, and found it soft and pliable. She pushed on it, trying to break through. It ballooned out, but would not break. She called to Jimmy on the other side of the barrier, but he didn't hear. She screamed his name as loud as she could, and tried to push through the elastic bubble, but no matter how much she struggled and yelled, she could not break through, or make Jimmy hear.

She kept crying his name and straining against the film until she finally woke up, confused about where she was. After a moment she calmed down. She was home.

ᘒ

It had been four months since David's sudden death, and Catherine was plagued with nightmares. In her waking hours she was mostly fine. She sorely missed her husband, but her life and work had been sufficiently separate from his that she was able to find comfort in returning to her daily routines. She was a teacher, and the joys and rigors of teaching were a healthy distraction from the pain and grief that might have claimed her otherwise.

But at night, in her dreams, things were different. And she often felt guilty upon waking, because the face that visited her most was not David's, but Jimmy's. She dreamed of Jimmy often. And her dreams were not always nightmares. Sometimes they were pleasant, even sexual, and those brought the most guilt, because her subconscious seemed to be longing as much for Jimmy as for David.

As much as Catherine had loved her husband, she had never stopped loving Jimmy. Seeing his face at David's memorial had been a shock to her system that she couldn't forget. She told herself again and again that it could not have been Jimmy, that it wasn't possible. But she couldn't convince herself to believe it—not completely, and especially not at night, while she was asleep. While she was asleep, her subconscious nagged and nagged and nagged her, telling her in no uncertain terms: Jimmy was alive.

ᘒ

Four months out, Hannah still experienced her father's death as a pain that greeted her when she woke up, and stayed with her most waking hours. Because she worked for a law firm that still bore her father's name, and vision, she felt his loss as a constant stinging sorrow that would not abate. Everywhere she turned, he was there. But, of course, he wasn't there, and she missed him relentlessly. The partners and other lawyers in the firm saw and understood the magnitude of her suffering, but there was little they could do to ease her pain. It was clear to everyone that the only thing that could help her was time.

Hannah was at her mother's house for dinner, and she planned to bring up the subject of taking a leave of absence from her job. Perhaps she would join the Peace Corps for a year, or work for a Bay Area law firm that one of her friends from law school had invited her to join. She needed to do something to remove herself, at least temporarily, from her father's domain. She hoped that her mother would understand if doing so meant that she would have to leave Los Angeles.

Dinner was finished and Catherine was searching the freezer for ice cream when Hannah finally broached the subject. "I'm thinking about leaving Southern California for a while," she said. "I already raised the possibility with the partners, and they told me that I can come back whenever I want. They've been patient with me, but I can tell they think it's a good idea."

Catherine, ice cream now in hand, seemed sympathetic. "Everyone understands how hard it's been for you," she said. She grabbed two bowls and began dishing out Rocky Road. "School's almost out, and I'll be off for the summer in another week. How would you feel about maybe taking a short vacation with me before you go off and do whatever it is you decide to do?"

Hannah was intrigued. "What do you have in mind?"

"I don't know," Catherine said. "I was thinking of a couple of different options." She hesitated. "I've always wanted to see Bryce Canyon and Zion. I've also been thinking of maybe taking a trip back to Arkansas, which probably sounds a little strange. But if you want to go with me, that's another possibility to consider."

Hannah hadn't seen this coming. "Why on earth would you want to go to Arkansas? I would think it would be the last place you'd want to go."

Catherine placed a bowl of ice cream in front of Hannah, then sat down in front of a bowl of her own. "I don't really know how to explain it," she said. "I just feel like I need to go back there." She smiled and shook her head, seeming embarrassed. "Never mind. Forget I mentioned it. If I do go, it's something I should probably do alone. Or maybe with my dad."

"What would you do when you got there?" Hannah asked. "Do you even know anyone there anymore?"

"Not really," Catherine answered. "And I really don't know how to explain my desire to go back. I just know that some part of me feels compelled to go back and just *be there* again—just for a day or so. But really," she said, "forget I mentioned it."

※

They had finished their ice cream and were out in the backyard, enjoying the night air. Hannah studied her mother, who was across the yard watering some potted plants. She had thought a lot about her mother since learning about Arkansas, and she now saw her in a completely different light. Not that she hadn't always perceived a depth to her mother that was unusual. She'd always understood, growing up, that Catherine was different from most mothers. She was more serious, more tuned in to the dramas that seemed to play out nightly on the evening news. She and her father had both been different. They weren't exactly radicals, but they'd been socially conscious in a way that colored almost everything they did, including raising her.

They had raised her to pay attention to events and forces in the world that other people seemed to notice, but not feel as deeply. Big changes had swept the country during Hannah's earliest years, and her parents had experienced them intensely. Hannah had too. She'd understood that she had a stake in the Civil Rights battles that were regularly brought into their living room by Walter Cronkite, and Huntley and Brinkley. Many of Hannah's strongest early memories were scenes she watched with her parents on the nightly news: black demonstrators being struck with police batons; blacks being attacked by whites at lunch counter sit-ins; blacks being hit with water cannons, being attacked by police dogs...

She remembered her mother and father watching, enraged, as George Wallace stood in a schoolhouse door to prevent black students from entering an Alabama college. She remembered similar expressions of emotion when three Civil Rights workers were murdered trying to register voters in Mississippi. Though much of what they watched on the news was frightening, Hannah's parents had made her feel as if she were part of something that was important, historic.

She recalled watching Martin Luther King's *I Have a Dream* speech on television. It was one of her most indelible early memories. Another was seeing her mother cry after learning the terrible news that Martin Luther King had been murdered. Hannah had vivid memories of all the assassinations that occurred like a repeating nightmare throughout her childhood: President Kennedy; Martin Luther King; then Bobby Kennedy. Both Catherine and Hannah had cried through them all.

In addition to tragedies and protests turned to violence, Hannah also remembered events met with great jubilation. There was President Johnson's passage of the Civil Rights Act of 1964, which struck down the Jim Crow laws that were used to enforce racial segregation in the South. There was the Voting Rights Act of 1965, which put a stop to laws that prohibited blacks from voting. These great moments in history seemed to go unnoticed by most of the families in their quiet tree-lined neighborhood, but in her family, they were occasions for great celebration.

Contemplating her mother now, Hannah realized that besides her social consciousness, there had always been something else about her—a sadness that was sometimes expressed on her face when she thought no one was looking. It was something *not* about the nightly news, and it was there even during happy times. Now Hannah understood the sadness and pain she'd had to live with, and hide. Seeing her mother with new eyes, Hannah was amazed that she'd been able to live with the pain, and guilt, and still be a wonderful, loving mother and wife.

Hannah could easily picture her mother at twenty, falling in love with a handsome young Jimmy, winning his heart, dreaming of making a life with him, despite the obstacles. It pained her terribly to think about what she'd suffered as a result of her actions, and at such an early age.

Now finished watering, Catherine crossed the lawn and sat down on the patio next to Hannah.

"I might go back to Arkansas with you," Hannah said, suddenly in the mood to support her mother's idea.

Catherine's expression brightened. "Really?"

Hannah shrugged and smiled. "What the hell."

Catherine kicked off her grass-covered shoes. "I'll probably get there, feel like a fool, and then want to turn around and come back. But...I don't know, it just feels like something I need to do."

She thought for a moment, then looked into Hannah's eyes. "I guess I'm like one of those World War II veterans who wants to go back to the beach at Normandy."

Chapter 16

Arkansas, 1986

Two weeks later, Catherine and Hannah were in a rental car, looking for the turnoff that led to what had once been her grandparents' farm. Catherine wanted to take Hannah to the pond, and then to see where their house had been. Ben had long ago sold the land, but she was curious to see what was there now. Catherine had invited Ben to partake in their sojourn, but he'd firmly declined, stating that he'd *rather visit the seven circles of hell.*

Shortly they were entering town, and Catherine realized they'd passed the road she'd been looking for. "I obviously missed the turn," she said.

They were now driving slowly down a Main Street that was less tired than her recollections, but which otherwise seemed remarkably unchanged. Were it not for the modern cars that replaced the metal behemoths of the 50s', Catherine might have believed she'd entered *The Twilight Zone*, where sodas still cost a nickel.

They passed the movie theater, whose gentrified marquee now read *Top Gun*. Nearby, Catherine recognized the diner where she'd sat with her father and Mama Rae after Jimmy disappeared and their house had been savaged. The sign out front had been refurbished, but otherwise it looked the same, and it brought back memories that were so vivid and so terrible that Catherine realized her father might have been right. What was the point of revisiting a place where such awful things had happened? She suddenly wished she were anywhere else.

She might have turned around and headed back for the airport, but her attention was suddenly captured by a middle-aged white couple emerging from the diner. An elderly black woman was approaching just as they were exiting, and the white man politely held the door open as she entered. This was not 1955, she reminded herself, and the scene gave her a renewed sense of mission—though she was still not clear on exactly what the mission was.

She was hungry, and momentarily entertained the idea of eating in the diner, but decided it would be pushing her luck. "What do you say we find some food?" Catherine asked Hannah. "Then we can go back and find the road I missed."

"Sounds good to me," Hannah said. "What about the place we just passed?"

"I'm probably not up to visiting that place in particular," Catherine said, "but I'm sure that if we keep going, we'll find something." She looked sideways at Hannah, and could see that she understood.

As they continued slowly up the street, Catherine was fascinated by the people they passed, and by the simple normalcy of the people they saw on the street, both black and white. Her sense of being in *The Twilight Zone* slowly diminished and was replaced by a feeling of relative calm. She had her eye out for the barber shop where Jimmy's father had worked, but there was no sign of the antique barber pole that had once signaled its presence. At the location where she believed it had been, there was now a woman's hair salon with a flashy neon sign. They eventually passed the hardware store where, regrettably, her recollections of the charming old man and his train were overshadowed by the memory of her fateful encounter with JT. Hannah noticed the store and gave her mother a look with raised eyebrows, as if to ask, *'Is that it?'* Catherine simply nodded.

A little farther on, they came to a place called *Shorty's Barbeque*, with a hand-written signboard out front that advertised Barbequed Catfish, Sliced Brisket, and Pulled-Pork Sandwiches, boasting: *'All meals come with baked beans and coleslaw.'* Hannah pointed to the restaurant. "What about there? I wouldn't mind some authentic Southern barbeque. That alone might be worth the trip."

Barbeque sounded good to Catherine, too, so she quickly pulled over and parked. This would be their first real interaction with the town, and Catherine was glad to have found an establishment that held no memories.

଼

Catherine and Hannah were sitting towards the back of the surprisingly large restaurant, enjoying the mouth-watering smells and colorful atmosphere of the place, when Shorty himself delivered two delicious-looking pulled-pork sandwiches, complete with the promised baked beans and coleslaw. A roll of paper towels stood ready on one side of the wooden table, and by the looks of the sandwiches, they were going to need it.

"I bet you don't have barbeque like this where y'all come from," Shorty said, his broad smile punctuated by a gold-rimmed tooth. He looked from mother to daughter. "Where y'all from?"

"Los Angeles," Hannah offered, mirroring back his grin.

"Ah, LA," he said, his smile widening. "I have people in LA, but I've never been there myself. Always wanted to go, but this place keeps me pretty busy." He looked over his shoulder and expressed obvious disappointment at seeing a line of people waiting to place orders. "I'm short-handed today," he said, "so duty calls. But you ladies enjoy your meal, and just holler if you need anything."

Catherine and Hannah said thank you, and then quickly turned their attention to their sandwiches, which were spicy and even more delectable than they appeared.

"Oh my god, this is the best thing I've ever tasted," Hannah said after taking her first bite.

With her mouth full, Catherine signaled agreement with an enthusiastic nod.

About half-way through their meal, they became aware of an elderly black gentleman at a nearby table. Hannah noticed him first. "That man over there keeps looking at us," she said. "Do you know him?"

Catherine glanced over and gave the man a friendly smile, but she didn't recognize him. The only black man of his vintage that she'd had any real contact with was Will, and it was definitely not Will. But, in any case, she had a hard time imagining that even Will would recognize her after more than thirty years.

"He's probably just curious about the two of us," Catherine said. "I doubt they get too many customers in here that they don't recognize. This town isn't exactly a tourist hub."

Catherine was just taking another bite of her sandwich when the man was suddenly heading in their direction. In a moment he was standing next to their table. Catherine, who was sure her face was covered in barbeque sauce, pulled a paper towel from the roll and quickly wiped her mouth. Hannah did the same, then they both greeted the gentleman with embarrassed smiles.

"I'm sorry," the man said politely. "I don't mean to interrupt you, but I know you've noticed me looking over here, and I just thought I'd offer an explanation. I hope you don't mind."

"We don't mind at all," Catherine said. She raised her eyebrows. "Is there something we can help you with?"

"Well, this is a little awkward," he said. He turned to Hannah. "It's you who've captured my interest."

He hesitated, then said, "You bear such a strong resemblance to someone that I used to know...I just have to ask you: Are you related to the Emerson family?"

Hannah glanced quickly at her mother, then looked back at the man, not sure what to say.

"I'm sorry, I shouldn't have bothered you," he said, looking back and forth between the two of them.

"No, it's fine," Catherine said, trying to get her bearings. After so many years she hadn't expected anyone to recognize her, and it had never occurred to her that someone might recognize Hannah. But Hannah looked so much like Jimmy, *of course* someone might notice the resemblance. She felt like a fool for not having realized this and prepared for the situation. She was at a loss for how to respond.

"I'm sorry," the gentleman said, "I should introduce myself. My name is Jacob Harris. I used to be a teacher here in town."

He focused his attention on Hannah. "You remind me so much of one of my former students. When I saw you, I just...well, I wondered if maybe you and he were related."

Catherine recognized the name of the teacher who'd been such a good friend to Jimmy, and she was suddenly flushed with emotion. "Mr. Harris," she said. "This is very unexpected." She hesitated, then, on impulse, said, "Would you like to join us?"

Seeming pleased, he gave a warm smile. "If you don't mind," he said. "Let me just go get my things."

While he left to retrieve items from his table, Catherine spoke quietly to Hannah, who looked startled. "I don't know what the odds are that we'd run into him like this, but that's the teacher who helped Jimmy get his scholarship. I'm inclined to tell him the truth. Are you okay with that?"

"Well, you came here looking for something," Hannah said. "Maybe this is it."

Mr. Harris returned and took a seat opposite the wall, between Catherine and Hannah. "You're sure you don't mind me intruding?" he asked. He had the stately air of an English teacher, and Catherine tried to remember if she'd ever known what he taught.

"No, it's our pleasure," she said, moving a pile of used paper towels to her side of the table. "My name is Catherine, and this is Hannah."

Mr. Harris's face gave a subtle but discernible twitch, as if he were stifling a look of surprise, and Catherine could see that he was probably putting two and two together.

The teacher turned to Hannah once again, and seemed fascinated by her face. "So, I'm guessing you must be related to my student, or I wouldn't be sitting here."

Hannah looked to her mother.

"Hannah is my daughter," Catherine said. "And Jimmy Emerson was her father."

Mr. Harris, who had been leaning forward over the table, sat back slowly in his chair. "I never knew there was a child," he said. He turned to Catherine. "And of course, you're..."

Catherine nodded.

"I wondered when I saw you, and thought maybe, but..."

"I know how you must feel," Catherine said. "I'm sure it's a shock." She could see by the teacher's expression that he was processing the information. "We kept Hannah a secret, because after all that happened, we were afraid someone might try to harm her."

Mr. Harris was silent.

"It was my husband who wrote the book," Catherine said.

The teacher's expression slowly changed from bewilderment to understanding.

"We got married when Hannah was about a year old," Catherine said. "Almost no one knows Jimmy and I had a child, and I'd kind of like to keep it that way. I'm telling you now because I know you were Jimmy's friend."

"So Jimmy's family doesn't know?"

"Well, I'm embarrassed to tell you this, but no, they don't." Catherine looked down at her hands. "After I left, my father stayed in town until my grandmother died, and he decided not to tell them. I guess he felt it would make things more painful for them if they knew."

She looked up and straight into the teacher's eyes. "As you might imagine, I wasn't their favorite person. Just about everyone blamed me for what happened to Jimmy, including myself. There was no way, after Jimmy was killed, that Sally wanted to hear I was pregnant with his child."

"If you don't mind my asking, why are you here?"

"I know it sounds ridiculous, but I don't even know," Catherine replied, trying not to cry. She picked up a paper towel and began twisting it.

"You must have some idea," Mr. Harris said. His voice was filled with compassion. "What do you plan to do, who are you planning to see?"

Catherine shook her head, and she felt like a fool.

Hannah jumped in. "My father died suddenly a few months ago, and my mother has had a hard time adjusting. Both of us have."

She looked into her mother's eyes, then back to Mr. Harris. "She's been thinking a lot about the things that happened here—it's been a lot for her to deal with over the years." Her voice softened. "I think she just feels like she needs to come back here and touch base before she can move on." She turned to her mother. "Does that sound about right?"

"I don't know," Catherine said. "I guess that's as good an explanation as any."

"Also," Hannah added, "she saw someone who looked like Jimmy at my father's memorial, and it kind of stirred her up."

"You thought you saw Jimmy?" Mr. Harris asked.

"I'm sure it was my imagination," Catherine said. "But yes, I thought I saw him."

The teacher's face took on a strange expression, and he seemed to be thinking. "There are a couple of things I want you to know," he said. "First, your husband was a courageous man. That book, and all that came out as a result, was important. I'm sure I don't have to tell you.

"And your grandmother..." He shook his head and smiled. "Now she was something. *Old Mama Rae...* I'm surprised we don't have some kind of monument or something to Mama Rae—except, I guess, maybe the white folks might not take too kindly to it." He laughed, and then his face got serious again. "And Jimmy..." he said. "Jimmy was an extraordinary young man." He looked at Hannah. "Your father was the best student I ever had. I don't blame your mother one bit for falling in love with that boy."

He turned to Catherine. "It was just the wrong time."

"What was he like when you had him as a student?" Hannah asked.

Mr. Harris took off his glasses and began wiping them with a cloth he pulled from his pocket. "That boy could change the temperature of a room just by walking into it," he said. "He had something very special. A spirit, intelligence, determination...humor..."

He put his glasses back on. "I had lots of bright students over the years, but there was something really special about Jimmy." He grinned at Hannah. "And he was a *handsome* young man. Just look at you. You're a beautiful woman—stunning—and you look so much like him, you about stopped my heart when I first saw you."

He turned back to Catherine. "Don't get me wrong. You're a beautiful woman too. She didn't get all her good looks from her father."

Catherine smiled, moved by Mr. Harris's kindness, and charm.

"Do you think you might go see Jimmy's family while you're here in town?" Mr. Harris asked. "It's my understanding that Will died a few years back, but Mary, his aunt, still lives here, and one or two of her kids might still be around. I've kind of lost track. Mary is well up into her seventies now—like me—but as far as I know, she's still healthy. I see her around town from time to time, and we sometimes exchange words."

Catherine and Hannah looked at each other. "We'll have to think about it," Catherine said, turning back to the teacher. "Like I told you, I was not their favorite person, and the fact that I kept Hannah a secret all these years might not go over too well."

Catherine considered the situation, but was uncertain what to do. "I'm sure it seems crazy to you that we would come all this way and not want to see Jimmy's family." She shook her head. "I'm just not sure."

Mr. Harris gave Catherine a look of understanding. "I can imagine how you might feel. But I hope you'll give it some thought. I think it might be all right."

He looked back at Hannah. "If you don't mind my asking, what do you do for a living? I assume you're a career gal, because I don't see a wedding ring on your finger."

Hannah answered his question with obvious pride. "I'm a lawyer," she said. "I've been working for my father's law firm, and our main focus is Civil Rights law."

Mr. Harris beamed. "Well, I see you inherited more from your father than his good looks. He'd be very proud of you."

He turned to Catherine, who was suddenly struggling not to cry. "He'd be proud of you both," he said. He tipped his head towards Hannah, as if to say, 'look at this wonderful daughter you raised.'

"You're very kind," Catherine said, moved by the old man's gesture. "I can't tell you how happy I am that we came in here and bumped into you. It's an incredible coincidence."

"Well, I'm not a big believer in coincidence," Mr. Harris said. "I think maybe our meeting was meant to be. And I hope you don't mind me telling you this, but I really think you should consider paying a visit to Mary. She still lives in the same little house. I can tell you how to get there."

Just thinking about seeing Mary again gave Catherine the shakes, but it occurred to her that Hannah might want to meet her. She glanced at Hannah, who looked equally unsure.

"We'll see," Catherine said. Then she asked, hesitantly, "Do you happen to know if Sally is still alive?"

Mr. Harris squinted his eyes. "I'm sure I recall hearing that she died a few years back. I believe in Chicago. It's maybe been two or three years now." He paused to think. "I don't think I ever knew any of the details, but I'm certain I heard she passed."

Catherine was hit with a familiar sense of anguish. To survive over the years, she'd been forced to suppress a lot of her feelings, but now some of the old pain and guilt were flooding back in.

"I can see that you're distressed," Mr. Harris said. "I'm sorry if I've upset you."

Catherine was embarrassed. "No, you've been wonderful. There's no need to apologize. It's just hard thinking about Sally. It's been terrible all these years, living with what happened. Thinking about Sally has always been one of the hardest things." Once again, Catherine fought back tears.

Mr. Harris had a pained expression on his face, and appeared to be at a loss for words, when Shorty suddenly materialized and reeled them all back to the present.

"Jake, you old devil!" he said. "Look at you sittin' here like a king between these two fine women!"

He looked back and forth between Catherine and Hannah. "Is this a friends of yours, or do I need to call Security?" He followed up with a big belly laugh.

"No need for Security," declared Hannah, who was clearly happy for the light-hearted intervention. "Mr. Harris was just telling us that he used to be a teacher here in town."

"And he was one fine teacher, too," Shorty said, with obvious sincerity. "He was the best there was."

He grinned. "The day this man retired, we had a party for him right here, and half the town came out."

He paused for effect. *"The black half!"* More laughter.

"We had so many people come out, they were spilling out into the street. White folks in town didn't know *what* was happening. They probably thought it was an uprising!"

Shorty's good humor was infectious, and soon Catherine and Hannah and Mr. Harris were all laughing and joking with him. When he finally had to leave to take more orders, they were all happy to let the new tenor stand, preferring to finish up their sandwiches in an air of light conversation.

Before Catherine and Hannah eventually said good-bye to Mr. Harris, they exchanged both addresses and hugs. Mr. Harris promised that he'd refrain from discussing what he'd learned with anyone in town. But he did offer a few more words of encouragement on the subject of visiting Mary, as well as carefully printed directions to her house.

On their way out of the restaurant, Catherine and Hannah said good-bye to Shorty, thanking him for the best barbeque they'd ever tasted. The last thing they saw as they were leaving was the flash of his big gold-toothed smile.

"You ladies best come back and see me again," he called after them as they disappeared out the door. "I'll be saving y'all a table."

◌

Back in the car, Catherine made a U-turn and headed for the highway, where she was determined to find the road that led to where their farm had been.

"Do you think we'll go see Mary?" Hannah asked.

"Well, I won't pretend I'm not scared to death just thinking about it, but we probably should. What do you think?"

"I think it's going to be pretty strange showing up at her doorstep after all these years, but, on the other hand, we're here. What else are we supposed to do?"

Catherine glanced over at Hannah, who had the backdrop of Main Street passing behind her head, and she knew they'd go. She wasn't sure what they'd accomplish, or what to expect, but her instincts told her to listen to the teacher and see what happened.

"I think we'll probably go," Catherine said, "but first I want to find the road to the farm."

When they were back on the highway, it wasn't long before Catherine found the turn, which was now surrounded by a small development of modest prefab houses. "No wonder I didn't see it before," Catherine said. "This used to all be open."

She turned left onto the road, which was now paved, and soon the new houses thinned out and the scenery became familiar again.

"This is better," Catherine said as they progressed towards the pond.

She pointed to a tidy white farmhouse with several horses grazing nearby. "That used to be a shack," she said. Farther on they passed additional small houses that were new, but the area was largely unspoiled.

Finally, they came to the pond, and Catherine was struck, as always, by its quiet beauty.

"This is almost exactly like I pictured it," Hannah said as her mother pulled off the road.

Catherine parked in the same spot where her father had parked the first time he'd brought her to the pond in 1955. The tree that had towered over his truck then had been majestic; now it was positively epic.

Catherine and Hannah got out of the car. "This is incredible," Hannah said. "You talked so much about this pond, I feel almost like I'm stepping onto the set of a movie."

A truck drove past, and the driver slowed down to take a look at Catherine and Hannah, but he kept going. Several children were fishing on the pier across the pond, and they looked up. One of them, a boy of around nine or ten, waved, and both Catherine and Hannah returned his greeting.

The old pier was gone, replaced with something wider and sturdier. There was also a sign posted on one of the trees that warned bathers to 'Swim at your own risk.' But otherwise everything looked pretty much the same. It was still early in the summer, so the heat was not intense, but the air was hot and fragrant, and the sounds of birds and insects transported Catherine back in time. She had so many vivid memories of this place—going all the way back to catching tadpoles with Jimmy—that her head was practically spinning.

"This place is definitely as beautiful as you said it was," Hannah said.

"I can't tell you how happy I am to see it so unchanged," Catherine said. "It's almost too bad my dad isn't here with us. I think he'd enjoy it. He'd have enjoyed Shorty's, too."

She picked up a small rock and skipped it over the pond. "If nothing else comes out of this trip, at least I'm having the chance to replace some of my terrible memories with good ones." She smiled. "It's not 1955 anymore."

She was suddenly filled up with sorrow. "I think the three of us could have been a family and done just fine," she said. "Obviously not here, not back then. But I think we'd have been okay in California." She smiled across the pond at the children, who'd just caught a fish and were squealing with joy.

She turned back to Hannah. "Please don't think that any of this means that I didn't love your father. I loved him dearly, and I'll never stop missing him."

"You don't have to worry, Mom," Hannah said. "I understand. I really do. You can love them both." She picked up a small rock, examined it, and then tossed it into the water. "I didn't even know Jimmy, but after everything I've heard about him, I feel like I love him too."

⅓

A few minutes later, Catherine and Hannah waved goodbye to the children and headed for the farm. They decided it would be pleasant to walk, so they left the car parked where it was and struck out on foot.

"Everything looks the same," Catherine said as they progressed up the road. She pointed into the trees on the right. "It was somewhere just in there that Jimmy and I had our fort."

Soon they came to the entrance of the now-paved driveway they were looking for. A large sign stating *'Private Property'* was nailed to a nearby tree, but they decided to ignore it, and cautiously ventured forth.

The house that stood at the end of the winding approach was exactly where the old house had been. It was larger than her grandmother's house—with two stories and an attached garage—but a wrap-around porch, complete with porch swing, was eerily reminiscent of the old structure. Nearby, two old-looking horses stood munching weeds near the gate of the pasture, which was surrounded by a modest wire and wood fence that replaced the rough-hewn plank fence Catherine remembered. A large gray barn with an overhang shelter built off its right side now marked the spot where the old barn had been.

"Things don't look that different," Catherine said, stopping with Hannah a good distance from the house. "All the structures are new, but the basic layout of the place is the same."

Catherine and Hannah stood quietly under a dramatic cloud-filled sky and took the place in. Green hills and trees, the sweet smell of hay and horses, and a gentle breeze brought memories to Catherine that were both fond and frightening.

Shortly, an elderly man with pants pulled up high over a pot-belly appeared on the porch and called over to them. His voice was not friendly. "Can I help you?" he hollered.

In another second he was joined by an old woman with a tousled pixie haircut. She offered no greeting, but had a bearing that was similarly inhospitable.

Catherine's instinctive reaction was alarm, but she told herself she was being silly. "I'm sorry," she called in a friendly tone. She walked closer to the house so that she wouldn't have to yell, and Hannah followed. "We were just taking a walk, and wanted to take a peek and see what's up here. You have a lovely place."

"Well, it's private property," called the old man. "Didn't you see the sign?"

"I'm sorry," Catherine said, stung by the hostile response. "I guess our curiosity just got the better of us. We'll be on our way, and I apologize for bothering you."

The couple stood as still as statues, and Catherine had the uncomfortable feeling that they were focused on Hannah.

"Y'all from around here?" called the man, suddenly coming back to life.

"No, we're just visiting," Hannah chimed.

"We'll be going now. You have a nice day," Catherine added with just the tiniest hint of sarcasm.

"So much for Southern hospitality," Hannah commented as she followed her mother back towards the road.

"Well, we do look like a couple of pretty dangerous characters."

"Was it my imagination, or were they glaring at me?" Hannah asked.

"I'd say they were glaring," Catherine said. "But, you never know, they might be unfriendly like that to everyone. With the pond so close by, they probably have a lot of people bothering them."

"Well, anyway, I'm glad I got a chance to see the place, even if we weren't welcomed with open arms," Hannah said.

Nearing the pond again, Catherine and Hannah could see that both a truck and another car were now parked next to their car. When they got closer to the water, they began to hear laughing and splashing, and soon they discovered that a group of teenage boys, mostly white, but two black, had supplanted the smaller children, who were now gone. A couple of the boys looked over as they approached, but most paid them no mind, intent as they were on swimming, horseplay, and cannon-balling off the end of the pier.

As Catherine sat down behind the wheel of their now extremely hot car, she exchanged a smile with Hannah, pleased that this happy scene was the last thing in her mind before heading to their next destination.

ʚ

Before leaving Shorty's, Jacob Harris had given Catherine and Hannah directions for getting to Mary's house. He'd also given them his phone number, and encouraged them to call if they needed anything, or wanted to get together again before leaving town.

"I still can't get over running into Jimmy's teacher," Hannah said, examining the meticulous handwriting on the paper in her hand.

"It was a pretty crazy coincidence," Catherine said. She glanced at Hannah. "I believe in coincidences, by the way."

"So you don't have the feeling that this was all meant to be?" Hannah asked. "Running into Mr. Harris; him telling you to go see Mary?"

"I don't know," Catherine said. "I think we probably just got lucky. Or maybe unlucky. We still haven't seen Mary. For all we know, she'll slam the door in our faces."

"I don't think that's going to happen," Hannah said. "Mr. Harris seems to know her, and I don't think he'd send us there if he thought she'd respond badly. Do you?"

"I'm sure he meant well," Catherine answered, "but he may not have any idea how she'll respond. On top of getting Jimmy killed, I had his child and never informed the family. That's a lot to forgive."

Catherine stopped at the intersection with the highway and turned to her daughter. "I hope you can forgive me," she said.

Hannah reached for her mother. "Of course, I forgive you."

"Well, I wouldn't blame you for being angry."

"You know, I used to fantasize that Sidney Poitier was my real father," Hannah said. "I can remember when I was, I don't know, maybe nine or ten, fantasizing that he was my father, but, because he was a big movie star, you weren't allowed to tell anyone."

Catherine laughed. "I remember how much you loved Sidney Poitier."

"But seriously, Mom," Hannah said. "I'm not mad at you. I mainly just feel bad for you. But I am happy you finally told me. And I'm glad to be here with you." She smiled reassuringly. "Really."

As they were nearing town, Hannah consulted Mr. Harris's directions. "Towards the end of Main Street, we need to look for Green Street, then turn left."

When the sign for Green Street appeared, Catherine turned, and soon she began to recognize the shops, churches, and small houses that characterized what was still the black part of town. The neighborhood and people looked somewhat more prosperous than they had in the 50's, but, once again, Catherine was surprised by how little things had changed.

"Turn left up here," Hannah said, pointing to the next corner. After one more turn, Catherine and Hannah were on the sleepy residential street where Mary lived. There were still no sidewalks, and some of the homes were in serious need of paint, but large trees that shaded many of the tiny houses gave the neighborhood a natural beauty that was heartening.

As they neared Mary's house, Catherine's pulse began to quicken. "Remind me why we're doing this?" she said, nervousness starting to overtake her.

"I don't know, Mom. You tell me, why are we doing this?"

Catherine drove past Mary's house and parked in front of an empty lot. Her heart was beating so hard now that she was practically incapacitated. She turned to Hannah. "I'm sorry, but I can't do it. I don't know what I thought I might accomplish here, but I physically can't do it." She tried to calm herself with slow breathing.

"It's okay," Hannah said. "I'm not going to push for anything you don't want to do. If you like, we can turn around right now and go back to our motel. Then, tomorrow, we can fly out of here, and it will have been a nice trip. I saw the pond, and the farm, and we had a wonderful time eating barbeque at Shorty's. We can leave it at that, and it'll be fine. Really."

Catherine broke down. "I don't know why we've come here," she cried. "What can I possibly say to Mary? *Hi, remember me? Here's the daughter I got from Jimmy the day I got him killed.*"

She turned to Hannah, realizing how terrible her words must have sounded. "Oh Hannah, please forgive me for saying that. I'm so sorry I said that. I love you more than anything in the world. You know that, don't you?"

"Of course I do," Hannah assured. "Of course I know."

"This whole thing is ridiculous!" Catherine cried. "The only thing I can possibly accomplish by visiting Mary is stirring up old pain. I'm a fool to have wanted to come back here."

Suddenly there was a tapping at Catherine's window that made both Catherine and Hannah jump. They looked over and were surprised to see Mr. Harris.

Embarrassed to be caught in such a panicked state, Catherine quickly wiped her face, then rolled down the window.

"Hello," the teacher said. "I'm sorry I scared you." He seemed nervous. "I'm sure you're wondering what I'm doing here, and I'd just like to explain if that's all right."

"Okay," Catherine said, at a loss for what else to say. She shot Hannah a surprised look, then turned back to the teacher, curious to hear what he would say.

"Would it be all right if I got into your car for a minute?"

Catherine nodded. Then, while she and Hannah were sharing another look, Mr. Harris opened the door to the back seat and got in.

"I hope you don't think this is a terrible intrusion," he began. "After I left you, I was sorry I hadn't offered to come to

Mary's with you, so I decided to come over here and wait for you, hoping you'd show up this afternoon."

"Well, we were just having some second thoughts," Hannah explained. She looked at Catherine, who was struggling to pull herself together.

"Why did you want to come with us?" Catherine managed. "Is it because you're afraid Mary won't react well? Because I'm wondering now what we're doing here. I can't imagine that she'll be happy to see us."

Mr. Harris sighed. "There are some things you need to be told," he said. "I wanted to tell you back at Shorty's, but I don't know that it's my place. That's why I encouraged you to see Mary. But I've been thinking about it, and I want to make sure she tells you. Because if she doesn't, I will."

Catherine's already-racing heart began pounding harder in her chest, and her face flushed hot. "I don't understand," she said, struggling to gain composure. "What is it we need to be told?"

"Let me just go see if Mary will see us," Mr. Harris said. "If she doesn't want to talk to you about this, I'll tell you everything. I promise."

He paused for a moment, as if collecting his thoughts, then got out of the car, leaving Catherine and Hannah in a mutual state of bewilderment.

Catherine remained in a fog of confusion for several minutes, then began a regimen of deep breathing, hoping to somehow steady herself for whatever surprises might come. Just as she was regaining a semblance of calm, Mr. Harris returned and leaned into her window.

"I think you'd better come in," he said. "Mary's a little upset, but she'll be all right."

"Are you sure?" Catherine asked, once again fearful.

"It'll be fine," Mr. Harris assured. "But take your time, there's no rush." His eyes were kind, and his voice was filled with sympathy.

After taking several more slow deep breaths, Catherine nodded to Hannah, who looked a little unsteady herself. Then the two of them got out of the car and followed Mr. Harris to Mary's doorstep.

When Mr. Harris knocked on the door, there was initially no response. Standing behind the teacher, Catherine and Hannah were frozen in a shared state of nervous suspense. The teacher knocked again, this time with greater urgency, but there was still no response. He knocked a third time, and pushed on a doorbell to the right of the door.

Finally, the door opened to reveal a large woman with a surprisingly youthful face. Her expression was hard to read, seeming to be somewhere between sadness and fear. She said nothing, but pushed open the screen door.

Catherine and Hannah clasped hands, then followed Mary and Mr. Harris through a small living room and into a dining room, where Mary nodded to a table with four place settings. A pitcher of water sat at the center of the table next to a small plate of cookies.

Catherine and Hannah pulled out chairs and sat down on one side of the table. Mr. Harris and Mary settled on the other side. Mr. Harris cleared his throat, and Mary proceeded to look down at her hands, occasionally stealing a glance at Hannah.

"Maybe I should start," Mr. Harris said. "I had a short conversation with Mary, and I believe I may be able to explain most everything to you. Some things I knew already, others I've just learned today." He looked at Mary and his expression was one of disappointment, if not anger.

The walls of the dining room were covered with dark flowered wallpaper, ornaments of various kinds, and framed family photographs. It wasn't long before Catherine's eyes were drawn to one photo that all but stopped her heart. Ignoring Mr. Harris, who was just starting his explanation, she abruptly stood up and went to the picture. There was no mistaking it. It was Jimmy, maybe forty years old, standing next to a wife and two children, a boy and a girl.

All at once Catherine was incapable of thinking straight. She struggled for equilibrium as a dam inside her burst, flooding her senses with the weight of thirty-one years of agonizing guilt and heartache. She remained in a state of trembling confusion for a time, then slowly calmed to a sense of relief as her mind settled on the one thought that floated high above the emotional torrent: Jimmy hadn't been murdered after all—he was alive.

She looked at Hannah, whose expression indicated she understood the meaning of the photo. Then she turned her gaze to Mary and Mr. Harris, who sat stone still. "I don't understand," she said, suddenly finding it hard to breathe.

Mr. Harris jumped up from the table and slowly guided her back to her chair.

"I don't understand," Catherine repeated, struggling to find her voice. "So that wasn't Jimmy's body in the fire at Sally's house? Jimmy didn't die?" Tears streamed down her face and she wondered if she were dreaming.

"But if Jimmy was alive, why wasn't I told?"

The teacher's voice betrayed both regret and anger. "It was my understanding that both you and your father were told," he said. "I'm certain Jimmy believed you were told."

Feeling light-headed, Catherine fell into Hannah's arms as Mr. Harris and Mary looked on in silence. When she regained a measure of equilibrium, she sat up, squeezed her daughter's hand, and looked straight at Mary, who was frozen in place.

Turning back to the wall, Catherine fixed her attention on Jimmy, then forced herself to look away. "Okay," she said to Mr. Harris after taking some deep breaths. "Go ahead with what you were going to explain. I'm ready."

೮೩

Mr. Harris took a moment to compose himself, then began. "It's a little hard to know where to start," he said. "I guess I'll start at the beginning, as I know the story, and we'll go from there."

He turned to Mary with a look of subdued distaste. "Please correct me if I get anything wrong."

Mary, who'd been avoiding looking at Catherine, looked at her now with an expression that offered a glimmer of something that seemed like sympathy, or possibly regret. With her first real acknowledgement of Catherine, she seemed finally to be integrating the reality of what had shown up on her doorstep. She sighed heavily and nodded, signaling to Mr. Harris to go ahead and start.

"My memory is not that great anymore," he began, "but I believe I recall everything pretty well. It was an awfully bad time." He looked at Catherine. "I don't have to tell you."

He poured some water into his glass, took a drink, then put the glass down on the table. "So many of us were frantic about Jimmy. And there was the business with the girls being taken. Thank God they came back unharmed. Then George was arrested..."

He paused, took a deep breath, then exhaled. "From the start, Will enlisted practically everyone in the black community to try and figure out what to do. We'd seen things like this before, and we were all terrified that they'd find Jimmy and kill him, or possibly put him in prison for years."

He shook his head. "For days, we didn't know where he was, or if he was even alive. By the time we knew he was safe, George was in jail, and then we were all worried about what they might do to George..."

Catherine interrupted. "Wait. So you're saying that people knew Jimmy was safe when George was in jail?" She looked at Mary, who averted her eyes, then back to Mr. Harris.

"Well, I don't recall exactly when it was we found out Jimmy was all right, but I believe it was right after George was arrested." He thought for a moment. "Yes, it would have to have been right after."

"So where was he?" Catherine asked, not bothering to hide her distress.

"I understand how you must feel," the teacher responded, "and I'm truly sorry you were never told."

Catherine was interested in answers, not apologies. "Where was he?" she asked again.

"Well, it turned out that almost immediately after the two of you got yourselves into trouble, he ran off and jumped a freight train. When word finally came that he was safe, he was in Chicago."

Catherine looked back and forth between Mr. Harris and Mary, stunned that no one had felt it necessary to tell her, or her father or grandmother. She looked at Jimmy's picture on the wall, so little changed from the way she remembered him, and once again found herself fighting off tears.

Mr. Harris gave Catherine a look of sympathy. "It's inexcusable that no one let you know Jimmy was safe. But, according to what Mary told me, and also some of the things I know about what was going on at the time, there were good reasons to keep his whereabouts a secret—although I would argue not from you and your family. I don't agree with the decision that was made not to tell you."

"So who made that decision?" Catherine asked. "Sally?" She looked at Mary, but Mary remained silent. In fact, she hadn't said a word since they'd entered the house.

"Before we get into all that," Mr. Harris said, "let me try to explain some things, because there's still a lot you don't know." He took another drink of water.

"Like I told you, Will had involved a lot of people in trying to figure out how to find Jimmy and keep him safe. When George was grabbed, everyone figured the sheriff and his bunch might be just as happy to punish George if they couldn't get their hands on Jimmy. So when Jimmy turned up in Chicago, Will and some others came up with a plan to make it look like Jimmy was dead, hoping that if they thought they'd killed Jimmy, they'd be satisfied and let George go."

Catherine interrupted. "But it was my understanding that the railroad gave George an alibi, so wouldn't they have had to let him go anyway?"

"Well, that may be what you and your father thought," Mr. Harris said, "but black folks don't have a lot of confidence in things like alibis. From what we knew, if they'd wanted to get George, they'd have got him. They might have hung him in his cell, and called it a suicide, or shot him, claiming he was trying to escape. That's the way they did things in those days."

Mary was nodding.

Mr. Harris acknowledged her with a look and went on. "So there wasn't a lot of confidence that George would be let go once they had him in jail. As far as we were concerned, he was in grave danger, and no railroad alibi was going to magically save him."

"All right," Catherine said. "But what about the body they found at Sally's house?"

"Well, okay, let me explain. And this is where things get kind of complicated, because there were several people involved in what was done, and protecting them was a big part of why everything was kept so secret. If it had gotten out what all was done to make everyone think Jimmy was dead, some folks would have been in serious trouble. And you have to remember, besides the sheriff, and eventually the FBI, there was a journalist—your husband, I guess—running around trying to dig up information, so there was a lot of fear that what they'd done would be discovered."

"But David was Jimmy's friend," Catherine said. "He wouldn't have done anything to harm the people who were trying to protect him."

"Well, no one could have been sure of that," Mr. Harris said. "All they knew is that they had to make sure no one found out the truth."

He folded his large hands in front of him and paused, seeming to search his memory. "Originally, I believe there was an idea to make it look like Jimmy was killed in the barn that burned on your grandmother's property. But then the Klan went and burned Sally's house, and that made everything easier."

"So where did they get a body?" Hannah asked. "And how did they convince people it was Jimmy?"

"Well, remember, in those days, everything was segregated, including mortuaries. So Will and some others, including some of the local clergy, cooked up a scheme to enlist the help of the black mortuary in town. Originally, I think their

idea was to dig up a body, if they had to, but it turned out tha̶
someone in town had just died. It was an old man, but he didn't
have much family. I think there was just one brother, and he
agreed to let them use his body to try and save George." He
made a face. "I know it sounds ghoulish, but they were desperate."

Catherine and Hannah looked at one another in disbelief.

"The body was burned, and they got Jimmy's dentist to go
along and identify the teeth as Jimmy's. So you see, there were
people in town who went way out on a limb. If what they'd
done had been discovered, they'd have been in serious danger
themselves. And, keep in mind, your grandmother *shot* a deputy sheriff thinking he'd killed Jimmy."

Mary spoke up for the first time. *"Your grandmother killed a
man,"* she said. "Once that happened, Sally didn't want Mama
Rae knowin' the truth. She killed that man because she thought
he and his boy murdered Jimmy.

"And, I'm not gonna lie," she continued. "Sally was also
worried about you and Jimmy takin' up together. After all
she'd been through, and all she'd suffered, she didn't want you
havin' *nothin'* to do with Jimmy. She *wanted* you to think he
was gone. And, I'm sorry to say, we didn't argue with her."
She looked at Hannah. "We didn't know nothin' about no
child."

"But what about Jimmy?" Catherine asked. "I can't believe
Jimmy would have wanted me to think he was dead?"

Mary noticeably flinched, but offered no response.

"Jimmy was told that you and your father were informed,"
Mr. Harris said. "And I'm certain of this, because I spoke to
him about it. As a matter of fact, I spoke to him this afternoon,
and he's very upset."

The teacher looked straight into Catherine's eyes. "He's anxious to talk to you."

Catherine's heart began racing again at the thought. She'd hoped that by some miracle she would discover that Jimmy was alive, but she realized now that she'd never really expected it to be true. Understanding now that he was just a phone call away, she wondered what they might say to each other, and was struck with an emotion resembling fear.

"You might as well tell her about the letter," Mary said, her voice filled with dread.

Catherine looked back and forth between Mary and Mr. Harris. "What do you mean? What letter?"

The teacher sighed. "Well," he said, "after Jimmy arrived in Chicago, he sent me a letter and asked me to make sure you got it." He frowned. "I regret this now more than I can say, but I gave the letter to Will, and he told me he'd give it to your father."

He looked at Mary. "I gather from talking to Mary that the letter was destroyed. Sally insisted on it. But, of course, Jimmy never knew that."

"We all knew it was wrong," pleaded Mary, "but Sally was just so fearful. She loved that boy more than you can possibly imagine, and she was terrified that if y'all got together, he'd come to harm."

Her face was trembling. "If you could have just seen how much she suffered thinkin' he'd been killed."

∞

After learning about the letter, Catherine sat in stunned silence, staring at the photograph of Jimmy and his family. When she was finally able to speak, her first words were a request to use the bathroom.

"That'll be fine," Mary said. She stood up and led Catherine into a narrow hall, then pointed her to the bathroom.

Catherine was rinsing her hands, staring at the dazed reflection in the bathroom mirror, when she heard the phone ring. Frozen at the thought that it might be Jimmy, she strained to hear what was being said, but could hear nothing.

In a state of nervous anticipation, she left the bathroom and walked back to the dining room. As soon as she arrived, she saw Mary standing in the doorway of the kitchen, holding the phone. She knew instantly by the look on her face that it was Jimmy.

Mary raised the phone to Catherine. "He wants to speak to you."

Catherine turned to her daughter, who appeared to be holding her breath. Then she looked at the teacher.

"Mary and I will leave you alone," he said.

Mary handed Catherine the phone, then she followed Mr. Harris into the living room. Hannah remained at the dining room table as her mother took the phone and stepped into the kitchen.

Catherine took a deep breath and tried to steady her nerves. She raised the phone to her mouth and attempted to speak, but her emotions combined with a knot in her throat made it difficult. "*Jimmy*," she whispered.

"*Catherine*," rushed a familiar voice through the wire. The worry in his tone brought Catherine immediately to tears, and despite her best efforts to remain calm, she was soon sobbing.

"Oh Catherine, I'm so sorry," Jimmy said. "I'm so sorry."

She tried to respond, but hearing his voice, she became so overwrought that she was unable to talk.

Hannah, who was now standing in the doorway, went to her mother, and Catherine passed her the phone. She took the receiver and put it to her ear. "This is Hannah," she said. "Your daughter."

"*Hannah*," Jimmy said. He spoke her name with reverence. "Hannah. How's your mother? Is she all right?"

Hannah looked at Catherine, who was now sitting in a kitchen chair, trying to pull herself together. "I guess you know she's thought all these years that you were killed in that fire, so she's feeling pretty overwhelmed right now. But she'll be fine."

"Hannah," Jimmy said, "I just can't begin to express how sorry and upset I am to learn this. I just don't know what to say." He sounded beside himself. "How long are you planning to be in Arkansas? I'd like to see you both as soon as I can, if it's all right. As soon as I get off the phone I'll make arrangements to fly to wherever you want to meet me."

"We're flying back to LA tomorrow evening," Hannah said. "So maybe the best thing would be to meet us there." She locked tear-filled eyes with her mother, who was now listening.

"I look forward to meeting you, Hannah," Jimmy said. "I look forward to seeing both of you."

"Were you at my father's memorial?" Hannah asked.

Catherine heard the question and held her breath.

"Yes I was," Jimmy said. "But I had no idea he'd been married to your mother."

Hannah nodded to her mother and Catherine quickly stood up. "I think my mom is ready to talk to you," Hannah said, "so I'm going to say good-bye and give the phone back to her now. But I look forward to meeting you."

"Good-bye, Hannah," Jimmy answered, his voice filled with affection. "I look forward to meeting you, too."

Catherine took a deep breath, exhaled, then took the phone. "Okay, I'm going to try this again," she said.

"Are you all right?" Jimmy asked. *"Oh, Catherine, I just don't know what to say..."*

"I'm fine," Catherine said. She smiled tearfully at Hannah, and took a couple more deep breaths. *"This is just ..."* She hesitated, wanting to say so much, but not knowing how to begin.

"Catherine," Jimmy said, "Saying *'I'm sorry'* just seems so monumentally inadequate."

Even after three decades, Catherine could picture Jimmy's face with perfect clarity. She visualized it now, filled with pain, and was hit with a familiar sense of longing. "I know you didn't know," she said. "I don't blame you."

"I can't even begin to tell you how I feel," Jimmy continued. "I'm so sorry, and so...*angry*...mostly at myself. I should have *made sure* you knew. I just never imagined that my mother could do such a thing. But I should have made sure you knew. There's just no excuse for not making certain."

"Please don't blame yourself," Catherine said. "And, really, despite everything, I've had a good life. Wait until you meet your daughter. She's amazing. And she looks just like you."

"I know she does," Jimmy said with unmistakable affection. "I saw her at David's memorial."

"How did you happen to be at the memorial?" Catherine asked. "And why didn't you come talk to me?"

"I saw David's obituary in the New York Times," Jimmy said, "and, just by coincidence, I was going to be in LA the day of his memorial, so I decided to go. I had no idea that you and ꞁe had married, so it was a shock to see you there. But the bigger shock was Hannah. I knew immediately that she was mine. She looks a lot like my daughter Elizabeth. But I was confused about why you'd never told me about her."

Catherine came to a sudden realization. Of course Jimmy had been confused. He might even have been angry.

"I wanted to talk to you," Jimmy said, "but David's memorial didn't seem like the right place for it, so I just left." His voice betrayed deep feelings. "I've been dying to talk to you, but I wanted to give you some time. It didn't seem right to hit you too soon after David's death."

There was a long silence, as though neither Catherine nor Jimmy knew what to say.

"I hope you can forgive me, Catherine."

"I keep telling you, there's nothing to forgive," Catherine whispered. *"Jimmy, none of this is your fault."*

"I want to see you as soon as possible, and meet Hannah," Jimmy said. "Would that be all right?"

"Yes, please," Catherine said. She looked at Hannah, who was wide-eyed. "We want to see you too."

Chapter 17

Los Angeles, 1986

Catherine was now back in LA, anticipating Jimmy's arrival, and she was so nervous that she could barely contain herself. She and Hannah had managed to take an earlier flight back from Arkansas, so she'd had two days to prepare herself for their reunion. But now, just minutes before Jimmy would show up on her doorstep, she did not feel prepared. Not even close. She was anxious to see him, but so filled with fears and questions that she was having a hard time calming herself. Her greatest struggle was trying to subdue her excitement, and accept that Jimmy was not the same person she'd loved when she was twenty years old. He was now in his fifties, with a wife, and a family, and a whole history she knew almost nothing about. She understood this intellectually, but not emotionally, and she felt off balance by the power of her desire to see him again.

It was early afternoon. They had all agreed that it would be best for Catherine and Jimmy to see each other first, so Hannah wasn't going to meet Jimmy until that evening, for dinner. Catherine now wondered if this decision had been wise. If Hannah were there, perhaps it would be easier for her to behave with the reserve that was called for. Perhaps she would feel calmer.

Catherine walked to the bathroom and looked in the mirror for about the fifth time that hour. *"Calm down!"* she commanded herself out loud. She stared at her face, and cursed herself for caring so much about her reflection. She knew that er interest in the mirror was both inappropriate and shallow, and yet she couldn't help herself.

She left the bathroom and turned her thoughts to some of the things she'd been told by Mr. Harris after talking to Jimmy in Mary's kitchen. She'd learned that Jimmy's children were now both in college. She'd learned that he hadn't become a lawyer after all. Instead, he had earned an advanced degree in American History from the University of Chicago and become a professor at Columbia. When Mr. Harris had told her this, she'd cried. It still choked her up to think about it.

As Catherine sat in her living room, waiting for a knock on her door, she imagined Jimmy captivating students in a lecture hall, working in an office stacked with papers and books, attending faculty dinners and events... She also tried to imagine what Jimmy's wife was like, and wondered if she, too, was an academic.

Catherine was a sixth-grade teacher in a mostly black elementary school, and she was anxious to tell Jimmy about her work, and her students. She began an imaginary conversation with Jimmy on the subject. Since learning that Jimmy was alive, she'd had multiple *'conversations'* of this kind—while driving, while taking her morning bath, while trying unsuccessfully to sleep. But she always did most of the talking. She looked forward to a conversation where he actually talked back. And there was so much she wanted to know, so many things she wanted to talk to him about. She was just starting to compile a mental list when she heard four light knocks on the door.

Instantly, her pulse sped up. *"Okay,"* she whispered aloud. Then she stood up, took a deep breath, and walked slowly to the front door. After pausing for one more long breath, she pulled it open.

She had hoped she'd be able to remain reasonably cc
posed, but the instant she saw Jimmy's face she was struck k
a tsunami of emotion. Standing in front of her now—hand-
somely dressed in a blue shirt and khaki pants—Jimmy looked
equally struck. For a moment, they both stood frozen. Then, all
at once, they came together in an embrace that spoke of feelings
so powerful that words were neither adequate nor necessary.

When they finally let go of one another, Catherine beckoned Jimmy inside, where he uttered his first word. "*Catherine.*" The look in his eyes and wrinkles on his forehead signaled both joy and pain.

Determined not to fall apart, Catherine reached for Jimmy
and they hugged once again. When they finally separated, they
were both so tongue-tied that they had to laugh.

"Jimmy," Catherine said, trying to sound calm. "You have
no idea."

"I think I have an idea," he said, and there were tears in his
eyes.

Jimmy followed Catherine into the living room, and they
sat down next to one another on a large, comfortable couch.
Jimmy was the first to speak. "Driving over here, I was thinking about all the things I wanted to say to you, and now that
I'm here, I'm drawing a blank. All that comes to mind
is...*Wow.*"

"I understand," Catherine said. "I've been talking to you
non-stop in my head for days, but now it's kind of hard to
know where to begin. There's just so much."

They sat in silence for the next few moments, simply taking
each other in. Neither seemed to know where to start. Finally
Jimmy began. "I'm so sorry about David," he said. "I've followed his career, and I know about his work. His death must
have been a terrible shock to you and Hannah."

Catherine was already brimming with emotion, and at the
ention of David, she had to struggle not to cry.

"I'm sorry," Jimmy said. "I'm sure it's been difficult."

"I'm fine," Catherine said. She took a deep breath and
breathed out slowly. "I miss David a lot. But I'm so happy to
see you. I can't even tell you what it's like to have you sitting
here next to me now. It doesn't even seem real."

"You haven't changed at all," Jimmy said, finally flashing
his smile. "*Seriously*. When I saw you at David's memorial I
recognized you instantly. You look almost exactly as I remember you."

Catherine was pleased by the compliment. "You haven't
changed much yourself," she said. "And I saw you at the memorial, too. I about had a heart attack, and then you were gone.
I thought I was going crazy."

"I'm really sorry about that," Jimmy said. "It was such an
awkward situation, I wasn't quite sure what to do."

"It's all right, I understand. The important thing is you're
here now, *and you're alive*." She took his hands and squeezed
them.

Blushing, and not sure what to say next, Catherine turned
the conversation to Hannah. "I guess I should show you some
pictures of your daughter." She stood up and went to the fireplace mantle, and Jimmy followed her. She pointed to a picture
of Hannah in a cap and gown. "That was her college graduation."

He picked up the photograph and studied it. "You must be
so proud of her," he said. "And she's beautiful." He turned to
Catherine with a look of affection. "Like her mother."

Catherine was amused. "Let's face it," she said, "if anyc gets to take credit for her good looks, it's you. She's looked lik you from almost the day she was born."

Jimmy laughed. "Well, I see some of you in there, too." He put down the photo and picked up another one in a small faux-jeweled frame. This was Hannah dressed as a princess for Halloween when she was six. He stared at the picture, and it was obvious that he was moved by the precious image.

"She was the most adorable little thing you've ever seen," Catherine said. "I wish you could have seen her." She was struck by a moment of deep sadness. "If only I'd told your family..."

Jimmy looked into Catherine's eyes and mirrored back her regret. "It's not your fault," he said. "*Seriously.* It's not your fault."

He put down the princess photo and continued perusing the mantle, studying each picture with intense interest. Soon he made his way over to more pictures on a bookcase. Just that morning Catherine had framed the old photo of the two of them and placed it there. The moment Jimmy spotted it, he picked it up. Catherine was standing next to him. "I never thought I'd see this again," he said. He shook his head and smiled, and Catherine wondered what he was thinking.

"You know, I did eventually try to contact you," he said, "but you were already engaged."

"What do you mean?" Catherine asked, trying to hide her alarm. "When was this?"

Jimmy looked into her eyes, glanced back at the photo, and then placed it carefully back on the shelf. "Well," he said, "I know now that you never got the letter that I wrote to you, but I didn't know it then." He paused, seeming to be uncertain how much to tell her.

Catherine waited silently for him to continue. After a few moments he went on. "In the letter I promised I'd contact you after everything died down. So eventually I did. Unfortunately, I just waited too long." His voice was filled with regret.

Catherine stared at Jimmy with questioning eyes, struggling not to reveal how impacted she was by his words.

He sighed. "After I left town, there was a lot of fear about the situation I'd left behind, and things were very hectic in Chicago. We had to find a place to live. I had to figure out how to make some money. I eventually had to find a way to get myself back in school. Oh, and my name is James Turner now, by the way."

Catherine smiled and secretly mourned *James Emerson*, which had always struck her as a great name.

"Anyway," Jimmy continued, "it took time to get my bearings. When I finally started to feel solid, I looked up your parents' phone number, and I called. I actually talked to your mother, but I didn't tell her who I was." He shook his head. "That was obviously a mistake." He thought for a moment. "I guess I was a little afraid to talk to her, so I just told her I was an old friend. When I asked about you, she said you were getting married." He frowned and shrugged his shoulders. "I figured the best thing would be to just let it go. Your mother didn't say anything about Hannah."

Catherine had a vague recollection of her mother mentioning a call, and cursed herself for treating the information so carelessly.

Jimmy picked up a photo of Catherine, David, and Hannah at Dodger Stadium. "I had no idea you were marrying David. Obviously, it was a mistake not telling *him* I was alive." His

forehead wrinkled in remembering. "It was all just so comp[
cated, with him writing about what happened, and people te.
rified he'd find out they faked my death."

He studied the photograph in his hand. "I can understand
the two of you getting together, and I'm glad you had someone
to help you through everything. I know all of it was really traumatic for you. And Mama Rae killing the deputy! I don't even
know what to say about that. That was..." He shook his head.
"I don't know, that was unbelievable. I'm sure it was a terrible
trauma for your family."

"It was pretty awful," Catherine said, holding back tears.
"All of it was awful, from start to finish. It was like the nightmare that wouldn't end."

"I'm so sorry," Jimmy said. "I know how much you must
have suffered. And you probably blamed yourself for everything. I'll never forgive myself for that." He put his hands
lightly on Catherine's shoulders and looked into her eyes. "I'd
do anything if I could go back and do it all over again differ-
ently."

"I'm all right," Catherine said, trying to remain steady. "As
hard as it is for me to come to grips with some of the things I've
learned, nothing is more important than the fact that you're
alive. *That good news trumps absolutely everything.* And look at
you," she added brightly. "You're a professor at Columbia."

Jimmy smiled and followed Catherine back to the couch.
He sat down and sighed. "What a story you and I have. I still
have nightmares about some of it." He shook his head. "There
were a lot of years after, when I was living in a small apartment
with my family in Chicago, when I had terrible nightmares—
about the Klan, about being hunted, being trapped. I used to
sometimes dream that men were hurting you, and there was
nothing I could do to stop it."

He smiled and looked down at his hands. "I had my share good dreams, too." He looked back up. "I spent a lot of years thinking about you, Catherine."

Catherine looked into Jimmy's eyes, frightened to reveal the depth of her feelings. She had wanted to ask him what he was thinking when he'd tried to contact her, and now she worked up the courage. "When you finally called me, what were you going to tell me?"

"Well," he said, holding her gaze, "I had it in my mind that maybe I could come to San Diego, like you'd talked about. If you still wanted me to."

Once again, Catherine fought back tears. She'd have done anything to know about that phone call. "Were you angry when you found out I was getting married? You must have felt betrayed."

"No," Jimmy said, "I wouldn't say I felt betrayed. But I'd be lying if I said I wasn't upset. I was definitely disappointed. But I was mainly mad at myself for waiting so long to contact you. I figured if I'd gotten in touch sooner..."

He paused, seeming to measure his words. "I eventually convinced myself that it was all for the best. I'd always worried about the kind of life you'd have with me, even in California. So I tried to put you out of my mind. What else could I do? But it wasn't easy. To be honest, in all these years, I've really never stopped thinking about you." He smiled. "I think about you every time I see an interracial couple, and you see those more and more. These days, in New York, people barely bat an eye."

Catherine closed her eyes and debated with herself about how to respond. She wanted to tell Jimmy that she'd never stopped thinking about him, either. That, despite her marriage to David, she'd never stopped loving him. How could she have stopped loving him? *She had his child.* But she wasn't sure it was wise to say too much. What would be the point after so many years? Yet she wanted to tell him the truth.

When she opened her eyes, he was looking at her intently. "Jimmy," she said, her heart speeding up. "There are things I want to tell you, but I'm just not sure, after all these years, if I should, or if you would even want me to." She hesitated, uncertain. "Things happened the way they did, and there's no changing any of it."

"Well, that's true," Jimmy said. "But we've both lived with pretty profound memories of one another, and we have a daughter, so I wouldn't consider anything you want to tell me to be out of bounds. And I can assure you that there's nothing you could say that I wouldn't want to hear."

Catherine took a deep breath. "All right," she said. Then she began talking, not knowing exactly what was going to come out.

"When I found out that you'd been killed, *that those maniacs had murdered you*, I didn't know how I was ever going to find the strength to go on. I was so grief stricken, and I felt so responsible for everything. By the time my mother showed up to take me back home, I was totally out of it, and I was in bad shape for weeks afterwards. I was like a zombie, barely able to function at all.

"And, Jimmy," she pleaded, "please know that I don't blame you for *anything*. I know you're mad at yourself for not making sure I knew what really happened, but I don't want you to blame yourself. You were living through your own nightmare, *and you trusted your family*. So, please, no more guilt for either of us. Okay?"

Jimmy nodded, but the look on his face made it plain that he found her story painful.

"So, anyway," Catherine went on, "I was in bad shape. I dropped out of school, and was just living at my parents' house in kind of a vegetative state. And then suddenly I realized I was pregnant. And that added a whole new dimension to everything.

"At first, I was terrified for all the reasons you can imagine. But eventually it woke me up, and made me realize that I had to pull myself together. I didn't have a choice. And, of course, I had my mom telling me that I should put the baby up for adoption, that it would ruin my life, that it wouldn't be fair to condemn a black child to having a single white mother, etc., etc. But I never listened to any of that. All I could think about was the fact that I would be raising *your* child. And, Jimmy, I loved you so much. It meant everything to me that I would be raising your child. It felt like a way to have a part of you back, and a way for you to live on through our child."

Catherine took a deep breath in an attempt to calm herself, and she could see that Jimmy was struggling with emotions as well. When she went on, there were tears in both their eyes.

"Once I started having those thoughts," she said, "I never for a second regretted that I was having your baby. And when Hannah was born, she was the whole world to me. And it *did* feel like I had a part of you back. I saw you every time I looked into her sweet little face. I still see you when I look at her." She smiled through her tears. "When she was first born, I was disappointed that she wasn't a boy. I'd been fantasizing about having a little boy that looked just like you. But, in about two seconds, I was completely in love with her. And she *did* look like you..."

She paused to take some more deep breaths, and Jimmy remained silent. "It was a weird balancing act," she continued. "I was so in love with our baby, but, at the same time, I was still dealing with so much grief, and guilt, and longing for you. Tears began flowing down her cheeks. "Jimmy, if I'd taken that phone call, I would have begged you to come to San Diego."

She wiped her face, struggling for composure. "When David started coming around, he was so kind. And he'd been your friend, so I had someone to talk to who'd known you, and understood how special you were, and that meant everything to me. But..."

Jimmy interrupted. "You don't have to apologize for David, Catherine. I don't blame you for marrying David. I'm glad he was there for you." He took her hands in his and kissed them. "We both know how it might have been for us, but, under the circumstances, what you did made perfect sense."

They looked into each other's eyes, and it was obvious that what they'd once had was still there. Unfortunately, there was nowhere for it to go.

Battling strong emotions, Catherine stood up. "I know it's a little early, but I have some good red wine. If I open a bottle, will you drink some with me?"

"I'd love to," Jimmy said, giving her a look of understanding.

"You sit right here," Catherine said. "I'll be back in a minute. When I come back, I want to hear about your kids, and I'll tell you some more about Hannah."

Catherine headed for the refuge of the kitchen, where she used the time alone to try to pull herself together. She hated herself for seeming to minimize her feelings for David. *And in his house.* But she couldn't help herself. She wanted Jimmy to know how much she'd longed for a life with him.

ଓ

Catherine handed Jimmy a glass of wine, then rejoined him on the couch. "Okay, so tell me about your kids," she said, trying to sound casual.

Jimmy gave her a look as if he were reading her mind.

"I'm fine," she responded. "*Really.*" She raised her glass and met his gaze with a smile. "To your resurrection."

Jimmy raised his glass and returned the smile. "Okay, so I'll tell you about my kids." He put down his glass, pulled his wallet from his back pocket, removed a small trimmed photograph, and then handed it to Catherine.

She studied the picture. It was his two children, teen aged, aboard what was clearly the Staten Island Ferry, with the Statue of Liberty visible in the background. They had their arms around each other, and were grinning joyfully. "They're beautiful," she said. "I can definitely see a resemblance between Elizabeth and Hannah. And your son looks a lot like you looked the last time I saw you."

"Thanks," Jimmy said. "That picture was taken a couple of years ago around Thanksgiving. Jacob had just started college, and Elizabeth was still in high school. Jacob is twenty-two now, and Elizabeth is almost twenty. Jacob just finished his third year at Queens College. He's majoring in Economics, and doing very well." His face lit up. "I'm sure you're going to love him."

Catherine was touched and a little surprised to learn that Jimmy assumed she'd be meeting his children.

"Elizabeth has a four-year scholarship to NYU," he continued. "She'll be a sophomore in the fall. I think she and Hannah might be a lot alike, because she's talking about becoming a lawyer, also." He chuckled. "I know she'll be a good one, too, because that girl can put up an argument."

"What made you decide not to go into law?" Cather, asked.

"Well, there were a number of factors," Jimmy said. "Money was one of them, I guess, but when I was at the University of Chicago I got interested in history, and decided to stick with that."

"Mr. Harris told me you'd gone to the University of Chicago."

"Yeah, well I obviously couldn't go back to Oberlin after what had happened, so I ended up going to a two-year college in Chicago, and then transferring to the University of Chicago. I put myself through by working a series of menial jobs." He took a drink of his wine. "I thought about law school after I graduated, but by then I'd gotten deep into Post-Reconstruction American History. I had a professor at the University of Chicago who was encouraging me to pursue it, so he helped me get into graduate school, and I worked for him as a teaching assistant while I got my Masters and then eventually a PhD."

Jimmy leaned back on the couch, closer to Catherine than before. "That professor is actually one of the only people outside of my family who knows my own little place in history. He mentioned David's book one day when we were having a beer, and I couldn't resist telling him." He grinned. "Believe it or not, I've listed that book as recommended reading for some of my classes. It's all I can do sometimes not to stand up in front of the class and reveal my secret identity."

"Why not do it?" Catherine asked. "By now, most of the people you'd have wanted to protect are probably dead. And, even if they aren't, do you really think they'd have to worry after all these years? If anything, I think they'd be considered heroes."

"You might be right," Jimmy said. "I may go ahead some-
ay. I've definitely thought about it."

"Well, let me know beforehand if you do. I'd get a kick out
of attending that particular lecture."

"How about this? After I reveal my identity, you can stand
up and reveal yours. I bet we'd get a standing ovation."

"How bittersweet would that be?" Catherine remarked,
struck by the sad irony. "Times have definitely changed."

"Yes they have," Jimmy said, and there was regret in his
eyes.

"Speaking of history," Catherine said, "I want to hear what
happened after my father and I left you in the rafters. That's a
part of our story that's missing from the history books."

"Sure. But first, tell me, is your father still alive?"

"Yes he is. My mom died a few years ago, but my dad's
doing fine. I'm sure he'd enjoy seeing you, if you have the time.
He was *so* happy to hear you're alive, although not too thrilled
with your mother." Immediately regretting the remark, she
touched Jimmy's knee. "I'm sorry, forget I said that. I don't
want to get into that. I want to hear what happened after my
father and I left you."

Jimmy patted Catherine's hand. "It's all right. I understand
exactly how your father feels. *Believe me.*" He paused for a few
moments, then exhaled. "So, okay, after you and your father
left me, it wasn't long before I realized that there was no way I
could stay up there in the roof. It was too hot, and I could
barely breathe. It smelled terrible, and there were rat feces everywhere." He made a face. "Your dad meant well, but I was
actually better off under the house. It was awful. Also, I knew
they'd come back to the house looking for me, so I decided to
just take my chances and run for it."

He leaned forward and poured more wine into his glass. knew about people riding freight trains. I went to high schoo. with a couple of kids who used to talk about jumping trains, and I figured that if they could do it, I could. So I made a run for the tracks in a spot where I knew the trains slowed down." He laughed nervously. "When it came time to actually jump on, it was terrifying. I could easily have gotten myself killed."

Catherine shuddered at the image that came to mind.

"I eventually ended up in a boxcar with three old black men, and those men are actually one of the reasons I ended up pursuing history instead of law."

"Really? Why is that?" Catherine asked.

Jimmy smiled. "You might not want to get me started."

"No, go ahead. I want to hear."

"Well," Jimmy said, "one old guy in particular told me some pretty horrific stories about his life growing up in Alabama in the late 1800's. His name was Isaac. When he was around nine or ten, his father was arrested for vagrancy, hit with a bunch of fines he couldn't pay, and sent to work in an Alabama coal mine, where he was essentially worked to death. In the meantime, his family all but starved. Isaac said he and his brothers and sisters used to go out in the yard and eat dirt to fill their stomachs when they were hungry."

Catherine reacted viscerally to the image, and Jimmy noticed the expression on her face. "It gets much worse. When Isaac was sixteen, he and a group of his friends were arrested for playing a game of dice, and they were sent to the same mine where his father had died." Jimmy shook his head. "I don't even want to tell you some of the things he described to me about the conditions there. The conditions in that mine were horrendous. Unimaginable. He would surely have died there, just like his father, but a white man his mother had worked for tervened, and they finally let him out. But his friends died in that mine, and they were all just teenagers."

Catherine was silent, moved by both the story and Jimmy's pained expression.

"In those days," Jimmy continued, "a system called *convict leasing* was widely employed as a means of pulling Southern black men back into forced labor. All kinds of ridiculous laws were invented to essentially allow Southern sheriffs to arrest anyone they wanted right off the street, and then make money leasing them out as slave labor. Vagrancy and loitering were two of the most commonly used *'infractions,'* but there were others. This was absolutely a new form of slavery, and, in some ways, it was even worse than antebellum slavery, because there was no incentive to keep men healthy, or alive. If they worked a man to death, they could just order up a new one. There was no punishment if someone died. This new version of slavery started up very shortly after Reconstruction and persisted, in some states, for eighty years, right up until the Second World War. Much of the Southern economy was predicated on it."

Catherine was horrified. "I can't believe this history is not well known!"

"Well, I'm trying to help make it known," Jimmy said. "I'm writing a book about it that'll be out soon. I've been researching this now for years."

Overflowing with both admiration and affection, Catherine resisted a strong impulse to move closer to Jimmy. "It probably won't surprise you that I'm a teacher," she said. "I teach in South LA—sixth grade, mostly black—and I see the byproducts of our terrible history every day in the classroom." She touched his arm. "What you're doing is really important. This country needs to own up to all the harm we've done to

people if we're ever going to find the will and compassi
needed to solve some of our problems." She thought for a mc
ment. "What you describe is so shocking; I think your book is
going to be a big deal."

"Well, we'll see," Jimmy said. "I hope so. And I'm not the
only person interested in this. There are other people working
on it, so hopefully we'll get a discussion going. But it's not a
discussion that a lot of people really want to have, so it may
make less of a splash than you think."

"You know," Catherine said, "I read the essay you wrote
for your college scholarship, and I remember telling my father
afterwards that you were going to do great things." She took
his hand and squeezed it. *"I was right. You are."*

For the next few moments Catherine and Jimmy shared a
silence that felt both physically and emotionally charged. It
was clear that beneath the veneer of their conversation, they
were both feeling the old bond, and attraction, but they had no
idea what to do with the feelings.

Catherine finally spoke up and broke the spell. "Now
maybe you can tell me some more of your escape story. I really
do want to hear more about what happened."

"Okay," Jimmy said, seeming happy to oblige. "So I didn't
actually ride the boxcar the whole way to Chicago. We jumped
off midway when the train stopped, because we heard some
men farther up the tracks getting thrown off and beaten up.
That was another pretty scary episode, and a pretty close call."
He raised his eyebrows. "You haven't lived until you've been
stalked in a dark railroad yard, then forced to hide under a
train that might start moving again at any moment."

"Oh my God," Catherine said, horrified to picture Jimmy
in such terrifying straights. "Did any of the men you were with
get caught?"

"I don't think so," Jimmy said. "But it was the last I saw of any of them, because we all ran off in different directions."

"So then what?" Catherine asked. "You jumped back on the train before it took off again?"

"No. After that experience, I'd had enough, so I ended up buying a ticket on a passenger train with money I got from working for your father." He smiled. "I'd like to tell you that I rode the rails like an outlaw all the way to Chicago, but the truth is, as soon as I had the opportunity, I opted for a more comfortable ride. But I've never forgotten the stories I heard on that train, or those men. Another thing I'll never forget is the sound of rain and hail beating on the top of that boxcar. It started to pour like hell not long after I jumped on, and the sound was deafening. It was like being on the inside of a snare drum."

Catherine reached for her wine glass on the coffee table, then took a drink. "I remember that storm," she said. "It started up just after we got back to our house, when we thought you were still inside. The place was crawling with men looking for you. I'll never forget sitting in the truck in the pouring rain, expecting them to pull you out of the house at any moment. It was terrifying."

She felt suddenly shaken by the painful memory. "Thank God you ran off. If they'd found you, they probably would have killed you." Her voice trembled with emotion. "When they burned your house, and *thought* they'd killed you, *they were proud of that*. That deputy that Mama Rae shot, he came over to crow about burning you to death. He wanted to rub our noses in it."

Catherine looked down at the glass in her hand, trying, once again, to fight back tears. When she looked back up, Jimmy was staring at her with a pained expression. "I know

we said no more guilt," he said, "but I'll never forgive mys
for letting you believe all these years that I'd been killec
Never."

Catherine tried to smile, but the effort of holding back a
sudden rush of emotion was expressed as a grimace. She
wanted to say that it was okay, that it wasn't his fault, but
when she tried to utter the words, she found that she was too
overwrought to speak. Horrific memories, and the weight of
decades of guilt and grief were suddenly bearing down on her,
and there was no pretending otherwise.

Jimmy put his wine glass on the coffee table, took the glass
from Catherine's hand and placed it next to his, then pulled her
into his arms. Embarrassed, and frightened to reveal the depth
of her emotions, Catherine initially resisted, but she quickly
succumbed to Jimmy's embrace and let her tears flow.

"It's not the first time I've held you while you cried,"
Jimmy said, smoothing back a strand of her hair.

"I remember," Catherine whispered.

Fearful about becoming too comfortable in his arms, she
began to pull away, but Jimmy held tight. "Please," he said.
"Let me hold you for a while. I think, under the circumstances,
we can be forgiven for indulging just a little."

Catherine wanted to express so much to Jimmy, but she
didn't dare. Instead, she rested quietly in his arms, wishing she
could stay there forever, but understanding the danger in re-
maining too long.

After a few minutes, she carefully disengaged, resuming
her previous position on the couch. "I'm all right," she said,
giving his arm a squeeze. Jimmy was looking at her with affection, but she tried to ignore its impact, forcing herself to think,
instead, of Jimmy's wife—whose name had not yet even been
mentioned.

CB

They spent the next couple of hours in the same spot on the couch, drinking wine and sharing stories from their respective lives. Jimmy talked about his early life and struggles in Chicago, and Catherine told Jimmy about Hannah, and about her own career as a teacher.

Jimmy listened intently while Catherine talked about Hannah, and he seemed equally moved by her devotion to her students. After hearing her describe *'going on the warpath'* when one of her students was suspended for stealing milk from the cafeteria, he remarked, "You're still an Abolitionist."

"The day I met David he told me you'd called me that," Catherine said. "I've liked thinking of myself that way ever since." She thought about reaching for Jimmy's hand, but resisted. "It gives me goosebumps to hear you say it."

She put her wine glass next to the now-empty bottle on the coffee table and stood up. "In a little while I'll start working on dinner," she said. "But how about, in the meantime, I get us something to snack on, and maybe some water. I don't know about you, but after all that wine, I feel like I could probably use some."

Jimmy stood up and followed Catherine into the kitchen, where he was immediately drawn to the refrigerator, which was covered with scores of class photos.

"Some of those go back quite a few years," Catherine remarked, noticing Jimmy's interest. She handed him a glass of water, then pointed. "There's the boy who was suspended. *Ronald.* He's in middle school now. I hope he's doing all right." She pointed to another picture. "She was one of my absolute favorites. Sheryl Davis. She used to come back and visit me from time to time. She's in high school now, and she'll be going to college."

She pointed to another. "This one reminded me of you. *Jeffrey*. I was so crazy about that little boy." She smiled at Jimmy. "It's hard not to play favorites sometimes."

She looked back at the sea of faces. "It's rough having kids for only one year. You get attached to them, and then you have to let them go. And they have so many forces working against them."

She turned back to Jimmy, and he had a look on his face that she recognized. He put his glass down on the kitchen table, then stepped back to Catherine and looked into her eyes. She held her breath as he put his hands lightly on her hips.

"Jimmy," she said fearfully, her emotions rising.

"I know," he said. "I'm going to behave myself. But I have to be honest with you. Not kissing you over the last couple of hours is the hardest thing I've ever done, and that includes jumping onto a moving train."

They both laughed, but then Jimmy's face became serious again. "There's something I need to say to you. I hope you don't mind, but I feel like I just have to." His hands were still on her hips, and his eyes were locked onto hers.

Catherine began to tremble, and her legs felt like rubber. She nodded. "All right."

Jimmy sighed. "Seeing you again is both wonderful and really hard. I knew it would be hard, but I had no idea it would be this difficult." His wrinkled brow betrayed distress. "I'm married, and nothing is going to change that. But I don't want to have to pretend that it's easy seeing you again under these circumstances. It's *not* easy."

He hadn't moved his hands, and Catherine fought the urge to move closer.

"I'm not suggesting we do anything we shouldn't," he continued. "As tempting as it might be, I know it would be a bad idea, for a whole host of reasons. But I do want you to know that if things were different... Well, I think you know."

He removed his hands and took a step back. "I'm sorry," he said. "This is probably a little heavy for our first meeting."

"No, it's fine," Catherine whispered. "I can assure you that I feel the same way. I'm all but falling down I feel so weak in the knees right now." She smiled and fought back tears. "We just have to figure out how to channel our feelings in a way that makes sense, given the circumstances. And I hope we can find a way, because I'd hate to have you back, and then lose you again."

"You'll never lose me again," Jimmy said. "That's a promise."

"I almost hate to ask," Catherine said. "But what does your wife think about all this? She'd have to be a saint not to be bothered by it."

"Well, I'd have to say she's bothered by it," Jimmy said. "But I'm confident she'll adjust in time—especially because of Hannah. She wouldn't respect me if I didn't acknowledge Hannah. And she understands that I'm going to have to have some kind of relationship with you. But I won't lie. She's not overjoyed."

"I hope you know that I would never want to come between you and your wife," Catherine said. "As hard as this situation might be, I couldn't live with myself if I were to harm your family."

"Please don't worry about that," Jimmy said. "We'll figure it out."

"Well, I'm glad we're talking about it," Catherine said. "It may not make things easier, but I'd rather be honest than have to pretend. And, let's face it, we wouldn't be very good at pretending." She smiled and shook her head. "I don't know if it's a blessing or a curse, but even after all these years, I still feel the old bond. I don't think it'll ever go away."

Jimmy reached for Catherine and they shared a short kiss followed by an amused look acknowledging their restraint. Then, after a moment, they hugged so long and so hard, it was plain that neither of them wanted to let go.

Chapter 18

Hannah was on her way to her mother's house and was stuck in traffic on the Santa Monica freeway. Clearly, there was an accident up ahead, and there was no telling how long it would take for things to clear up.

Ordinarily, she would have taken a traffic jam in stride, this being a part of life to which she'd become accustomed since moving back to Southern California. But today she was losing patience, and angry at herself for not leaving her apartment earlier. She'd spent all day in nervous anticipation of meeting Jimmy, *her father*, and now, stuck in a line of cars that was barely moving, her nervousness was compounding.

She felt a fleeting longing for Northern California, where she'd attended law school, then pondered the suggestion from one of her friends that she apply to his firm in San Francisco. Suddenly the idea seemed ridiculous. She needed to return to her father's firm and get on with her life.

Hannah longed for the day when she could think of her father without anguish. It had now been over four months since his death, but she still felt his absence as a constant nagging pain. Her thoughts turned to Jimmy. *Would she call him Jimmy?* The name sounded so uncomfortably familiar, so boyish. And yet she couldn't imagine calling him *Dad*, or *Father*. Perhaps she would call him *James*, or *Jim*. Or maybe now he had a completely different name.

She shook her head, acknowledging to herself that she was avoiding the more serious questions raised by his unexpected injection into her life. Since learning the truth about her birth, she'd had a difficult time reconciling her feelings about Jimmy with her grief over her father's death. It was so strange to lose one father, and then suddenly discover another. She already felt an emotional connection to this man whom she'd never met. Her mother's story was so dramatic, and told to her with such passion, how could she not? And yet she was confused and conflicted by her feelings.

Now moving at the earthshaking speed of twenty miles per hour, Hannah contemplated Jimmy's kids, and wondered how they might fit into the picture. They were her half-siblings, so she imagined she would probably meet them. She wondered if they would accept her, or simply be alarmed by her existence, resentful at the prospect of her staking a claim on their father. And how would they, and Jimmy's wife, react to her mother? It was hard for her to imagine that she'd be accepted, much less welcomed.

Traffic was suddenly at a standstill, and Hannah began worrying about the cases and clients she'd abandoned in her grief. She thought about a party that had spontaneously erupted in her father's office shortly before he died. She and her father had just been successful in securing the release of a thirty-nine-year-old black man named Reggie Johnson who'd spent twenty years in prison for a crime he didn't commit. He'd been a promising nineteen-year-old college student with no criminal record and a solid alibi from friends. Nevertheless, he'd been railroaded by an overzealous prosecutor and convicted by an almost all-white jury, solely on the testimony of a petty criminal who'd been rewarded with a lighter sentence on a drug charge. A wave of guilt washed over Hannah as she remembered the look of joy on Reggie's face when he'd received the new verdict of *Not-Guilty*. It was suddenly clear that she'd be foolish to leave the firm, even short term. She needed to pull herself together and get back to work. Yes, her father was gone, but his legacy was intact, and she was part of that legacy. She resolved to call the now-senior partner and discuss returning to work. She wanted to continue in her father's footsteps and make her mother proud. *Make Jimmy proud.* She smiled at the thought.

Finally nearing her exit, Hannah wondered how her mother and Jimmy were doing. She'd been tempted many times during the day to call and ask, but she'd resisted, deciding to wait and see for herself. Now she was stuck in this damn traffic, and she felt like she'd never get there. Once again, she cursed herself for not leaving her apartment earlier. She looked at the speedometer. Three miles per hour! She had only a few more miles to go, but at this rate, it could take over an hour.

She glanced at herself in the rear-view mirror. "Calm down and be patient," she said out loud. "You'll get there."

ം

It was now six forty-five, and Hannah was well overdue. "She's definitely held up in traffic," Catherine said. "And I know she's in a state over it, because she hates being late. And today of all days."

A chicken was baking in the oven, Catherine was making a salad, and Jimmy, who was getting more and more nervous, was sitting at the kitchen table, flipping through an album filled with family pictures. "You'd think, after some of the things I've been through, I'd be made of sterner stuff," Jimmy said. "Maybe I should have another glass of wine."

Catherine turned around and smiled. "You have nothing to worry about. She's going to love you. I promise."

Jimmy stood up and reached for an unopened wine bottle he spotted on a counter. "Do you mind if I open this?"

294

"No, go ahead. The corkscrew is in the drawer right in front of you."

Jimmy opened the wine, poured himself a glass, and was starting to pace like an expectant father when he was suddenly stopped in his tracks by the sound of a car in the driveway.

Catherine met his startled expression with a grin. "There she is." She took his hand and led him to the front door. Then she gave Jimmy a last look of encouragement and opened the door to reveal her anxious-looking daughter hurrying up the walkway towards the porch.

"There you are!" Catherine exclaimed.

"I'm so sorry I'm late," Hannah said, kissing her mother in the doorway. "There must have been an accident on the freeway. I thought I'd *never* get here." Now looking past her mother, she smiled at a figure standing in the foyer. "Hello," she said, her voice softening.

Catherine moved aside, and Hannah extended her hands to Jimmy, who was beaming a look of exhilaration. She knew the moment she laid eyes on him that she would grow to love him. And her mother hadn't exaggerated—she immediately saw herself in his face, which, at present, was smiling broadly. "I'm so pleased to meet you," she said.

Jimmy took her hands and squeezed them. "I'm *very* pleased to meet you too." Still grinning, he cocked his head slightly and narrowed his eyes. "Do you think it's too soon for a hug?"

"Definitely not," Hannah replied, echoing his enthusiasm. Then she and Jimmy exchanged an earnest embrace as Catherine looked tearfully on.

Disengaging from the hug, both Hannah and Jimmy noticed Catherine's *'waterworks'*—as Ben would have said—and chuckled at her predictable response.

Catherine saw their looks of amusement. "Can you blame me?"

"Not at all," Jimmy said, pulling both Catherine and Hannah into his arms. "It's a wonder I'm not blubbering myself."

The three of them enjoyed a warm group hug, and Catherine and Hannah exchanged a look of loving accord. *This was a good thing. A very good thing.*

When Jimmy released them, Catherine nodded towards the living room. "You two go relax for a few minutes while I do a couple of things to get ready for dinner."

As she headed for the kitchen, she called back over her shoulder, "Hannah, can I get you a glass of wine?"

"Yes, please!" Hannah responded with a feigned air of desperation. Then she followed Jimmy to the living room.

A few moments later Catherine handed both Hannah and Jimmy a glass, then left them sitting, side by side, in a shared state of anticipation.

As Hannah was wondering how to start, Jimmy took her hands and looked at her with affection. "I'm sure all this is pretty overwhelming for you. I know it's been terrible, losing your father. I knew him when he was a young man, and I know about the work he was doing. That you were both doing." He smiled. "You know, I don't know if your mother's told you this, but your father and I talked about practicing law together, so it's wonderful to find out that I have a daughter fulfilling that dream."

Despite the sadness that always accompanied thoughts of her father, Hannah smiled, touched by Jimmy's sincerity.

"I hope I haven't upset you," Jimmy said. "But I thought I should say something." He nodded to all the photos around the room. "I feel his presence all around us, and I want you to know how grateful I am that he was here for you and your mother, and that he was such a great father to you."

Hannah focused for a moment on one of the pictures, then turned back to Jimmy. "I'm having a pretty hard time accepting that he's gone, but, believe me, learning about you is a welcome surprise. But, you're right, it's been a lot to deal with." She looked into eyes resembling her own. "You must be feeling pretty overwhelmed yourself. Finding out you have a daughter you didn't know about, seeing my mother again."

Jimmy nodded. "It's been...." He paused. "Well, yes. But, as you said, it's welcome." He smiled his easy smile, and Hannah couldn't help wondering what had transpired between Jimmy and her mother before her arrival.

"Does your family know about us?" she asked impulsively. An instant later she regretted asking the question so abruptly, and so soon. "I'm sorry," she said before Jimmy had a chance to respond. "That just came out. We don't have to talk about that now."

Jimmy looked sympathetic. "You don't have to apologize. It's a perfectly natural question, and the answer is that my wife knows, but we haven't told our son and daughter yet. But I have confidence everything will work out fine. You don't need to worry that you won't be accepted by my family."

"What about my mother?" Hannah asked. "I hate bringing it up, but I've been worrying about it. I honestly don't know if I can have a relationship with your family if they're not able to accept her, too."

猄

Catherine entered the room with a feeling of mild alarm. "I didn't mean to eavesdrop," she said, "but please, Hannah, don't worry about that now. For now, I just want you and Jimmy to enjoy getting to know each other." She sat down in a chair opposite the couch and leaned forward with a purposeful look. "Whatever happens in the long run, *tonight* the three of us are a family, and I don't want anything or any worries about the future to spoil it. *Please.*"

"I'm sorry," Hannah said. "You're right."

Jimmy took Hannah's hand and fixed his gaze on Catherine. "I'm in agreement," he said. "But, no matter what, we're always going to be some kind of family. And that's a promise."

Catherine and Jimmy locked eyes and shared a feeling of warm certainty. Despite all the other realities of their lives, they *were* family. There was no denying it, and no changing it.

Moments later Catherine announced that dinner was served and getting cold, so the three of them filed into the dining room, where they were met with a beautiful table lit with candles. Catherine sat at the head of the table, with Hannah on her right, and Jimmy on her left. They spent the first part of the meal in thoughtful conversation about some of Hannah's most challenging cases, and Catherine could not have been prouder. Sitting in the flickering light between Hannah and Jimmy, and with David's picture prominent on the sideboard, she felt as though she were dreaming.

Eventually, and inevitably, the conversation turned to Arkansas, and they shared memories—carefully avoiding the worst—from all three time frames, starting with Hannah's fond recollections of Shorty. They were back in 1955 when Hannah turned to her mother and asked, "Did you ask Jimmy what was in the letter he left you?"

"No," Catherine said. "We haven't talked about that yet." She turned to Jimmy. "You left a letter for me in the woods before you disappeared, but, unfortunately, it got soaked in the rain and was completely unreadable. Do you remember what you wrote?"

Jimmy's face broke into a half-smile. "Actually, I do re-member," he said. "Maybe not the exact words..."

Catherine's pulse quickened, and suddenly she was back in Mama Rae's kitchen, desperate to know Jimmy's thoughts.

"Some of it was what you might expect," Jimmy said. "I apologized for running off, and told you that I was going to try to get to Chicago and find my brother. I think I also promised to write you when I was safe." He frowned and shook his head.

"It's all right," Catherine said. "No more guilt, remember?"

Jimmy sighed. "All right... Anyway, I remember writing that I'd rather die trying to save myself than be found up in the attic, cowering like an animal. And I meant that." He hesitated for a moment, then continued. "I didn't have time for anything particularly poetic, but I believe I also told you that I loved you, and that I had faith we'd see each other again." He shot Catherine a grin. "That was quite a day you and I had before all hell broke loose."

Catherine grinned back, and they shared a long moment that made her blush.

"I think my very last words were something like, '*Who knows what the future might bring?*'"

He looked at Hannah and there were tears in his eyes. "It occurs to me that this is the perfect moment for a toast." He picked up his glass and raised it—first to Hannah, and then to Catherine. "To this miracle the future has brought. And to her mother."

They clinked glasses, and now all of them were in tears.

"One more," Hannah said, her eyes sparkling in the candlelight. She pointed her glass to the photo on the sideboard, and then to Jimmy. "*To my fathers.*"

✳ ✳ ✳

Author's Note & Recommended Reading

The Civil Rights Movement of the Sixties had a profound impact on my psyche. I was born in 1957, and raised by parents who talked openly and often about racial inequality, and about the civil rights marches and battles that we followed with great interest on the evening news. In 1964, my paternal grandfather severed his relationship with my family after an argument over civil rights. Thus, by the age of seven, I already knew that an epic struggle was taking place, and there was no question as to whose side we were on. I went to an integrated junior high school and high school, and benefited not only from interracial friendships, but from seeing, up close, how some lives were shaped by a history of racial discrimination. In college, my interest in racial inequality and social justice intensified, and from there it has never abated. *Arkansas Summer* is my humble attempt to both express this interest, and shine a spotlight on history about which I have deep feelings.

I had the idea for writing *"Arkansas Summer"* after reading *"Devil in the Grove: Thurgood Marshall, the Groveland Boys, and the Dawn of a New America,"* by Gilbert King. This Pulitzer Prize-winning book tells the tragic true story of four young black men who were falsely accused of rape in Lake County, Florida in 1949. It also provides fascinating insights into the early career and heroism of Thurgood Marshall, who risked his life to defend the "Groveland Boys" as a lawyer for the NAACP. I highly recommend this book to anyone who wants to learn more about the terror perpetrated by some Southern sheriffs in the Jim Crow era.

I also recommend *"The Warmth of Other Suns,"* by Isabelle Wilkerson. This beautifully-written book tells the touching true stories of a handful of men and women who were part of

300

the "Great Migration" of African Americans who fled the Jim Crow South for the hope of a better life in Northern cities.

Another wonderful book for book clubs or readers who want to learn more about life in the Jim Crow South is *"Remembering Jim Crow: African Americans Tell About Life in the Segregated South,"* edited by William Henry Chaffee, Raymond Gavins, and Robert Korstad. This oral history contains scores of fascinating personal stories, told by black men and women who not only suffered under the oppressive Jim Crow system, but managed, within that system, to maintain dignity in their daily lives.

Two of the most stunning books I read while doing research for my novel were *"Worse than Slavery,"* by David Oshinsky, and the Pulitzer Prize-winning *"Slavery by Another Name,"* by Douglas Blackmon. Anyone who is interested in learning more about the shocking practice of "convict leasing" should read at least one of these books. An excellent documentary can also be located and viewed on the web by searching for *"Slavery by Another Name."*

Another book that I highly recommend is the well-known and highly-acclaimed *"The New Jim Crow: Mass Incarceration in the Age of Colorblindness,"* by Michelle Alexander. This amazing work is a powerful indictment of our current "Justice System," which disproportionately targets, convicts, and incarcerates persons of color, trapping millions of Americans in a race-based underclass.

Finally, I have to recommend *"Just Mercy,"* by Bryan Stevenson, who is the founder and Executive Director of the Equal Justice Initiative, in Montgomery, Alabama (www.eji.org). This book is the deeply touching memoir of a brilliant lawyer who has dedicated his life to freeing innocent persons from death row, challenging injustices in our Criminal Justice System, advocating for the poor and disenfranchised, and publicizing forgotten racial history. To my mind, Bryan Stevenson is America's best and most inspiring champion for social justice. To see his Ted Talk go to: http://eji.org/videos/bryan-stevenson-ted-talk.

Acknowledgements

For approximately a year, I worked on this novel as though it were a job. At the end of each writing session, I sent new pages off to several persons who had generously agreed to be first-tier "readers." Like clockwork, they wrote back with words of encouragement and/or advice for improvement. Thus, I had constant constructive feedback as the book progressed, which was wonderful for keeping wind in my sails, and for helping me to see how I could better the story as it steadily unfolded. To say that I'm grateful to these readers for their commitment and constant loving support is an understatement. From the bottom of my heart, "*Thank you!*" to David Silva, Barbara Lekander, James Moose, Beth Moose, and Jim Eberle. You will never know how much your devotion and thoughtful advice helped and nourished me as I worked.

I owe additional gratitude to others who read "installments" on a less regular basis, but whose encouragement and feedback were also invaluable. Thank you to Gale Jesi, Carolyn Hammel, Martha Casey, Paula Berggren, Katy Culver, Virginia Moose, Sue Grether, Tracy Laughlin, Anita Vermund, Lisa Redd, Susi Allison, and Yvonne Sheer. Thank you also to Paul Dingus, John Dingus, Olivia Weeks, Avery Yu, Susan Schlickeisen, Irwin Sheer, Jimmy Moose, Cathy Boggs, Julie Didion, Elizabeth Baker, Andrea O'Brien, Robert Egan, Senta Ludwig, Ruti Lovitt, Excetral Caldwell, Sarah Maclay, and Richard Turner—for reading drafts at different stages and offering helpful and heartwarming reactions.

Special thanks to Pamela Schneider and Ara Grigorian, who provided me with invaluable criticism, guidance, and enthusiasm towards the end of the process.

Finally, I want to thank my husband, Peter Dingus, for his constant love and support, and for encouraging me, for as long as I've known him, to write a novel.